To Helen Singer,
a fellow teacher,
Best wishes.

Stan Seaberg

Loose Cannons

Loose Cannons

BY *Stan Seaberg*

Pentland Press, Inc.
England • USA • Scotland

Loose Cannons is a work of fiction. Except for the necessary use of real persons, events, and place names to give historical authenticity, all of the characters and incidents are creations of the author's imagination. Any resemblance to real persons living or dead is completely coincidental.

PUBLISHED BY PENTLAND PRESS, INC.
5122 Bur Oak Circle, Raleigh, North Carolina 27612
United States of America
919-782-0281

ISBN 1-57197-093-2
Library of Congress Catalog Card Number 97-075506

Printed in the United States of America

Several people have made important contributions to the completion of *Loose Cannons:* Pete Heilman, English teacher *extraordinaire*, first gave me the confidence to write fiction; incisive critiques by colleagues Richard Livingston and David Alford were helpful at several stages; two interactive writing seminars taught by novelist and gifted teacher Donna Levin provided the most essential criticism, support and empowerment; my typist, Barbara Dale, provided dozens of helpful suggestions and corrections in addition to unsurpassed professional competence; two culturally rich and event-filled alternative tours organized by Barbie and Vic Ulmer of Our Developing World provided both context and inspiration for the novel; finally, and most importantly, two beautiful adventurers, my daughters, Sylvia and Sonja, have endured their father's repeated mid-life crises with astonishing support and constancy. I, of course, take full credit for the book's shortcomings as well as my own.

Table of Contents

Foreword

Generations—and the way we think of them—are marked off not so much by round-numbered years as by the pivotal events that shape them. Gertrude Stein's "Lost Generation" was disillusioned by the Great War; depression-era children grew up with a healthy belief in the possibility of poverty; the men and women who lived through the uncertainty of the Second World War eagerly embraced the conformist Eisenhower years.

And my generation was shaped by Vietnam. It turned us against authority; it made us believers in the power of television; it forced us to reevaluate our image of ourselves as Americans and our role in world politics. Just as the stock market crash left a generation unsure of the economic future, Vietnam left a later generation unsure of their moral terrain and determined to take the high ground.

Of course, it wasn't quite that easy. The popular media was full for many years of macho men like Chuck Norris and Sylvester Stallone acting out a collective fantasy that we "woulda-coulda-shoulda" won it, if only those darned bleeding-heart liberals in Congress would have let the military have its way. In films like *Missing in Action* and *Rambo II*, Norris and company go back to Vietnam and set free the prisoners against tremendous odds, thus winning one permanently for the Gipper.

Other films like *The Deer Hunter, Coming Home*, and *Platoon* dealt more realistically with the scars of war, although they also helped give rise to the stereotype of the post-traumatic-stressed veteran, a stereotype that persists today (and which is not exactly helped by studies showing that a high percentage of the homeless are also vets).

Literature is usually a little more self-scrutinizing than Hollywood, and at the same time that Rambo was shooting up the Vietcong, authors like Tim O'Brien and Tim Mahoney were looking at the experience of the young and innocent sent to fight.

As years pass, a second wave of literature is emerging, literature that examines many other aspects of the war, including its effect on those whose lives we were ostensibly trying to save. Robert Olen Butler has written about the Vietnamese adjusting to life in America. Le Ly Hyslip, a Vietnamese woman, has written a personal memoir of the upheaval of the war years and their aftermath.

And now Stan Seaberg.

In *Loose Cannons*, Seaberg tells the story of a ragtag bunch of veterans who make the journey back to Vietnam as part of a "reconciliation tour." But it's also a journey of redemption and discovery.

As literature, *Loose Cannons* has roots that go as far back as *Canterbury Tales*, in which a group of pilgrims tell their individual stories. Here, the pilgrimage is to Vietnam, and the master narrator is Specialist Parker, whose driving ambition is to find out what happened to Annie Binh, the independent young Vietnamese woman he worshiped from afar.

Specialist Parker is the unifying force, but he is also able to tell us, through a variety of narrative devices, the stories of his fellow travelers. The result is a collection of interconnected short stories that has more recent roots in books like Amy Tan's *The Joy Luck Club*, Gloria Naylor's *The Women of Brewster Place*, and Fenton Johnson's *Scissors, Paper, Rock*.

The structure is perfect for what Seaberg aims to accomplish: to assemble a mosaic of the American serviceperson's experience in Vietnam. Because instead of this being just one isolated drama, everyone's here: the diehard patriot disillusioned, the seeking son, the seeking father, the witness of atrocities, the young woman looking for love.

Although they have many different ambitions, they share at least one hope—a hope that's expressed by Kate Noonan, a middle-aged nurse, who says, "Putting this group together . . . reminds me of the way we patchworked bodies together in Vietnam. If the heart was still ticking we could sometimes find enough body parts to glue the guy together . . . This group has a lot of heart . . . I hope we can find the missing parts of our lives in Vietnam."

There's a lot of heart in the book, too, and enough twists and turns to make both O. Henry and Aesop proud. There's also the whiff of magic blowing through these tales, as when a young man named Steve Solberg is visited by a masseuse who may or may not be Ms. Hung, the lovely teacher he met earlier that day. Like her country, Ms. Hung's beauty is marred by the scars inflicted by outsiders. And like her country, she suffers, yet endures.

This sense of the magical is most subtly created in the many reunions that take place. The vets of the reconciliation tour are charmed in their ability to find both their lost loves and antagonists. Vic Carlson finds the mother of his children.

Ben Hubbard finds the woman who betrayed him. And Tommy, the homosexual in "Tunnel Vision," finds "the ex-Vietcong tunnel rat and sniper" who killed the only man Tommy ever loved.

When the sniper turns around and rescues Tommy, Tommy discovers that the only way to put the war behind him is to put the war behind him. As he and many other characters put to rest the past and move on, there's a sense of being reborn into a new life.

Magic and rebirth are also associated with things female. And unlike O'Brien and many other American authors (and filmmakers like Francis Ford Coppola and Oliver Stone) who have concentrated on the male experience in Vietnam, Seaberg looks at the particular sacrifice that both American and Vietnamese women made.

As one Mr. Hu observes, "From the time of the Trung sisters who led the resistance against China in the first century up to the present, Vietnamese women have sacrificed themselves for family and country."

Ms. Hung (the mysterious teacher from "Out of Body—English") advises Solberg to read *The Tale of Kieu*, which tells the story of a woman who gives up everything dearest to her for the sake of her family. It may be hard for Western readers to admire Kieu as a role model, since she "endures as her fate a life of mostly abuse and betrayal." Yet in her stoicism she does stand for the notion that "reconciliation, not revenge, must be the ultimate closure to war and violence."

In wartime, the rule of law is suspended, and women are especially vulnerable. Seaberg doesn't shy away from the stories of torture and rape, but does not dwell on them unnecessarily, either.

But not all of the women in *Loose Cannons* are helpless victims. May Ly Chung, Cao Nu Lien (now Sybil Patterson) and, most charmingly, Annie Binh, all rise like phoenixes from the ashes of their ravaged country to make lives and identities of their own. Kate Noonan, the American nurse, exorcises her demons as well. It's inspiring to read about these strong women, women who likewise inspire the men to start again.

Good fiction is never preachy, and *Loose Cannons* is no exception. Seaberg doesn't proclaim either the evil or the rightness of the war, or of any of the governments involved. Bad things happen to a lot of innocent people, and many of those things are done by bad people—but there are bad people on all sides, and often those bad people have in turn been victims themselves: forced to join the VC to protect their families, or so numbed by atrocities that their moral compass is circling out of control.

So the paradox is that this is a highly political book, and yet not a political book at all, only a human one. There's even comic relief in the form of a Vietnamese Elvis impersonator and the American gospel singer who loves him—not to mention the woman guerrilla fighter who moonlights as a "Kickboxing Spider Woman."

Of course, what makes any book worthwhile is that it's about more than just its own subject. These stories aren't just about Vietnam, or the vets themselves, but about forgiveness, and about moving on. If the vets—the pilgrims—of Seaberg's reconciliation tour can do that, then maybe the whole generation can.

Donna Levin is a writer and teacher of fiction in San Francisco, California.

Prologue:
Loose Cannons

I once heard a veteran say, "Vietnam sucked the soul right out of me and I've been searching for it ever since." With me, it was my heart that got sucked out—sucked out by the death of Annie Binh. When I left Vietnam in 1965, I never wanted to smell its sickly sweet, rotting humidity again. Vietnam had the stink of death for me. I wanted life, a new life—not realizing Vietnam was a region of the heart and mind, as well as a country.

Re-entry into the "real" world was totally unreal, especially entering college and trying to communicate with fellow students who were mostly teenagers. I felt surrounded by aliens from another planet—our worlds were so different. I was in for a bigger shock: self-recognition, the realization of how little I knew about myself, Vietnam, and the larger world. I didn't want to die like Steve McQueen in *The Sand Pebbles* or the grunts in Vietnam yelling, "What the hell happened?" So I pursued a degree in Asian studies and began questioning my assumptions about the Vietnam War. I survived the maelstrom of late '60s protests, strikes, riots and assassinations, stripped of every patriotic platitude I'd learned in high school civics—except my faith in the Bill of Rights. A policeman's billy robbed me of that faith along with a hunk of my head.

The war was still on when I started teaching high school history, and students were still being drafted. So I joined Vietnam Veterans Against the War, started draft counseling and taught politically incorrect history, meaning my version of the unvarnished truth.

After fighting a guerrilla war with an asshole principal, I quit and moved to Santa Cruz to surf, read history, and write novels. I flopped as a writer, but I made a bundle rehabbing old Victorians (the '88 quake was a windfall)—enough to retire on in twenty years. Surfing was always a great escape, which is partly why two marriages and a half-dozen relationships got wiped out. I say partly because consciously or unconsciously I measured every woman against Annie Binh, and the tall Birkenstock babes invariably fell short. Annie was always there, in a region of my heart and mind and in my dreams.

With early retirement, the onset of male menopause, and time to muse, Annie appeared more often in my dreams. Always posed as in a black and white photo of her arrest, she stood in the foreground looking straight into the camera with a frightened yet brave smile. Behind her stood grim-faced *Huoat Vu* (security police) with dark glasses and combat helmets. When the silent, still figures began moving, I woke up screaming, unable to face the finale—Annie's torture and murder by Nhu's security police.

Driven by dreams or demons, I cruised several times a week on my Harley 1200 over the mountains into San Jose's Eastridge Mall looking for Annie Binh in the mid-life faces of suburban Vietnamese matrons. But with my flattop and twisted grin, my only hits were on aging valley girls prowling for Ricky Nelson look-alikes.

My obsession, I'm sure, drove me to join an adult education class in Vietnamese—maybe to exorcise my ghosts in their native tongue. By happenstance, the class overlapped with a seminar on the Vietnam War taught by two longtime friends. So I audited the class mainly to please them. At the time, I had no intentions of returning to Vietnam.

Phil and Betty Volsted were wrinkled and stringy with years, so spotted by the sun they looked like a couple of aging leopards instead of card-carrying Gray Panthers. But at sixty-plus years they had more high octane, piss and vinegar in their veins than most teenagers. So instead of moving into one of California's elder sanctuaries after retirement, they backpacked around the Third World off the beaten tracks from Nepal to Nicaragua, and it changed their lives forever.

Back in the States they formed Global Educational Enterprises, a nonprofit corporation specializing in unconventional education projects and alternative travel. Phil was an easy-going, shaggy, bearded giant with a zigzag nose, whose baby-blue eyes could freeze into Swedish ice when necessary. He'd been a boxer, union organizer and journalist before he turned to teaching to make sure America's high school students got some color and grain in their white-bread curriculum.

When Phil romanced Betty into marriage, she was a nail-thin, freckle-faced Okie girl working in a San Jose cannery. She responded to Phil's mind and body tutelage as voraciously as she devoured his gourmet cooking. By the time she'd worn Phil to a thin nail with her physical awakening, Betty was fat with child. She then channeled her energies into child-rearing as totally as she'd thrown herself into Phil's mind and body dialectics.

When their two kids entered school, Betty completed high school and took a college degree at San Jose State. She spent her adult years teaching ESL classes to Latino and Asian immigrants.

Betty and Phil had energetically opposed the Vietnam War inside of class and out, so it was not surprising that they should organize an adult education course called Vietnam—Twenty Years After. They were planning a tour for the following year but, as it happened, some aggressive vets hounded the Volsteds into an early decision. The tour, or prospect of a tour, probably salvaged the class.

The class was at first evenly split between vets and nonvets. But the vets took over and controlled the class with their arguments and bickering. They were still fighting the war and needed to lift a load of leftover trauma from their collective chests. By the second week, most of the civilians had left and the vets were still squabbling like a bunch of alley cats tied in a bag.

The first time I walked into the class, which was already in session, a feisty new guy, short and paunchy with wiry hair and the face of a bulldog, was introducing himself.

"Name's Tommy Neville; I was a medic with the 25th Infantry at Cu Chi. I was also a tunnel rat, one of the few who survived. After ten years of teaching middle school with no light at the end, I was willing to return to the Cu Chi tunnels. Instead I opened a bookstore and coffee shop called Iguana Dreams on upper Market—Castro Street, actually."

A tall, gray-haired man in suit and eye patch, wearing hand-tooled boots and spinning a Stetson, jerked his head around and half-opened his mouth.

"Yeah, yeah, I have a different sexual orientation from yours, old man. You gotta problem with that?" Tommy blurted.

The older guy laughed and spread his hands sideways, "I've got no problem. Point your cannon wherever you damn well please, just so it's not in my azimuth."

Neville snorted, "No problem, man, I know my azimuth from an asshole."

Phil looked confused and angry. His bald spot had turned red and his eyes were icing over. He fisted his right hand into his left like he wanted to shut up the feisty squirt with a knuckle ball. "C'mon you guys," he exploded, "cut the bullshit!" He looked at Betty giving him the evil eye and calmed down. She crooked a finger toward the straight-looking, dignified man with the eye patch who'd taken flack from Neville. Even in a school desk, the man sat tall in the saddle with a bemused smile on his handsome profile, as if he were playing the Marlboro Man in a Hathaway shirt ad. Betty thought he looked like Gregory Peck. Later she would call him Gregory Peckerwood.

"How about it, sir," Phil said. "Tell us who you are and why are you taking the class."

"My name is Ben Hubbard. I was head of supply at Bien Hoa airbase during much of the war. I've been a financial advisor and investment broker since the war. I currently reside in Morgan Hill."

"And why are you taking the class?" Betty asked.

Ben Hubbard thought for a minute. "Well, one reason might be that I probably spent more time in Vietnam than anyone." He looked at the Vietnamese, "Almost anyone else in this room. I thought I might serve as a kind of consultant, expert in residence so to speak."

A couple of vets snorted and Neville laughed. "If you were supply sergeant at Bien Hoa, man, I think you got more confessing to do than consulting."

Snorts of approval and several "Fucking A's" followed. The movie poster face suddenly flushed. He'd been drinking.

"Hey, all I said, goddammit, was that I'm here to contribute something."

"Well, sir," said Neville, "some of the rest of us may have something to contribute, too—maybe a hell of a lot more than you."

"Hey, I didn't say—oh, fuck off. Jesus!"

Neville jumped to his feet, but the nurse sitting next to him jerked him backwards.

At that point Betty intervened with an introduction that would change the course of the class—for me, at least. "I'm personally delighted," she said, "to have a Vietnamese friend with us. His daughter was in my ESL class at Eastmont High. I think he may provide some needed balance. Mr. Trang, please . . ."

Mr. Trang rose to his feet and bowed slightly. He was overweight and going gray at the temples. In spite of jowly cheeks, his face had a hard, square look. His ears stuck out like Spock's on *Star Trek*. He was overdressed in a three-piece suit with white shirt and tie. His voice, barely audible at first, picked up volume until, by the end of his talk, he was thundering like a frenetic TV evangelist.

"My name is Nam Van Trang. I served honorably as a colonel in the South Vietnamese army in our war for survival. I am here because Mrs. Volsted requested my presence. I had hoped I might contribute something to your class, but I don't think I can endure the bickering and stupidity I find among American veterans."

Then Mr. Trang unleashed a tirade in a tense, high-pitched voice that shocked everyone. "I am not only disturbed by the bickering here, I am shocked that veterans would have misgivings about a war to preserve democracy and to resist godless communism not only in Vietnam but in America. I am standing here because the same kind of bickering and fighting happened in Vietnam among your so-called leaders of the free world. This, more than the drug-crazed and sex-crazed American soldiers, lost the war. It was the failure of purpose and will that destroyed my country."

Mr. Trang turned and walked out the door. Betty started after him, but Phil grabbed her arm. A bomb burst of angry comments ricocheted around the room.

"Fuckin' ARVN still blamin' us for losing their war."

"And I thought I was frozen in time," someone said.

"Got his ass stuck in a time warp."

"Talk like that gonna get his ass kicked into a permanent time warp."

"Well, yes, he is frozen in time," said Phil. "All of the older generation Vietnamese in America are stuck in a time warp. They always will be so long as they live only in memory."

"As long as they live in this country."

"Send the fucker back to Vietnam," Neville growled.

"I'll do my best to get him back here," Betty said. "We need someone from the Vietnamese community."

Three or four people answered in unison, "Don't bother."

Mr. Trang would never return to the class. At the moment, I could have cared less because I was confused and in shock. I thought I recognized him as the man I'd talked with recently at the nearby copy mart. His kids had been helping me with Vietnamese until he horned in and insisted on tutoring me. Listening to his official voice and noticing the fresh haircut exposing his bat-like ears, I saw him now as Major Trang of ARVN intelligence, the third person in a love triangle that caused the death of Annie Binh and my commanding officer. But I still wasn't certain. The jowly face and paunchy gut belied the trim, hard body and sharp-boned face of the Major Trang I'd known.

"Hey! Can't you guys handle a little reality. Half of what the man said is pretty much on target." It was the nurse, Kate Noonan. She hadn't said much before, so everyone was surprised and tongue-tied. Kate was just as surprised when nobody answered her.

She smiled, her eyes crinkling like the Okie women in Dorothea Lange photographs. She was handsome in a middle-aged kind of way. Her reddish hair was cut short and turning gray. She had a strong chin, thrust forward when she talked, and steel gray eyes. She had arrived late from work with an Asian friend and gave a negative head shake when Phil first gestured in her direction. After her animated outburst, Phil looked at her and smiled.

"How about you, young lady," Phil said, "I think we need some feminine grace to counterbalance the male dominance in this class."

There were friendly snickers.

"Well, my name is Kate Noonan. By the way, call me feminist, not feminine. I'm currently serving as chief administrator of nursing at El Camino Hospital. No bedpans or IVs. I served with two emergency hospitals in Vietnam, first at An Khe and then in Chu Lai for six months. I spent my last three months at Bien Hoa filing papers after I'd run out of steam. I've been active in the Vietnam Nurses Association and with the Telephone Tree which, as you may know, tries to trace MIAs and POWs."

"Lotsa luck," someone said.

"Hey, the commies are no dummies," Ben Hubbard said. "The MIA thing is one of the few cards they can still play. They are not gonna dig up a lot of bones for nothing, not until Uncle Sam coughs up Nixon's promised forty mill."

"Hold it, hold it," said Phil. "Hold the discussion. Let Kate finish."

"I'm about finished," Kate said. "What I really want is to meet some Vietnamese officials face to face and ask them about our MIAs, I mean eyeball to eyeball."

"Why?" someone asked. "What good will that do?"

"Because," Kate's voice broke, "well, because our own government has consistently lied to us and opposed our efforts. Not on the surface, of course, but behind the scenes. I don't know the reasons, but I want to find out. That's why I'm taking this class. I'm hoping to meet someone who knows about this hidden agenda."

"You gotta crack the CIA," someone said, "and they can't be cracked."

"Hell, the CIA spooks are already half-cracked."

A chain of laughter whipped around the room.

Ben Hubbard threw his head back and slapped his forehead. "Jesus, the old conspiracy thing again. Will it ever stop?"

Neville challenged him. "Hey man, didn't you every hear of the Pentagon Papers? Get fucking real."

Betty intervened. "Okay, guys. We know you all have something to say and we want you to say it. But for purposes of dialogue and discussion . . ."

"I'm not finished," Kate said sharply, and everyone shut up.

"I'd like to introduce my friend, Lily Okada, who's been helping me with the MIAs, answering the mail, telephoning, running down hundreds of leads. She's unbelievable." Kate turned to her friend. "How about it, Lily, want to tell us about your work in Vietnam?"

Lily had to be in her forties, but she looked thirty, maybe because she had the figure of a younger woman and wore her hair shoulder length. Only when she smiled did lines appear at the corners of her eyes and mouth.

"Thanks, Kate," she said, "since I'm just a visitor, maybe I'll pass this 'round." She scanned the class and smiled, "I'm glad to be among friends."

Kate broke in, "I don't want to violate Lily's privacy. I'll just say this: She served two tours in Vietnam and has had more face-to-face contact with Vietnamese people than anyone I know."

Andy Fetzer, a muscular guy with his sleeves rolled up over his biceps, raised his hand. He was darkly handsome in a thick kind of way—thick straight hair pulled back in a small ponytail, thick eyebrows, cheeks, lips and neck, and dark, brooding eyes. He looked like a boxer. His talk was straight and humble. No frills.

"I was with a marine recon outfit, LURPs, out of An Khe. I've been a carpenter and building contractor since getting out of service. The war washed back on me pretty heavy last year, and I washed out—went bonkers. Lost my business and my family. I finally went to the Wall. That helped, just being with other vets. I'm living now in Mountain View doing part-time carpentry and taking therapy at the Vets Hospital. I'm also trying to reconcile with my wife and girls. I'm taking this seminar to get some larger perspective on the war. Basically I want to know why I fucked up—oops, 'scuse me, screwed up."

Several vets started laughing. "Hey man," Neville said, "no fucking big deal!"

"Agreed," said Phil. "In this class we want to be up-front and open. What comes out, comes out. Shit happens, as the kids say. No problem."

Hand claps and cheers abounded.

"How about a smoke break?" asked Kate Noonan.

"Let's all take a break," said Phil, "but watch out for Betty; she'll grab that cigarette right out of your mouth!"

After the break a slim guy wearing chinos and a golf shirt raised his hand. He was about as thin in his nose and lips and neck as Fetzer was thick. He was blonde all over, even to his eyebrows—a Wonderbread man. His hair was curling around his ears, but it was so thin on top that his scalp was freckled.

"Vic Carlson," he said, "currently teaching writing and American lit at Valley College. I was with the Third Marines in Danang. I guess you could say I was the ultimate REMF (rear echelon motherfucker). I never fired a gun in anger."

Andy Fetzer laughed. "This is my rifle, this is my gun; this one's for killing, this one's for fun. Your gun is your dick, man; you really were an REMF!"

Carlson turned red and angry, "Yeah, well, I did what I had to do."

"Like sitting on your ass and lubricating your gun?" Fetzer scored a direct hit.

Vic Carlson ignored the insult. "I also joined the class," he said, "because a friend told me you'd be going to Vietnam."

Betty and Phil looked at each other. "Well," Phil said, "we've talked about it, yes, but that's as far as it's gone. We'll keep working on it. This class will be first on the list for sure, front of the line. Anything else?"

"Yes," Carlson said, "I think I may have a son in Vietnam. I'd like to find him if possible."

Several vets laughed. "Impossible," Fetzer said. "We all have sons and daughters in Vietnam." He looked at Kate Noonan. "Nurse, there's where you'll find your MIAs—in the thousands of children of American soldiers abandoned in Vietnam."

Lily Okada raised her hand. "I'd like to say something after all since I'm Amerasian myself. For the record, there are lots of unsung heroes—private groups like the Quakers, who worked with orphans and street kids in Saigon, many of whom were Amerasian, the offspring of American males."

Lily paused. "Maybe I'd better say this now in case I join the group: My first tour in Vietnam, I was a Red Cross service worker, a Donut Dolly."

"Fun girl!" Vic was grinning as he said it.

Lily's face flushed and her voice crackled with anger. "You bastard! I knew some asshole would jump me with an insult. At least we weren't REMFs. We flew in and out of fire bases all the time and took a lot of incoming, too. And I didn't leave any kids in Vietnam. In fact, I took one home with me!"

There was a minute of total silence. Then Vic mumbled, "I apologize. I didn't mean anything by it."

Lily snubbed him. "I'm here," she said, "because of the tour; otherwise, I'm not sticking around."

Phil nodded to a younger guy in his thirties wearing an athletic suit with a headband wrapped around shoulder-length hair.

"I'm Steve Solberg," the young man said. "My dad flew phantom jets for the air force out of Danang. I'm here because I lost my dad when I was fifteen. I'd come to hate the war I saw on nightly TV and I came to hate my own father as a killer. I've got a terrible ache for my father and I want to find him, I mean find out what he was *really* like. I'm a tennis coach at De Anza College and a rec supervisor for the Sunnyvale Parks. I used to teach junior high, but I couldn't take all of the bureaucratic bullshit in the public school system."

Neville muttered, "Tell me about it."

"Hey," Neville shouted, "how about the tour? You wanna go to Vietnam, don't you, kid?"

"Hell, yes, I want to go to Vietnam. That's why I took the class."

Phil had to do some mental backpedaling. He and Betty had dressed up the class flyer with references to a tour. They had included the tour thing as a come-on, as an enticement to increase enrollment, to make the minimum cut; otherwise, no class.

Phil said, "We want to do a future trip if we can get enough people and cut through the red tape in Vietnam. But we still seem a long way from normalizing relations."

"Shit!" Neville exploded again. "I think you misled us, by God. You'd better get a trip on the road if you want this class to fly. You'd better normalize relations with us."

Several vets mumbled "right on." A couple of them slapped Neville on the shoulder.

Phil wondered if putting the class in a circle had been such a good idea. But Betty had insisted, "I want this seminar to represent a gathering, a healing. A circle represents a community that the war destroyed. We can at least try to patch some of the pieces together."

"Why don't we come back to this later?" Phil asked. "There's no way we can settle this right now."

"Goddammit," Neville insisted, "why can't we settle this tour thing right now?"

I'd had it with Neville. I stood up because I was a head taller than him and in lots better shape. "Hey little man," I said, "back off and listen up. I mean this is your first fucking session and you are climbing all over Phil and Betty, who are, incidentally, very good friends of mine. I think I can solve the tour problem if you'll settle down. I've got a good buddy in San Francisco, a travel agent who specializes in offbeat, low-budget tours. I'll meet with him personally this week and see what we can work out, okay?"

My reaction to Neville's harangue was spontaneous. All I wanted to do was shut his big mouth. I figured I would make an obligatory phone call to my travel agent friend and dutifully report his thumbs down. No big deal. Then I missed a couple of class sessions. I had a *mano a mano* encounter with ex-Major Trang that disturbed the hell out of me—mainly his version of events surrounding the deaths of Annie Binh and Colonel Rowe. That one conversation turned me completely around on returning to Vietnam. Now I *had* to go! I phoned my travel agent friend, an ex-AID worker in Vietnam. In less than two weeks he'd arranged a low-budget tour geared especially to the needs of veterans. I phoned the Volsteds immediately.

I returned to class a hero. Phil greeted me with a smile as wide as a piano keyboard. The entire class went out to the Gordon Biersch Brewery and drank ten pitchers of beer, and I got suckered into hours of organizing and planning for the tour to Vietnam.

Besides the vets and a couple of others from the seminar, two young women would come aboard the final week—a journalist-seminarian from New York and a Vietnamese dance teacher from San Jose.

Once the tour was agreed upon the group achieved a cease-fire. Most of the petty bickering stopped. Arguments were over substance, about the trip. The seminar was restructured around the prospective tour. Place names were linked to the geography of the veterans' war experiences. Tour planning responsibilities were assigned and seminar topics were linked closely with travel plans. Through this centering process the group achieved a rough solidarity.

For Betty and Phil, however, the hurry-up change in plans took a little getting used to. Betty, especially, thought the group resembled little more than a Chaucer's hodgepodge of loose cannon characters, a middle-aged wild bunch with grenades in their guts.

"I remember a song from World War II," Betty said, "*Coming in on a Wing and a Prayer*. That's how I feel about this tour. Only we're venturing out on a wing and a prayer which is even more uncertain."

"Putting this group together," Kate said, "reminds me of the way we patchworked bodies in Vietnam. If the heart was still ticking, we could sometimes find enough body parts to glue the guy together. Most of the guys didn't make it—too many missing parts. This group has a lot of heart; I hope we can find the missing parts of our lives in Vietnam."

Personally, I liked the protean possibilities and the ragged edges of our unpredictable group. Like Joseph Campbell's hero who "is the champion not of things become but of things becoming," they had the stuff which dreams and great stories are made of, the stuff I wanted to write about. Perhaps I could, while dodging the erratic shots of my loose cannon companions, piece together their stories and my own. That would be a trip worth taking. Like Chaucer's *Canterbury* pilgrims, I wanted to get moving at a "slightly faster pace than walking to Saint Thomas' (or my own) watering place."

I couldn't wait.

Hearts and Pawns

I think my disillusionment with the American adventure in Vietnam began the day my hero, Colonel Rowe, complied with a hamlet chief's offer to initiate his daughter into womanhood—which left him feeling pretty high and loose and me feeling tangled and tense. I should have been more upset by the callous violation of the hamlet chief's daughter, but I accepted the colonel's version that it was simply part of the cultural landscape, "like eating monkey stew or roasted rat," he grinned. "I'll do anything to win their fucking hearts and minds." The colonel's casual sex didn't bother me nearly as much as his bringing Annie Binh into the conversation. His question hit me like a rabbit punch.

"What do you think of Annie, Specialist Parker?"

"I—I—well, I think she's beautiful, sir, really beautiful."

When I first saw her in a white silken ao dai *I thought she was an Asian angel, a slender, curvaceous angel with breasts straining against her overblouse, and a neck so slender one could see her heartbeat pulsing in the lacework of throat veins. An oblique glance (I avoided her direct, challenging eyes) at her elegant profile reminded me of pictures I'd seen of Queen Nefertiti or the American dancer Josephine Baker, partly because of her high-bridged nose and close-cut hair, except that her cheeks and lips were rounded and full, the upper lip arching provocatively . . .*

"Parker!" the colonel said rather sharply.

"Yes sir, I'm sorry sir."

"About your age, isn't she?"

"Miss Binh, you mean? Yes sir, I reckon she is."

"And you never wanted to get into her pants. C'mon, 'fess up, Parker; it's good for the soul."

Army talk was down and dirty, but the colonel's crude reference to Annie embarrassed me.

"No sir," I said. "She's your girl."

The colonel looked away. "Forget it, Parker, I was just fooling around. She's driving me crazy. I'm twice her age, with a wife and kids in the States. I know I should drop her, but I can't. She's an obsession. You know what an obsession is?"

"I know what the word means, sir."

Then the colonel looked at me directly and said kind of aggressively, "You'll fucking know when an obsession starts to eat you up, Parker. It'll drive you into hell or the nut house or suicide. I feel like I'm heading for my fucking Waterloo. Sabe, Kimo Sabe?"

"Yes sir," I said with a straight face, "that's where Napoleon met Wellington."

Colonel Rowe laughed and knocked my hat off. "A history buff, no less. You dumb prick, Parker, it's only a figure of speech."

My answer was purposely indirect to cover my real feelings. I could no more tell my commanding officer I was madly in love with his mistress than I could have told my father I was in love with my mother. In a way, I treated Annie like my mother, as beauty personified, poised on a pedestal, untouchable. I was raised a rural romantic where the sacredness of womanhood was taken as holy writ. Now I was a closet virgin trapped in a military culture where sexual conquest was part of the macho creed.

I think it was this crude, colonial attitude toward the Vietnamese, especially women, that brought about the American disaster in Vietnam. This ugly hubris with its cultural blindness and lack of empathy was symptomatic of all our other problems. Most certainly it caused the deaths of Colonel Rowe and his beautiful Vietnamese mistress, Annie Binh. The shock of their deaths cut so deep that it took me half a lifetime to recover. I thought I had until I encountered the third person in the tragic triangle that included Colonel Rowe and Annie Binh. His business was right around the corner from where I was taking an evening class in Vietnamese—thirty years too late, but with early retirement I had the time and desire.

I was rapping with some Vietnamese kids who ran the photocopy-fax center, getting some free help with the language class, when an older Vietnamese guy in a beat-up leather jacket and porkpie hat walked in. He spoke sharply to the kids and they hustled back to business. Then he grinned, shook hands and introduced himself as the big daddy. He was all of five feet five. The big was in his waist and both sets of cheeks.

"My kids are American mongrels," he laughed. "They speak chop suey Vietnamese. How about I help you sometime—anytime?" He was so insistent that I agreed to meet with him during his weekly visits to the photocopy center, one of several he owned in the Bay area.

I didn't recognize him until we were three weeks into the program, not until I encountered him at a seminar where he'd had a haircut that exposed his ears. By that time I really liked the guy and, of course, I liked his kids as well.

In Vietnam we had called him Batman because of his pointy ears and bony face and his habit of traveling at night. I mean he had to have extrasensory perception to get from Saigon to My Tho and back again in the dark of night, especially with the countryside crawling with VC—if he wasn't with the VC himself.

In Vietnam he'd been Major Trang, an army intelligence officer who served as liaison with the head of security police, the notorious Ngo Dinh Nhu, brother of President Ngo Dinh Diem. He also served as liaison between the brothers Ngo and General Duong, commander of the 3rd ARVN in the Delta. General Duong was supposedly Diem's most reliable support in case of a coup. In 1963 I served as driver for Colonel Catlin Rowe, who ran the army's civic action program in the Delta, the program designed to win the hearts and minds of the Vietnamese people.

Major Trang made frequent trips to and from My Tho to confer with General Duong and Colonel Rowe and to check on the loyalty of various ARVN officers. Diem was paranoid as hell and rotated officers frequently; others simply disappeared. I figured Batman was also a hit man. Eventually, of course, Diem's paranoia would lead to his own downfall and execution—murder. Unfortunately, innocent people were caught in the web of deceit and intrigue surrounding Diem's death, including Colonel Rowe and Annie Binh.

In spite of his crude sexism, Colonel Rowe was one of the few Americans who not only understood the hearts and minds concept, but practiced it as well (or so I thought at the time). We were always on the go, driving through the boonies, checking the progress of civic action teams engaged in improving rice production, medical aid, sewage treatment and security.

The colonel's civic action program was continuously frustrated by the dictatorial policies of President Diem, invariably supported by the top brass at MACV. Hamlet chiefs, for example, were Diem loyalists (or lackeys), bureaucrats sent down from Saigon to villages with which they had no local affinities. "Goddammit, Parker!" the colonel groused, "If we don't learn from the mistakes of the French, we'll be trapped in a whole country of Dien Bien Phus. The French had their puppet emperor, Bao Dai; we've got the fucking loose cannon Diem, a combination Chinese Mandarin, Catholic priest, French bureaucrat and, worst of all, unmarried celibate—a fucking elitist who knows as little about village Vietnam as he does about women. Nada! Nada! Nada!"

Most of the village chiefs scurried out of their villages by sundown, before the VC moved in. Those who stayed were often assassinated, sometimes brutally. I remember driving the colonel to a village where the hamlet chief and his family were laid out with their throats slashed. A heavy rain had washed away the blood and paled the skin so they looked like white mannequins. Thirty or forty villagers, mostly women and children, circled at a distance. Colonel Rowe kicked at the dirt. "Look at them," he shouted, "the villagers should be furious but they aren't. They're scared shitless. They aren't angry because the chief isn't one of them; he's an outsider."

The colonel was furiously opposed to the strategic hamlet program in which entire villages were moved wholesale to distant strategic locations where they were enclosed in armed stockades. The purpose was to prevent the VC from taxing the rice crops and force drafting young males.

Together we watched the evacuation of Nam Suc village as a company of ARVN shoved and bullied villagers with their kids, pigs, chickens, utensils and farm tools into five ton trucks. Women and kids were weeping and screaming, tearing their fingernails into the ground as they were forcibly dragged to the transports. As soon as the trucks left, Rome plows scraped the huts and leftovers into piles for burning. Later, rice fields were sprayed with toxic Agent Blue and the ground was salted. The colonel cursed and shook his head. "We're creating a nation of rural slums, prison camps inside barbed wire. We bust our balls in civic action trying to create independent, self-supporting villages able to resist enemy propaganda and then we get this kind of shit—total dependency, living on handouts. Fucking American socialism. Jesus!"

Worst of all, we seemed to be losing even when we were winning. "Y'know, Parker," the colonel said after we'd left a village where a civic action team had doubled rice production and wiped out dysentery, "even the good things we do benefit the VC more than us. In villages where we've had the most success, the VC leave our people alone—no killing or hassling. You know why?"

"No sir, I don't. You'd think the VC would be kicking ass big time."

"Think, Parker. Simple arithmetic. We improve rice production, the VC get more taxes; we save babies, heal the kids, the VC draft more soldiers. Simple arithmetic. You ever hear of *Catch 22*, Parker?"

"I heard about it," I said, "a funny war novel, something like that."

"Read it, Parker. It's funny, but it's serious as hell. Describes our situation perfectly, a situation where you can't win." The colonel waved a sheet of paper. "Here's what I'm talking about. I've got a hit list of supposed VC agents; the CIA spooks tell MACV it wants them 'terminated with extreme prejudice.' At least half of them are informants for us, double agents, guys with families trying to survive by playing both sides. We knock them off because they're double agents and close off our pipeline to the VC. We can't operate without informants. Kaput, *Catch 22*. Can't win. Comprende, amigo?"

Unfortunately, Rowe's weakness, shared with most Americans in Vietnam, was his insatiable appetite for women and sex, sex in which forethought was as rare as foreplay.

I don't think Colonel Rowe knew what he was getting into when he picked up the gorgeous university student waiting at the curb for a taxi or family limo. Annie Binh was the nineteen-year-old daughter of Lu Duc Binh, the chancellor of Saigon University and an outspoken opposition leader in the South Vietnamese Assembly. She was probably just another adventure for him at first.

And why the tall, beautiful girl with the figure, face and even the hairstyle (with spit-curl ringlets) of the fabulous Josephine Baker was attracted to the hatchet-faced, balding forty-five-year-old is a bigger mystery. Rowe had a certain charisma, a bold confidence and devil-may-care quality that attracted adventurous women. And he certainly exuded a sense of power, his own and that of the American empire. In Vietnam, even the ugliest American male could make it with a beauty queen.

Annie was much more than a beauty queen. She was a vibrant activist, a brilliant student who attended the university, taught English classes on the side, spoke fluent French, performed in local drama and protested the corruption of the Saigon government at great personal risk. She resisted her father's restrictions and refused Colonel Rowe's offer of a luxury apartment.

I think Colonel Rowe enjoyed Annie's independent personality before he came to see it as dangerous. Early on, the colonel spent time romancing Annie. I remember driving them to Bien Hoa for weekend flights to Dalat and Cape Saint Jacques, and how they laughed and kidded each other, stealing kisses like a couple of newlyweds on a honeymoon. But with the escalating political crisis and Annie's bitter fights with her family and Colonel Rowe, their high spirits dissipated quickly.

Once he got wind of Annie's affair, Chancellor Binh raised one hell of a ruckus at MACV headquarters. He even forced a full brass hearing, but Colonel Rowe was not even reprimanded let alone court-martialed. Rowe was protected by the American press who had made him the hero of the war, and he was the indispensable prop for America's biggest propaganda ploy, the civic action program. Besides, most of the top brass shared Rowe's attitude about the rights of male conquest, since many of them also had Vietnamese mistresses.

Chancellor Binh tried to stop his feisty daughter. He even locked her inside the family's walled compound with security guards at the gate, but she crawled over the wall. Colonel Rowe and Annie continued to see each other against the claims of common sense, family loyalties, moral strictures and, for Rowe, military duty and common decency. They were obsessed with each other. Colonel Rowe's escalating romantic crisis was unfortunately caught in the web of a much larger crisis, the rising opposition to Diem by civilian and military leaders, the violent repression by Nhu's security forces, and the escalating protest by high school and college students who staged massive protest rallies in the summer of 1963. Annie, her older brother and younger sister were actively involved. She and the colonel argued loudly and bitterly over Annie's politics. He argued, rightly it turned out, that she was putting herself and her whole family at risk. Monasteries were being trashed and schools were being invaded by Nhu's security thugs. Opposition leaders were being tortured and killed or dumped in underground tiger cages. When Buddhist bonzes torched themselves in protest on Saigon's main streets, Madame Nhu dismissed them as barbecued monks.

Colonel Rowe should have dropped Annie Binh like a gob of burning napalm, but as with adhesive napalm he simply couldn't do it, physically, emotionally or otherwise. Instead, he turned for help to Major Trang to get Annie away from the violence in Saigon, the influence of her siblings and the clutches of her father. The colonel had Trang, supposedly a family friend of the Binhs, spirit Annie out of Saigon on his twice weekly liaison trips.

On at least one occasion, after taking fire coming into My Tho, Major Trang tried to warn Colonel Rowe about another kind of danger. "Sir," he said, "I feel I must warn you that we're putting Miss Binh's life at risk."

"I suppose so," Colonel Rowe replied, "but wouldn't her life be in even greater danger in Saigon?"

"At least there she'd be with her family," Trang responded.

"From what I understand about her family's politics, I think she's safer here," Rowe said.

"Her family's politics is what I fear might cause trouble for you and your mission here, colonel."

"I appreciate your concern, major, but given the circumstances, I think Annie is better off away from Saigon." The colonel paused for a moment. "If you can't handle the assignment, I'll have to get someone else."

When Colonel Rowe looked at me, Major Trang flushed. He replied rather stiffly, "Sir, I was just trying to be cautious."

"Thank you, major," Colonel Rowe said and turned away with a quick salute.

Once, just after Major Trang and Annie left for the return trip to Saigon, Colonel Rowe asked me flat out, "You got a girl, Parker?"

"Yes. Well, not really, sir," I said.

"Never had a girl in Vietnam you were goo-goo crazy over, a red-hot *mama san*?"

"No. I guess not, sir. I mean I met a couple of girls I really liked but . . ."

"What if you were really stuck on a girl, I mean you really loved her and she turned out to be a VC?"

"I'd have to toss her, sir, like a live grenade."

"What if she was pregnant with your kid?"

"That's different," I said, "I don't know . . ."

"You mean you wouldn't turn in the goddamn enemy, Parker, someone who might get us all fucking killed?"

When the colonel saw I was hawing around he kind of grinned and said, "You want the SOP on this, Parker?"

"Yes sir," I said.

"You fuck her first and then shoot her." The colonel's laugh was hollow and forced, like he didn't really mean it, like it was a cover for his own problems.

The trips to and from My Tho must have been hell for Annie because she always arrived looking puffy-eyed and distraught. Before meeting Colonel Rowe, she'd freshen up and change her face. Major Trang's persona changed even more. He was sullen and brutally short with Annie when Rowe wasn't around, but when the colonel showed up he was all respect and "yes sir!"

Even worse, the ARVN officers stared boldly at Annie as they would with a street whore and sniggered behind their salutes to Colonel Rowe as if he were growing a cuckold's horn. My confusion was compounded by twice having seen Major Trang escorting an elegantly dressed and smiling Annie to dinner dances at the MACV officer's club while I was on courier duty. At the time I simply marked it as an escort service Trang was performing for Colonel Rowe. Something didn't add up, but it was not a specialist's place to raise questions— not when relationships were so casual anyway. I may have sensed something was wrong, but I didn't know what was wrong or what I could do about it.

I could help, apparently, by playing chess with Annie, a game at which she excelled but for which the colonel had little time. "While you're waiting around for me, Parker," he said, "play her victim. She's unbeatable—a real killer." I was glad to play Annie's willing victim just to be near her and maybe rescue her from Major Trang. I was playing with a ghost. Annie's loss of weight accented her fine facial bones and luminous eyes. Her skin, beaded with perspiration, seemed almost transparent. She moved the pieces silently, not even looking at me or the small chessboard, but she still beat me easily. She looked so miserable and sadly beautiful I couldn't help asking, "Miss Binh, can't I help you? Maybe if you talk with Colonel Rowe he'd let me drive you to and from Saigon?"

"Look at your pawn," she said. "Any move you make you will lose. That pawn is me and all Vietnamese to you Americans. In the political game of chess we are the pawns."

"Driving you back and forth to Saigon would be no big thing," I said. "It's not part of some big political game."

"Yes, it is," Annie said. "You don't understand. It's part of a much bigger game I can't seem to escape."

"Is love also just a game?" I asked.

"Yes, and there, too, I am the pawn."

"I'm sorry," I said.

"And I too," she said, "much more than you."

For a brief interim, while Major Trang was away on special assignment, I served as Annie's driver. She told me she'd been named for Annie Oakley after her father had seen the American musical in Paris and loved it. So whenever we started the dangerous drive from My Tho to Saigon I always asked, "Annie got your gun?" Invariably she laughed and that brief moment was enough to make my day.

But nothing could change the ugly situation that seemed to doom Annie's relationship with her American lover. She was bored and unhappy. Rowe was frustrated by the factional politics that consumed his time and efforts. The two of them quarreled incessantly (with Annie a precocious student of American profanity) whenever Rowe could tear himself away from the crisis that was sucking him into the maelstrom of contradictory American policy over President Diem. The American generals at MACV were ordering Rowe to secure General Duong's support for Diem; the Ambassador (who secretly supported the rebel generals) pressured Rowe to guarantee Duong's neutrality in case of a coup.

Colonel Rowe was like a dog chasing its own tail. Because he was going in circles, trapped by opposing policies in a vortex of violence, Colonel Rowe failed to check on Annie. By the time he'd got around to it, she'd been arrested and was being held in custody by Nhu's security police. As with all violent explosions in Saigon, events moved with terrible swiftness. Before Colonel Rowe could intervene, Annie was dead—a victim of murder or suicide.

During those hectic hours before the coup, Colonel Rowe was on the phone continuously. Because Trang was tied up in Saigon, Annie hitched a ride to My Tho on her own. The colonel was furious and snubbed Annie, which made her angry and frustrated. "Talk, talk, talk—with everyone in Vietnam but me. Why do I come here? Why do I come here?"

I'm sure the colonel was even more frustrated, judging by the cursing and banging of fists that followed each phone call. Eventually Annie's whining brought the colonel barging out of the office door, tightlipped and fuming. He grabbed Annie by the arm and took her into a corner where he lectured her in tones a father might use with an unruly daughter. Annie glared at him and jerked away. "No! No! No!" she spat. "You promised me, never again." The colonel grabbed for her arm and she slapped him hard. The colonel just as quickly slapped her back and turned on his heel. "Parker," he ordered, "take her back to Saigon."

Annie cried all the way into Saigon. By the time we neared her family's compound in Cholon, it was already dark.

"Stop!" she ordered.

I stopped but kept the motor running.

"Miss Binh," I said, "this is really dangerous. Colonel Rowe gave me strict orders to never stop. Never. It's putting your life at risk."

"Give me a cigarette," she said. So I shook a Marlboro out of a pack I kept handy for Colonel Rowe and lit it for her. She sucked in so deeply I could see her beautiful wet face reflected in the burning ash. She was still crying.

"I'm sorry," she said, "It's so impossible to be with my family. My parents treat me like a whore. I feel so rejected by Catlin, too. He's lied to me so many times. I've suffered through our painful relationship because he promised me so much, a future with him in America. Now it's going; all the promises, all the plans, slipping away. Just when I need him most, he's slipping away."

I wanted Annie to stop crying. I wanted to take her home. "Miss Binh," I said, "I'm certain Colonel Rowe is trying to do what's best. He's an honorable man."

Then Annie laughed in a bitter, cold way that chilled and frightened me. "Honorable!" Annie spit the word out like it was a curse, something ugly and dirty. She held the lighted cigarette between our faces so she could look into my eyes. "You Americans love that word, don't you? Death before dishonor. Peace with honor. Medal of honor. So many empty words." She pulled heavily on the cigarette. "Look at me. Tell me—you must know— tell me how many times your colonel has dishonored me."

I turned away from Annie because I could not betray my commanding officer. It was a point of honor. "I know Colonel Rowe loves you," I said. "He loves you more than anything in the world. I know that much." I was speaking for myself.

Annie had finally stopped crying. She stubbed out the cigarette and then quite suddenly her fingers were behind my neck pulling me to her. She kissed me long and hard and desperately, like I'd never been kissed in my life. Then she pushed me away. "I would take you as a lover just to spite him. But it would be wrong for him, for you, for me. That's why I have to turn for help to a man I hate. Tell that to your honorable colonel!"

Annie was out of the jeep and into the darkness before I could stop her. For the moment I was stunned, immobilized by Annie's unexpected kiss. Then a car careened past. Someone shouted. I ground the gears and burned rubber. An explosion behind me rocked the jeep and splattered cobblestones against the rear end. I drove madly through dark streets and alleyways looking for Annie but she had vanished into the night behind the walls of her family's estate, so I made myself believe. As it happened, I would never see Annie again, but the taste of her kiss, the sharp teeth and burning tongue, the bitter sweetness of it all would be with me forever.

By the time I'd returned to My Tho the coup was already underway, the army was in revolt. Our compound reflected the tensions outside. Americans blamed Vietnamese for the crisis, Vietnamese blamed Americans. Both groups fingered rifles and pistols. I felt like I was in Tombstone, Vietnam closing in on the OK Corral. I started looking for cover. I slept on a cot in the HQ hugging an M-16 while the colonel fumed and drank the night away in his office.

By midmorning the next day, Colonel Rowe was desperate to find Annie. All of the phone lines were jammed or had been cut. We could get nothing by radio telephone either. I could hear the colonel stomping and cursing inside his office, getting steadily drunker. About every five or ten minutes he'd burst out of his office shouting.

"Where the fuck is Major Trang? He should be here with Annie!"

If an ARVN came into the headquarters, the colonel put his hand on his forty-five and cursed him from the room. "Fucking faggots, I'd like to shoot them all!"

At 1600 hours we received a message by radio telephone that President Diem and Ngo Dinh Nhu had been arrested, and further that General "Big" Minh was in command of the government.

Two hours later Major Trang arrived by jeep accompanied by two security policemen.

"Major Trang, what the hell's been going on? Where's Annie?" Colonel Rowe was blubbering drunk.

Major Trang, no longer intimidated, announced, "I've been appointed deputy provisional security chief with the temporary rank of colonel. Naturally, I've been extremely busy. I have a packet for you!"

He handed Colonel Rowe a large sealed envelope and then moved closer to speak quietly, inaudibly.

The colonel's cry was wrenched out of him in terrifying staccato. "No! No! No! No, goddammit, no!"

The colonel put his hand on his forty-five. For a moment I thought he might shoot Major Trang. Instead he glared at the ARVN security police, swept at them with his arm and cursed them as a fucking pack of fairies and sodomites!

Colonel Rowe crashed into his office and slammed the door. Major Trang walked outside to confer with some ARVN officers. I remember sitting upright, feeling a terrible chill and stiffness, almost as if it were possible to feel rigor mortis setting in. Then a single shot cracked through the building like a whiplash. Major Trang rushed in with his security aides, pushed me outside and secured the building.

Someone told me later that I walked around and around inside the fence of the compound like a zombie walking guard. Did I dream of several hundred Vietnamese pressing against the fence, peering through cracks, shouting insults, trying to force their way in? That's what I remember. Then an American officer grabbed my arm and shook me roughly.

"Loosen up, soldier, get hold of yourself. We need your help."

Two jeep loads of American CID officers had arrived with a meat wagon. They conferred with Trang and the Vietnamese and then interviewed each American one-on-one. A tough, jowly captain questioned me like I was some convict. Pure intimidation.

"You understand, corporal, what you saw here today never happened?"

"Yes sir."

"It's a closed book. You never ever gonna tell a fuckin' soul—not even your priest, favorite prostitute, or Jesus Christ himself. Understand?"

"Yes sir."

"Colonel Rowe died while fighting in the line of duty."

"Yes sir."

The captain started to leave the hooch and then turned suddenly. He was crying. "Goddammit," he cried, "a fucking tragedy took place here today, a fucking tragedy. We're up to our ears in a mountain of shit and Rowe got in over his head. We're all in over our heads."

"Yes sir," I said.

"Shit!" he yelled and slammed the door. "Shit! Shit! Shit!"

"Sir," I said.

"Yes, corporal."

"Do you know what happened to Miss Binh? You see, I knew her and . . ."

"That's restricted intelligence, corporal; you're out of line."

"Yes sir," I said, "I'm sorry, sir."

"Oh, hell," the captain said, "all I could see were headless bodies without hands, dozens of them. No fingerprints. No identification. Some shitty business. Nhu's finale."

I threw up before the captain was out the door.

Two weeks later I took a long overdue R&R to Honolulu where I encountered the CID captain in the Moana hotel bar. I should say he encountered or recognized me. I thought I could escape Vietnam in the Victorian hotel filled mostly with nostalgic seniors reliving their honeymoons and young Japanese newlyweds, but on this Saturday everyone was outside in the spacious *lanai* facing Waikiki listening to Webly Edwards and Hawaii Calls. My luck. Only the captain and I were drinking at the indoor bar. He was also on R&R but was at the moment in strategic withdrawal following a firefight with his wife.

"Can't fucking communicate with anyone in the world, including my wife. The stinking mess in Vietnam has screwed my head around, totally mind-fucked me. Civilians—Jesus! We couldn't help our friends, but we save the asses of sleazeballs like your buddy, Major Trang. Got him and his floozy broad out of the country with a bundle of money and a one-way ticket to the good ol' US of A. Gimme yer tired, yer poor, blah, blah, blah, shuttling assholes like Trang to the land of the free—shit! Ten years we gonna be the land of the gooks I betcha . . ."

Trang was no buddy of mine; he *was* the enemy. I ditched the captain before he finished his drunken litany. I didn't understand the politics at the time; I only knew Colonel Rowe and Annie Binh had been sucked into something dirty and vicious and it destroyed them. I knew Major Trang was somehow involved, and others I didn't know about. I wanted to bury it all and I thought I had until I encountered the past again in the person of ex-Major Trang.

I called Major Trang the day before my scheduled tutorial and asked if we could meet at a Brits pub across the street from the Copy Cat. I figured it would take several beers to loosen ex-Major Trang's tongue. I couldn't wait. I popped the question before we'd finished our first round.

"You are Major Trang, aren't you? I know you are Major Trang."

He smiled. "Wrong. Colonel Trang. That was my final rank, awarded just before the coup."

Temporary, Major Trang, temporary, as I remember. His coolness upset me for some reason.

"Well," I said, "I knew you as Major Trang; also as Batman because of your ears."

Trang smiled and started to light a cigarette, remembered the no-smoking ordinance and dry sucked it. "I heard that more than once," he said.

"Do you remember Colonel Rowe and the girl—a young woman named Annie?"

"Very well, yes, very well indeed, and now I can place you as well, Colonel Rowe's driver, a specialist, I think."

It was my turn to smile. "Wrong," I said, "sergeant, I made sergeant. Do you recall the events surrounding the deaths of Colonel Rowe and Annie Binh?" I asked.

"As if it happened yesterday."

"Do you mind, then, if I ask you some personal questions?" I asked. "I want to clear up a few things if I can. They've been troubling me for twenty-five years."

Trang shook his head in disbelief. "That's a long time. If I can help you I will, of course, but you must understand many of the events were unclear and confusing to me."

You said as if it happened yesterday, Major Trang.

"Understood," I said. That was my first hint that I might not get the full story. "The package that you handed to Colonel Rowe after Annie's death," I said, "the thing that pushed him over the edge into suicide—what did it contain? It must have been pretty potent stuff."

"I didn't know," Trang said. "It was sealed."

"But after Colonel Rowe shot himself, didn't you . . . ?"

"Open it? No. Maybe you don't remember. He had burned all of the papers."

Yes, I remember, Major Trang, I remember you rushed in with aides and sealed off the colonel's quarters for thirty minutes before the American CID arrived.

I didn't want to close off Trang with accusations. I needed more. I needed to draw him out with a new tack. I threw out an untested theory, a fish lure into Trang's stream of consciousness.

"How about the rumor that Annie was being used as a pawn, that Ngo Dinh Nhu wanted to use her as a hostage to force her father's support for Diem or to ensure General Duong's support of Diem by pressuring Rowe?"

"That's all speculation," answered Trang. "Annie's father was supposedly a neutralist and a moderate. He opposed Diem, but he liked the generals even less. I think he was terribly upset by the behavior of his children, the son who'd gone over to the NLF and even more with the daughter's sordid affair with Colonel Rowe. That's why he eventually committed suicide, or so I've heard. You may draw your own conclusions."

"About the packet you delivered to Colonel Rowe," I said, "you must have had some idea what it contained."

"The sealed documents were given to me by the ARVN intelligence chief to be delivered to Colonel Rowe."

"And you had no idea what the message or documents were about?" I persisted.

"No, certainly not. My opinion is that they contained evidence of Annie's connection with the NLF, and that Rowe himself had been compromised by his affair."

"You mean she was a spy?"

"Exactly."

"But surely as a top intelligence officer and knowing Miss Binh, you must have suspected her long before her arrest. Didn't you take her into custody?"

"No, I was trying to save her and her family during the crisis. I was returning Annie to her father's residence from the university when Nhu's security police intercepted us and arrested her. I was outnumbered. There was nothing I could do."

Major Trang, you are one slippery bastard, but you slipped up; I'm going to nail you yet.

"Look, *Colonel* Trang, I don't want to invade your personal life and your private affairs, but I have to ask this question. I heard on more than one occasion that you and Miss Binh were promised in marriage by your families. Is this true?"

"Not quite," Trang answered. "The marriage arrangement involved my brother, a captain in the infantry who lost an eye, two limbs, and his manhood fighting in the Highlands."

"I would suppose you and your family were very upset with Annie's behavior," I said.

"To answer your question, yes. I was as angry as hell. To me she was nothing more than a prostitute, worse than a whore because she was selling her body *and* her soul, willing to abandon her family obligations and cultural traditions for a sexual adventure."

"Body and soul," I repeated the phrase. "No wonder you were so hard on her. I remember when she arrived with you in My Tho, her eyes were puffed and red like she'd been crying."

"I was too easy on her," Trang snapped angrily. "I tried to warn her away from politics and getting in over her head, but she wouldn't listen."

Trang was shaking and angry, but I couldn't let him off the hook. "How did you survive?" I asked. "Weren't you one of Nhu's boys, part of the inner circle?"

"No!" Trang exploded, "I was simply an army intelligence officer doing my job." Then he lowered his voice, "If you really want to know, I was in the armored personnel carrier when Diem and Nhu were executed. I tried to save their lives as the Americans wanted, but the other officers prevailed and shot them both."

"What about Annie?" I asked. "You must have known how she died."

"No one really knew. The bodies could not be identified but all of them showed traces of strychnine. She apparently took poison like the others. Nhu's security men probably forced it down her. It was karma. Fate—that's what we Vietnamese believe."

"You don't think she was a victim?"

"We were all victims," Trang replied, "victims of American policy, government and military corruption, personalism, history. I can't feel sorry for her, or for him. Their deeds determined their destiny. Karma."

At that moment I could have killed Major Trang. I wanted to kill him, but I realized he was right. In a certain sense we were all victims, even Americans who felt themselves victimized by a war they didn't understand. But with victims there must also be executioners, and few Americans wanted to face that reality. Neither did the Vietnamese, and certainly not Major Trang.

"How about the family?" I asked. "Did any of them survive? I'm thinking of returning to Vietnam. I'd like to talk with them."

"I hear through the Vietnamese grapevine that Annie Binh's sister teaches in a new private college in Ho Chi Minh City called the New Freedom College." Trang's laugh was hard and bitter. "The New Freedom College," he repeated. "That's a laugh—or maybe irony, as you Americans say." Then he added a final thought. "I wouldn't wonder if her brother, if he survived the war, isn't as important in the new regime as his father was in the old."

After my encounter with ex-Major Trang, I knew for certain he was covering up. Trang had not returned Annie to her home that fateful night. I had. Trang had forgotten that I sometimes chauffeured Annie in his absence. I also realized Trang's hatred for Annie was sufficiently deep and bitter enough for him to have killed her. That he had lied about the marriage arrangement was almost certain.

I now had the final scenario in place. Trang had planned his revenge carefully, making his move at the moment of national crisis when those who might have intervened on Annie's behalf would be tangled in conflicts. I closed my eyes to reconstruct the final night: Trang lurking in the darkness for Annie, waiting with the evidence that would put her in the clutches of the security police who would torture and kill her, waiting in the murder car that had swerved to kill me. I also realized, willy nilly, that I had been an unwitting participant in Annie's torture and death. I might have, should have, saved her on that terrible night.

I arrived at the Copy Cat a few minutes early for my tutorial with Major Trang. I wanted to sharpen my pronunciations with his kids, with whom I felt more at ease. As I walked in, the laughter froze as if someone had opened an icebox.

"Hey guys," I said, "what gives?"

The oldest, Thom, mumbled something about being too busy to help me with my Vietnamese.

"Okay," I said, "that's cool, but you guys were just standing around; I don't understand."

"You don't understand what?" The voice behind me was clipped and business-like. It was Major Trang with two buddies, ex-ARVN I assumed, also in leather jackets and porkpie hats.

"You don't understand what?" Major Trang repeated his question like an army officer dressing down a subordinate.

"Man, I am really confused about what's going on here," I said.

"What's going on here is a business," Major Trang snapped. "It's not a social gathering place or a forum for political discussions."

"Okay, okay, I understand that. I wasn't—I mean you suggested the tutoring—"

Major Trang interrupted, "If you have business here, photocopy or fax, fine; state your business. Otherwise, leave."

The two guys in leather jackets stepped forward. I left in a hurry.

Later that week I received a letter from Major Trang (we had exchanged addresses during the first language session):

> *Mr. Parker:*
>   *I want to first apologize for overreacting at the Copy Cat, but I think you know how freely young people act without a tight rein. I have several Copy Cats in the Bay area. I need to*

ensure that everything is strictly business. I meant no discourtesy to you.

Secondly, the Vietnamese Council of this county, of which I am a member, thinks it advisable that you not inquire into the death of Annie Binh. Your investigation will only bring more pain and suffering to the few remaining family members not destroyed by the war. In light of this resolution, we ask you not to contact Binh family members in Vietnam. If you persist in your venture, we are prepared to discuss this with you further. If we fail in our efforts here, we have contacts in Vietnam who are ready to assist you.

I include a letter for my brother in Hue, who I think will answer your questions more than adequately.

Finally, because of pressing business commitments, I will unfortunately not be able to continue our tutorial.

Sincerely,

Colonel Nam Van Trang

If Major Trang had not dismissed me so brusquely in his shop and then followed his heavy-handed brush-off with a letter of crudely veiled threats, I might not have pursued my probe further. The Vietnamese Council thing sounded phony, like a bullshit intimidation number.

Trang's actions and attitude, especially his letter, changed my decision. I was angry and energized, like a tired fighting bull who gets jabbed in the ass with barbed banderillos. I would not be satisfied now until I returned to Vietnam and talked with Trang's brother and Annie's sister and discovered what Trang was still trying to cover up and why.

Karma is the Joker

I felt like I'd been slapped in the face, so curt and coldly efficient were the customs officials in Hanoi's Hoi Bai airport. As part of an officially approved friendship delegation, I expected more courteous treatment. But hell, I reasoned, why expect a generous reception from a paranoid regime that had imprisoned half of its southern population in re-education centers for more than a decade. Then came the first of many surprise flip-flops in our encounters with Vietnamese. Outside the customs building we were suddenly bathed in the sunshine smile and solar personality of our grinning guide-interpreter, Vinh, a chubby, hand-pumping Elvis look-alike with a soaring ducktail pompadour. His cornball humor and cackling laughter would serve throughout our tour as a constant antidote to Vietnam's humorless bureaucrats.

After a week of nonstop meetings with civic and public officials in Hanoi, enhanced by back-cracking drives to rural villages, the long train ride from Hanoi to Hue should have been a recovery. It wasn't. Our sleeping accommodations with narrowly spaced hardwood bunks seemed designed to inflict the maximum amount of pain on my recently dislocated back. By the time we arrived in Hue, I must have limped up and down ten miles of train aisles. I had expected Hue to be barely rising from the rubble—so totally devastated had it been by the war—but the former capital had been completely rebuilt with added luxury hotels. Its tarnished tombs and temples, scattered along the Perfume River in moldering collapse, were being restored by Japanese joint venture companies eager to seduce Vietnam into its new co-prosperity sphere. But as in Hanoi, my mind was elsewhere, recycling the past, trying to reconstruct events that seemed more contradictory and confusing with time. I wondered how I would be received by my prospective informants. Would Trang's brother hide behind a screen of Buddhist obfuscation or simply give me a blunt refusal. When I finally gave him a fearful call, he responded with a cheery, "Yes, yes, tomorrow, 2:00 P.M."

With the letter for Trang's brother in hand, I walked across the Trang Tien bridge from our hotel to the west side of the river, south past the Citadel, site of the most ferocious fighting of the war and on to the Thien Mu pagoda and temple where Trang's brother served as one of several Buddhist bonzes (monks). I wondered how many of the rust-colored splotches on the ancient walls of the Citadel were badges of American blood and whether I'd walked over the mass grave of two thousand Vietnamese slaughtered by vengeful VC. The ghosts of war seemed everywhere present. The seven-story pagoda appeared to lean like the Tower of Pisa, but, since it had been standing since the time of the Chinese, I risked walking under its shadow to the temple and living quarters behind. I saw under a shed the Austin car used to transport the monk Thich Quang to the site of his 1963 self-immolation in Saigon. Photos of that horrifying protest against Diem's repressive policies seared through the world's consciousness and conscience like burning phosphorus.

Trang's brother was expecting me. He arrived on a crutch wiping his one good hand on the stump of his left. He'd been weeding in the vegetable garden. "Good afternoon," he said in carefully chopped English. "I receive your message; have been expecting you. Please come." The bonze shook the dirt crumbs from his frayed saffron robe, but the pungent aroma of mulch laced with manure remained. The monks' living quarters stood behind the temple and off to the side facing a large vegetable and flower garden. The dormitory was a simple box structure of unpainted wood with screens all around. The cells were separated by three-quarter-high walls so that the voices of other monks drifted in and out in tonal Vietnamese. We sat lotus-like on ragged mats in the unfurnished cell. A small shelf held all of the monks' possessions. A calligraphic scroll and a single flower in a small jar provided the only embellishment. A novice served us a rich, frothy green tea.

"Delicious," I said, "like nothing I've had before."

"Yes, come from tender top leaf, very special, healthy," explained the bonze.

He was much thinner than his brother and had sharper features, but he wore the family ears. His skin was weathered brown from working outdoors. His blind eye was simply an empty socket and he used a crutch to hobble about rather nimbly. He said he had learned English during his long hospitalization during the war, but it still sounded like pidgin.

The bonze rubbed his shaved head, pointed to my flat-top and grinned. "You wanna be bonze; already got head start."

I laughed, handed him Trang's letter and answered, "I'll think about it."

As the bonze read his brother's letter I tried to describe the three children, their work, and some sense of their life in the U.S., but it was as if I were describing life on Mars.

"Nothing about wife," the bonze said.

"I've never met her," I said, "but judging her by the children, she must be a wonderful woman."

"My brother, I think, is big success in America. He was, as you say, a go-getter."

"And you," I said, "You had no desire to go to America with your brother?"

The bonze laughed easily. "No," he said, "Buddhists (he winked with his good eye) believe in cessation of desire." He paused. "I want to see my brother and his family, but I belong in Vietnam."

"Even under the communists?" I asked.

"Even under communists, yes, but Renovation will bring many changes. Maybe my brother and family will visit me some day."

"I sincerely hope so," I said. "I never thought I'd ever see Vietnam again."

We sat in silence as the bonze finished his tea and then lit a cigarette. "But," he said, "you come to ask question about war."

"Yes, I have," I said. "I hope you will not find it too painful."

The bonze smiled, "Perhaps our talk will ease pain. To heal we must confront source of pain."

"Yes, I believe that," I said. "I want to find the truth about a matter involving your brother and the Binh family."

"And death of Annie Binh." The bonze stumped out his cigarette.

"Yes," I said, "and the circumstances surrounding her death, because it involved my commanding officer, Colonel Rowe."

"And my brother."

"Yes, your brother," I said. "I want to know if it is true that he was promised in marriage to Annie Binh."

The bonze didn't answer at first. He sat very still and closed his eyes. He rubbed his forehead and motioned for a cigarette. I shook one out and lit it for him. Still he said nothing. He cleared his throat. "Difficult question," he said. "Long time before American war, before French war, both fathers are students in Paris. Because they are close friends they make agreement: children of two families will marry. As children we understand. We talk and joke sometime."

"But who was promised to whom?" I asked.

The bonze shook his head. "It was family agreement, not personal."

"But I understood that Annie was promised to your brother."

The bonze replied, "Not really. Older brother have strong character, how you say, ego? He want Annie for himself. He want to possess her, but Annie fight back. She also have strong mind."

"So Trang simply assumed a relationship that did not exist," I said.

The bonze exhaled a series of smoke rings that floated to the ceiling. "There is family understanding, very important to Vietnamese. My brother very jealous, possessive. I know, because I too love Annie. She always daring and wild, different from mos' Vietnamese girl."

"And how about the sister?" I asked. "Where does she fit in?"

The bonze laughed. "I believe Americans call her jilted lover? She is madly in love with my brother before she get so involve in politics. Then she hate us because we are in military."

"Did your fathers maintain their friendship and family ties?"

"No," the bonze replied, "complete separation, like enemies even."

"Why?" I asked. "What caused it?"

"Politics, always politics." The bonze snuffed his cigarette. "My father support military as best hope for stable government. Chancellor Binh, no. He hate military in politics."

"You knew," I said, "that Annie had taken an American colonel as her lover."

"Yes. My brother visit me in hospital. He tell me."

"Did you know about the circumstances of Annie's death?"

"No, I only hear. I am long time in hospital. Brother must flee country. This letter is first contact since war."

"Did you ever question your brother's actions or motives?" I asked.

"Yes, I think he arrange my transfer to combat unit so I am out of his way."

"No, I mean did you question your brother's actions in regard to Annie's death?"

"Yes, I blame him for not protecting her. I think he can do something. Wrong of me, I know, but I am very upset."

"From what you've said, your brother must have been insanely jealous of the American colonel."

"Yes, yes," the bonze replied, "as I would be. But I know my brother will give his life to save Annie, not let her die if he can save her. I believe that."

"What if she had been a courier, a spy for the NLF?" I asked. "Her brother had gone over to the VC, at least your brother thought so, and he was a highly-placed intelligence officer."

"Something you not know," the bonze said. "Annie's brother is double agent. My brother is main contact, he tell me."

"Then Annie must have known that as well."

"Perhaps. But everything is secret, undercover. So much I never know. I am young, train to believe and obey. Now I think NLF is different from NVA, more democratic. I serve in re-education camp with many VC. They are angry and bitter about end of war, hate cadre from North."

At this point a tiny novice, barefoot, with shaved head and saffron robe, entered the room, put his arms around the neck of the bonze and whispered into his ear. How different was this child of peace, I thought, from the tough street urchins of wartime Saigon who chain-smoked cigarette butts, pimped for their sisters and tossed hand grenades into GI bars.

The bonze rose with surprising ease on his one good leg. "Time for meditation," he said. "Even monks live by clock." Then the bonze surprised me. He came stiffly to attention, saluted smartly and snapped, "Captain Trang requests permission to leave, sir!" He grinned. He held my fingers in a hand as calloused as leather, bowed and then hobbled off quickly. I sat in stunned silence, not so much at the bonze's unexpected theatrics as with his use of the word "captain," the way he said it. I repeated the word as buried memories brought flashbacks of a Captain Trang, as I'd known the major during my first months in My Tho, a Captain Trang who was at times soft-spoken, considerate, smiling. I recalled how much more at ease Annie seemed—relaxed, laughing, even exuberant. At the time I thought Trang's changing moods reflected the pressures and dangers of the war. Now I wondered. The bonze had briefly mentioned his disastrous transfer which he thought was probably engineered by Trang. Had Trang been using his brother as a double so he could pursue his devilish machinations and then, in a paroxysm of jealousy, had him transferred to a fighting unit and probable death? Or was I simply concocting scenarios I wanted to believe out of my imagination or mental confusion in trying to reconstruct the past? I felt like a frustrated kid forcing wrong-sized pieces into a difficult puzzle.

The conversation with the bonze provided new and important insights into the character of Major Trang. The revelation that Annie's brother may have been a double agent was a stunner, but that, of course, was Trang's version. The bonze verified the existence of a verbal marriage agreement and the subsequent splintering of the two families, disagreeing only on who was promised to whom. I accepted the bonze's version. Then I realized how clever Trang had been in steering me to his brother. He knew his brother would be in general agreement with his version of events simply because the brother's knowledge of particulars would be so fuzzy. He'd either been away from Saigon fighting in the Highlands or isolated in a hospital during the crises in Saigon.

For several nights, in fact, through several cities, I was plagued by splitting headaches and dreams that left me exhausted. Most nights I was at a water puppet show, similar to one we'd attended in Hanoi where the stage is a lake and the puppets are manipulated by underwater mechanisms controlled by hidden puppet masters. The puppets in my dream, as real as the characters from My Tho, were swimming in fear and confusion inside a ring of fire. Some nights the puppets would be fluid and amoeba-like, as sloppy as objects in a Dali painting, with weird Picasso figures and faces, changing and interchanging body parts until I didn't know who was whom, except for the puppet master, Major Trang. Only Major Trang popped to the surface and escaped the ring of fire, laughing in a coarse, cackling rhythm like some diabolical *Doppelganger* laughing in my face.

An unexpected encounter with the American Vietnamese dancer, Sybil Patterson, probably added to my confusion. She had become a shadow presence, virtually invisible after she failed to trace her relatives in Hue. I overheard Betty complain about her absences from group activities to Phil. "She claims to be a practitioner of Zen and insists she needs to spend time in retreat. *Zazen*, she calls it."

After my meeting with Trang's brother, I sat in the shade of a temple pool to reflect and softly chant a mantra I'd learned from a Vietnamese friend in

America. A burst of laughter, resonant as a temple bell was followed by a challenge: "Do you know what you're chanting? It's a profane song that was chanted by soldiers on the Ho Chi Minh Trail!" Sybil had been hiding in the shadows.

After my surprise encounter at the temple pool, Sybil somehow got mixed into my images and dreams of Annie Binh, an alien presence intruding into the private room reserved for Annie and me.

I arrived in Saigon in a troubled state of mind. The sights and smells and suffocating heat of Ho Chi Minh City (Saigon) were so familiar that it was almost like coming home: the pleasant aromas of flower and vegetable markets, of sidewalk cafes, sucking in the rotting stench and varietal mix of effluents, rasping for breath in the heat and monoxide. But the shaded Saigon streets I once knew had been raped of their trees by Rome plows as a military measure after I'd left, and the brassy street whores who sprouted in the rotting political mulch either had disappeared or were servicing in the shadows.

But central Saigon, with its spacious boulevards, was as beautiful as Paris, more impressive because it was so clean and fresh-looking. New coffee shops, boutiques and bakeries were geared to the recent surge of French tourists who must have felt very much at home. I bought a double chocolate ice cream cone on Le Loi Boulevard, strolled the four-block length of Nguyen Hue, and turned left along the Saigon River to the former Majestic Hotel. The fifth-floor restaurant provided a marvelous view of the waterfront and city below. I drank three Singapore-Saigon Slings in slow sips and then wandered back along the river to the Nguyen Tat Thanh Bridge. I had just leaned out to get a bird's-eye view of the sampans and barges below when someone rammed me so hard from behind that my ribs cracked. The railing nearly broke me in half, but it saved me. By the time I'd got my breath, my short, stocky attacker had jumped on a Honda and disappeared into traffic.

"Fuck you!" I yelled after him. "Fuck you!" I hadn't come six thousand miles to be intimidated by a two-bit henchman of the ex-ARVN Tong or Yakuza, or whoever they were.

Through an older academic friend of the Volsteds who ran a crafts rehab center for street teens, I was able to locate Professor Truy Duc Binh, who taught sociology and social welfare at the New Freedom College. The new college was housed in an old two-story military barracks near the former *Cercle Sportique*. I pushed up a narrow stairwell through a stream of slender girls in flowing *ao dais* and skinny guys with sharp elbows. They responded to my "*Chao* (hi!)" with "Hello, how are you. I am fine, thank you."

Truy Duc Binh was closing on fifty and looked it. She was wearing dark slacks and a white blouse. Her face was tanned with wrinkles fanning off of her eyes and mouth. She wore no makeup, not even to cover the scar that slashed across her neck and seemed to enter an ear that was partially gone. But her dark eyes were lively and she smiled easily. Tea was already waiting.

Madame Binh's office had been freshly painted a battleship gray which she had enhanced with bright yellow curtains in a paisley print. The wall behind

Madame Binh's desk consisted of bare shelves except for a dozen books and several stacks of paper. An official photo of Ho Chi Minh and a Vietnamese flag completed the decor, along with a few small desk photos.

"I like your curtains," I said.

Madame Binh laughed. "I made them from a childhood dress I found in a chest of old throwaways. The curtains remind me of a happier time."

My first thought was that this is what Annie might have looked like had she lived. Then a second image intruded—or rather a series of images, as on a police computer screen where a person's face is made older or younger. Madame Binh's face was progressively transmogrified into the image of the girl I had once seen laughing and talking with Annie outside the university, the girl who was Annie's sister. Then another image intruded, the beautiful, stylish young woman I saw at a distance being escorted by Major Trang to the MACV reception, the woman I thought was Annie but might have been her sister.

Madame Binh flattened a hand high overhead. "I'd forgotten how tall you Americans are. Please sit down so I can look you in the eye."

We talked for a while about her work at the college, about the problem of obtaining up-to-date teaching materials, the lack of resources and the enormous difficulties of opening Saigon's first private college since the war. I took notes and promised to have a close friend who was a sociologist at Chico State University ship her a box of books and journals in her field.

"Cai told me the real reason for your visit," she said. "You must know it's a painful remembrance for me." She rose to close the shutters against a sudden squall. From outside the shouts and squeals of students running for cover filled the room.

"I understand," I said. "I want you to know how much I appreciate your willingness to share a past that is also painful for me."

"Let me tell you a bit about myself so you'll sense how much I know or don't know about those times." Madame Binh coughed and paused to sip some tea. She took several deep breaths. "Asthma. This Saigon smog will eventually do me in."

"I'm used to it," I said. "I live in smoggy California."

"You know," she continued, "I was in the university when Annie was murdered. My parents moved to France to live with Mama's father's family after the coup. As a neutralist and anti-militarist my father's life was in danger." She paused to light a cigarette. "Ironic, isn't it? My father and brother were on opposing sides, yet both of them would have been killed by the military regime. To complicate things we had several cousins serving in ARVN."

"What happened to your family after the war—if it's not too painful?"

"Father got so depressed in Paris that he committed suicide, not only because of Annie's death but because he witnessed the death of *his* Vietnam, of the society and culture that gave meaning to his life, of everything he believed in. As dangerous as it was he still wanted to be in Saigon. After the war, elder brother administered several re-education camps for a decade and now promotes joint venture programs." Madame Binh smiled for the first time. "Mama is returning to Vietnam next month."

"And how about you?" I asked.

She laughed with a cynical edge. "Yes, me; how about me? I became a courier for the NLF as a kind of rebellion, I suppose, but mainly because I idolized my brother who had gone underground and was disinherited by Father. One could say I joined out of idealism, but that's so trite.

"In my teenage idealism I believed in democracy and freedom. After the war I found myself in strong disagreement with the new regime. Instead of democracy and freedom we got—well, something else. I criticized what was going on and was sent to a re-education camp for six years. In many ways I was like Annie—feisty, strong-willed and independent."

"That can get you into trouble in America, too," I said. "How did you finally get out of the re-education camp?"

"Elder brother got me released. But I never saw him, still haven't. Someone told me—another official."

"Sounds to me like he feels guilty about something," I said.

"I don't know," she said. "It's like the ideological barriers are still there. Maybe Mama's return will bring us together. I hope so."

"I hope so, too," I said. "How about Annie; was she also in the NLF?"

"No, I'm sure she wasn't. She was too much of a Bohemian or yuppie, as you Americans might say. She was captivated with the good life, an adventuress living on the edge. She was spoiled, catered to as a child. She always seemed to get her way while I struggled for acceptance."

"There were compromising documents which a Major Trang delivered to Annie's lover in a sealed packet," I interjected, "documents that, along with news of Annie's death, caused Colonel Rowe to shoot himself. I assumed they linked Annie in some way with the NLF."

Madame Binh's gentle face was suddenly tortured with a fury she couldn't control. "That's a pile of *merde*! With Trang it had to be a setup or a cover-up. The only letters that might have compromised her were letters from my brother to my parents, family stuff only. I'm certain of that."

"You don't think she might have carried other information, political or military?"

"Absolutely not," Madame Binh retorted. "My brother would never have put Annie's life at risk or compromised our father's shaky position, even though Father had cut him off."

"How well do you remember Major Trang?" I said. "He lives in California near where I live. I've talked with him about your sister and Colonel Rowe."

Madame Binh's face became an expressionless mask. Her voice and language turned harsh and bitter. The scar on her neck had turned bright red. For a moment I saw in her the young, tough survivor she must have been.

"He's truly an evil man, totally without principles, a chameleon who would eat his enemy's shit and call it *pate fois gras* to save his skin!"

"At the time I always thought Trang was tied in with Nhu, his right-hand man, but Trang insisted to me he was only the ARVN liaison," I said.

"Like piss is rain. Trang *was* Nhu's arm twister and hit man. I've talked with people in the re-education camps who were tortured by his henchmen. They clipped electrodes to women's nipples and shoved cattle prods between their legs. And worse, much worse!"

"I don't understand," I said, "how he could hurt Annie. He told me that his younger brother, an ARVN captain, was promised to Annie in marriage. He portrayed himself as Annie's protector and advisor. Colonel Rowe trusted Major Trang to drive Annie from Saigon to My Tho twice weekly."

Madame Binh started crying. "This is too painful, just too painful. Yes, my father had gone to school with Trang's father in Paris. Our families were very close at one time. But Annie's engagement, if you want to call it that, was to Major Trang, not to his brother. I believe even a wedding date had been set, but the arrangement was dissolved by political differences. Major Trang, I'm sure, felt humiliated, as men often do."

"Jesus!" I said.

"I don't know how to say this. It's so awful," Madame Binh continued, "but when Major Trang drove Annie to and from My Tho, he exacted a heavy price for his humiliation. I believe she may have been carrying his child."

"Why? How can you say that?"

"Because Trang had power, the power of life and death. Annie was in his power because she had no other choice, no other way to be with her American colonel."

I remembered then my final conversation with Annie Binh, her anger and sense of humiliation, of being trapped, of having to rely on a man she despised.

"And you think she was murdered?" I asked.

"Yes, it may have been suicide, technically, but I'm sure she was forced into it. Who knows what happened to her in detention—torture, rape, so many kinds of humiliation. If she took poison, as the official report says, she took it gladly." Madame Binh fumbled for a cigarette. I pushed a pack of menthol Kools (a Vietnamese favorite during the war) her way. "Keep it," I said. "I've got more."

Then I said something I knew would hurt, even anger her, but I had to say it. "You, too, I think, were once close to Major Trang and must have suffered humiliation at his hands."

Madame Binh jerked her head sideways as if I'd struck her and covered her face with her hands.

"I saw you with him at the MACV Officers Club," I said. "You were elegantly dressed. There was, I believe, a dance."

Madame Binh's mask disintegrated. She burst into tears and began a quiet moaning. "Why do you do this to me? Why can't you leave me alone? Why do you need to know all of this? What's your purpose, simply to inflict more pain or satisfy a morbid curiosity?"

I reached out to her. She jerked away, wiped her tears, and spoke brusquely. "Yes," she said, "I was in love with Major Trang, crazy for him even after he was in the military. Major Trang, you see, was a double agent. It was easy for me to accept him when I thought he was working for the NLF. It seemed very dangerous and romantic and heroic, like the French underground during World War II. I was so young, so naive . . ."

"So you became his contact," I said.

"Yes, my brother was the NLF contact in the countryside and I became the courier in Saigon. Major Trang was the conduit, the go-between. It was crucial to maintain communication between village and urban leaders."

"But how did Annie—?" I started to say. Madame Binh cut me off.

"It was a mistake, Annie's death. Because of the turmoil and arrests in Saigon, I was unable to make contact with Major Trang. He must have given a packet to Annie to give to me. She was picked up by the security police with the packet. I was the one who should have been caught and executed."

"Do you think Major Trang set her up?" I asked.

"Yes, I think he did. That's why I came to hate him, but I don't know for sure. I've always blamed myself."

"Trang might just as easily have set you up to save his own skin," I said.

Madame Binh stood up to open the shutters. The rain had stopped and the air seemed fresher. She stared out of the window without answering. Then she looked at me and said, "Whatever conclusions you arrive at, don't romanticize something as ugly and dirty as this. Don't make your Colonel Rowe a victim. He victimized Annie, compromised her, forced her to have an abortion—yes, an abortion, and she was pregnant again when she was murdered. Annie was no saint, either, I know that."

She paused, breathing heavily, trying to get more air. "You have to give Trang cold-blooded credit for using Annie's death to facilitate Colonel Rowe's. That must have been a double satisfaction."

"Triple," I said, "Trang told me he was in the armored vehicle when Diem and Nhu were executed."

"The chameleon. I don't doubt it. He probably pulled the trigger in order to save himself." Madame Binh rose from her chair. "No more questions," she said, "no more questions. You understand?"

"Yes, I understand," I said. "You've been most generous with your time. I wonder how or why men like Trang escape justice, fate, karma, whatever?"

"I think you have a proverb, 'The mills of God grind slowly,' or something like that."

"But they grind exceedingly fine," I said, finishing the quote.

"Let the gods take care of Trang; don't become his executioner," she said.

At my request, Madame Binh reluctantly gave me the name of the government-sponsored joint venture program administered by her brother, Bao Duc Binh. "I wish you success in a venture that has no chance of success," she said. "I don't think he will add anything to your search."

Out of nervousness or impatience, Madame Binh began rubbing the pencil-thin scar that crossed her neck like an enlarged vein. There was something familiar in that—Annie—Annie rubbing her neck after arriving in My Tho with her face scratched and bleeding. Major Trang grinning and laughing, and me so furious I didn't give a damn about rank, his or mine.

"What happened?" I demanded and pushed against him.

Trang, laughing so hard he could barely stand, sputtered, "They fight like wildcats; never see anything so fierce, better than kickboxing."

"Who—what are you talking about?" I demanded and pushed him harder.

Trang, angered now with my tone of voice, snapped, "Who you think? Annie's sister. They fight like wild animals."

I stepped back. "Her sister did this?" I didn't believe Major Trang.

"Yeah, sister do it," Trang grinned. "If I don't come between, they kill each other."

Captain Trang walked away, still laughing. I wanted to kill the son of a bitch.

My conversation with Truy Duc Binh was both clarifying and confusing. Several comments, taken in context with her emotional reactions, supported or reinforced those of the bonze, the sibling jealousy and her role as jilted lover.

Madame Binh's virulent hatred of Trang strongly laced with jealousy, both of which may have derived from being rejected, certainly colored her testimony. Her suggestion that Annie may have been sexually exploited by Trang may have reflected her own experience.

Why had Truy Duc Binh tried to put me off her brother's track? Did he know something that might compromise her version of events, perhaps even tell the lie? Madame Binh's dramatic mood change in response to a suggested liaison with Trang reminded me of a Bunruku puppet play I'd seen in which the simpering sweet face of a demure princess consumed by jealousy became instantly grotesque. However skewed her comments, she certainly did not exonerate Major Trang. My feelings and convictions concerning his character and role were only reinforced.

Between the tours and meetings of our final week in Ho Chi Minh City, I made a dozen calls and misfired on every one. The hell with it, big brother Binh would have to remain an enigma. With two days remaining, I took a taxi downtown to make some final purchases.

I returned to the hotel by pedicab. We had just passed the War Crimes Museum and turned right on Dien Bien Phu Street when a taxi swerved over a full lane to sideswipe the pedicab. Both of us, driver and passenger, were pitched into the gutter like a couple of bowling balls knocking down cyclists as if they were tenpins. The pedicab driver suffered a concussion, bruises and a broken arm. I, along with several cyclists, was scraped and bleeding but not seriously injured.

I licked my wounds that evening over a bottle of Suntory scotch. Something, maybe the combination of whiskey and smacking the pavement, gave me a flash of insight, call it Suntory *satori*. I realized the Vietnamese had the answer to all unanswerable, unsolvable questions: karma. Fucking karma. Forget Colonel Rowe, Annie Binh and Major Trang. *Que sera, sera*. What will be will be. Shit happens. In the game of life, karma is the final arbiter. Karma is the joker.

I woke up sober, mad as hell and also scared. The second warning by invisible hit men backed me off—that and the frustrating interviews that seemed to always end in the mills of the gods. I determined to escape my own obsession by exploring the obsessions of my fellow travelers.

Out of Body-English

Ms. Hung, the English teacher, was late for class. She skidded her rattletrap bike to a stop in a twister of dust and slid off the seat with a dancer's flourish. On this hot and sticky day she looked as cool as Venus on a half-shell, as slender and supple as a bamboo shoot in her form-fitting *ao dai*. The headmaster's frown didn't faze her one whit, nor was she intimidated by the obvious voyeurism of three gawking Americans. Her untypical flair and pizzazz left Steve Solberg, especially, stunned and salivating. When she lifted a stylish sun hat, he was surprised to see almond eyes as big as saucers set boldly in a fine-boned face with complementary decor—an elegant nose, determined lips and a strong chin. Ms. Hung's challenging look, a kind of fetching sneer, put him off at first but when she smiled his way and flicked her incredibly long lashes, his knees nearly collapsed. The smile and wink were involuntary, meant for all of them, but he took it personally. He smiled in return and kept smiling as Ms. Hung skipped up a flight of stairs as nimbly as a ballet dancer.

When Steve Solberg emerged from his trance, his buddies, Vic and Tommy, were signaling digital eroticisms and trying to muffle their laughter. "Assholes," he muttered. Headmaster Khanh was still frowning. "Miss Hung," he said, "is one of our finest teachers, but she's rather a tragic case. Not only is her family's background politically tainted, but three older brothers were killed during the war, so she provides for her parents and brothers' families on a meager salary.

How she does it," Mr. Khanh threw up his hands, "I don't know. Of course, we all work part-time jobs to survive. Even I have to tutor on the side."

Steve wanted to dance up the stairs after Ms. Hung, but the headmaster shoved the three of them gently into the bare-bones faculty room for an obligatory orientation, a hustle served with cigarettes and tea. They had selected the Quoc Hoc Secondary School as their day's assignment for Global Educational Enterprises. Theoretically, they were on a reconciliation tour but, in fact, they were also on personal journeys into their own dark histories. Vic, the ex-marine grunt, was tracing a son he'd fathered in Danang; Tommy, who'd been an army medic, was looking to reunite with an ex-VC tunnel rat, and Steve Solberg was trying for some kind of reconciliation with his father's ghost. As an antiwar teenager he had blamed his fighter pilot father for the war's atrocities. After his father's death, he was overwhelmed by feelings of remorse and guilt.

The three of them discovered their compatibility as loose cannon expatriates from California's public school system, which explains why they had short-fused attention for the verbal reams and streams of statistics, achievement scores, academic prizes and other bureaucratic claptrap Headmaster Khanh was inflicting on them and his subservient faculty clique, all of whom chain-smoked and genuflected on cue. The three of them drank gallons of tea and coughed on cue, to no avail, the toxic pollution did not abate. Steve escaped by dream dancing with Ms. Hung of the musical hips.

Actually, they were all dream dancing. Their Vietnamese hosts anticipated something more tangible than expressions of goodwill; the Americans expected to be welcomed as brothers, even with their pockets turned inside out and not one pack of cigarettes to share with the nicotine heads. When Mr. Khanh made a desperate plea for funding and got stonewalled, the dream dance collapsed. Warm clichés of friendship and solidarity turned to icicles in the frozen silence. A kind of nuclear night was rapidly descending when Vic, the gangling ex-marine suggested what they'd wanted all along. "Headmaster Khanh," he said, "you've got three excellent English speakers and teachers here for free; why not put us to work."

Mr. Khanh frowned as he listened to the interpreter. The frown broke into a broad smile, of relief probably. He quickly dispatched his yes-men to facilitate the proposal. Within ten minutes the visiting Americans were hustled off to several advanced English classes. Steve was assigned (he made sure) to the heavenly Ms. Hung.

The class of mostly girls in elegant white *ao dais* stood to attention when he entered. He was stunned. They all seemed to be cut from the same mold—slender, smiling and disarmingly attractive. The biblical phrase "lilies of the field" came to mind. Ms. Hung introduced him in formal, textbook English.

"Please class, I am deeply honored to introduce a teacher from America. Perhaps he will assist us with our lesson on American cinema." She turned Steve's way and smiled, "You might be interested to know that most of the students have recently viewed *Home Alone* and *Born on the Fourth of July* on their family television sets."

Steve was shocked that so many kids had home TV and that with an embargo in force they'd been able to view American films. It was another reality check.

Serving as a substitute teacher was, in Steve's mind, strictly secondary to seducing Ms. Hung, but he was, after all, a teacher on a goodwill mission. He turned to the gorgeous Ms. Hung and felt the rush of adrenaline. "Why don't we put the students in circular groups so they can share with each other what they've learned about America from these films. At the same time, I can check their English speaking skills." His suggestion was both educationally sound and subversively creative. He wanted to waltz around the room with Ms. Hung, not stand stiffly behind a lectern.

Ms. Hung, still formally correct, smiled and said, "I think that would be satisfactory with the headmaster." Then she smiled, "Let's do it."

Freed from their cocoon of formalized instruction, the students began to talk more freely in English while Steve buzzed about like a bumblebee sucking nectar from a field of flowers—listening, correcting, questioning—always with Ms. Hung at his elbow. She stuck with him like Velcro, in his face, reading his lips, repeating phrases, lip-synching his pronunciations with an intensity that was— well, it was damn erotic, dancing a kind of tango, teaching cheek to cheek. Talk about the *Scent of a Woman*—she exuded an aromatic mix of garlic and sandalwood that made him dizzy.

They repeated their act three times running. He was exhausted and soaked in sweat. Ms. Hung had a single bead of perspiration on her pert little nose, a pearl which he had the temerity to harvest with his little finger. Miss Hung, in all innocence, did not realize the disabling effect her proximity had on his physical and emotional state. He was getting totally stoned on her sandalwood perfume, rising higher than the *Hindenburg* and just as ready for disaster, like maybe suddenly biting Ms. Hung's edible garlic lips.

Fortunately the lunch break intervened, an *interruptus* that gave him breathing space. Steve foolishly anticipated his own *Home Alone* with Ms. Hung, but that event was not scheduled for the lunchtime matinee or any other time. Across a wide table in the faculty room he shared with Ms. Hung and her colleagues a most professional discussion on teaching and literature. To his embarrassing admission that he knew nothing about Vietnamese literature, Ms. Hung urged him to read *The Tale of Kieu*. "It's all there, everything, even the story of my own life and that of other Vietnamese women."

He wanted desperately to keep their connection alive, exchange addresses and at least write to her, but the tyranny of time, schedules and protocol intervened. Ms. Hung was through teaching by noon and left as quickly as she'd arrived. He stood by helplessly and watched Ms. Hung pedal her delightful derriere into the suffocating embrace of noon-hour traffic. "I'll read *The Tale of Kieu!*" he yelled after her. How ironic; he had wanted to romance Ms. Hung and failed. She had, in all innocence, seduced him completely.

"Hey, Captain Kirk," someone yelled, "come out of the clouds."

"Yeah, buddy boy, your *Mission Impossible* just ended. Crash landing. Stage left, jerk off. C'mon, we gotta go eat!" His two friends each grabbed an arm and hustled him off to join the rest of the tour group in a waiting minibus.

In retrospect, the bizarre events of that evening and the day following seemed to belong to a time-space dimension beyond his cultural experience and comprehension. At the time the events seemed accidental, but that's how Americans explain events they can't fit into their pragmatic world.

Steve supposed his experience with Ms. Hung that morning, combined with his mixed-up mood and the accidental way it happened, made him vulnerable to the young woman who bumped into him (actually knocked him on his ass) in a darkened stairwell at the Bac Man Hotel where they were staying.

"Excuse me," he said, just as their interpreter, Vinh, stopped by on his way to dinner.

The young woman laughed and said something in Vietnamese.

"What's she saying?" Steve asked.

"She wants to know if you'd like a massage," Vinh replied.

"Hell, yes," he said and jumped to his feet so quickly he bumped her against the stairwell "accidentally." "Just tell me where and when." His quick response was inspired by legitimate necessity as much as by kinky fantasies. Severe back and neck injuries from a motorcycle crash had turned him to massage as other victims seized on drugs and alcohol. He'd had several massages already in Vietnam, all strictly legit. At five dollars a rub-a-dub, it was a steal.

While Vinh conversed with the mystery woman in Vietnamese, Steve tried to get a closer look at her, but in the semi-darkness all he could see was a shadow figure in loose pantaloons and blouse with a sheen of black hair cascading down her back that caught slivers of light in mirror flashes. She exuded a feline athleticism, tense and tensile, as if ready to spring.

"She says she'll come to your room at eight o'clock." Vinh smiled and walked down the stairs to the dining room.

"Okey-dokey," he said.

"Okey-dokey," she mimicked. Then she added softly "boom-boom, ten dollah." He figured boom-boom must be a special kind of massage like rolfing, especially when she laughed and gave him a quick *Taiko* drum pounding on his back—boom-boom-boom. She laughed again, gave his triceps a painful twist and disappeared into the night.

"Okey-dokey, eight o'clock," he yelled into the darkness.

Her reply, barely audible, in childish singsong, came from a world away, "Okey-dokey. Okey-dokey. Okey-dokey."

Steve's arm had turned completely numb. He skipped dinner, went up to his room on the third floor and drank several beers while listening to Chris Isaak on his Walkman. Not that he wasn't hungry. He was. But the mysterious masseuse had mainlined his emotions. He needed to harness the wild horses in his groin, subdue the fantasies ricocheting around his skull. The last thing he needed was a salacious ribbing from his two older buddies.

Vinh came by and said he was going to cruise the waterfront with Vic and Tommy. Steve laughed and waved him off. Vinh was sucking up '50s slang like the words were Vietnamese noodles. He was, unbelievably, an Elvis Presley impersonator with the largest collection of rock and roll pirate tapes in Vietnam. He even sported a ducktail and drapes.

"That's cool, man," Steve said.

"Yeah, cool, man," Vinh replied. "Adios, Daddy-O."

Steve threw a beer can at him. He must have fallen asleep because a rapping on the window jerked him upright so suddenly that he spilled beer all over his undershirt.

"Come in," he said.

The masseuse slipped in silently and turned off the overhead light before he could clearly see her face. But he saw enough to nearly make him wet his pants along with his undershirt. He flopped back on the bed. Jesus! It couldn't be Ms. Hung. But it was Ms. Hung or her double. They'd been close enough to rub noses for most of that morning.

"Hi," he said half-jokingly, "long time no see."

Ms. Hung or whoever she was didn't say a thing. No reply, no laugh, no smile, nothing. In the dim light filtering through the curtains, she was again a mystery woman, or maybe just a working masseuse doing her job. She stripped off his wet undershirt, turned him on his stomach and dribbled oil up and down his back *a la* Jackson Pollock. He relaxed immediately. Then her steel fingers dug so deeply into his back muscles that he groaned with pain, and when the spasms relaxed he groaned with pleasure.

"Just don't fucking stop," he babbled to no one in particular, "just don't fucking stop."

She didn't stop. From his scalp to his toes, every muscle, sinew, joint and tendon was worked and reworked, pulled and pummeled until he felt he was becoming a boneless primordial, oozing back into the ooze.

Not quite. She was kneading his calves and thighs like bread dough when the yeast started rising—an erection so hard it hurt worse than when he was a pimply teenager with a one-track mind inside tight Levi's. He tried to go limp by testing the theory of mind over matter, but his mind was still apparently in tight Levi's. He embraced the bed mattress like a man hugs a raft in white water, but the masseuse outmaneuvered him. She scratched the soles of his feet until he giggled and relaxed his arms. Then she flipped him over as easily as a Tokyo fish seller turns a tuna, unzipped his shorts and slipped the condom on in a single, swift move, a preemptive strike designed perhaps to render his weak and gibbering protests irrelevant.

"Boom-boom," she said softly and slipped off the bed leaving a whiff of garlic and sandalwood.

She was across the room undressing in the dark when he did something stupid. He flipped on the overhead light. In the split second before she turned in a crouch and covered her face he saw the bright red burn scar with ugly lumps that seesawed across her back like a twisted bandoleer. Then, as if to flaunt her naked vulnerability and challenge his shock and disbelief, she stood and flung open her arms and body in a kind of tortured crucifix. The front of her was as badly scarred and disfigured as her back. It was Ms. Hung. It had to be Ms. Hung.

He looked into her great dark eyes, as big as obsidian mirrors, which seemed to grow larger and larger until they were as big as TV screens. He saw what he'd witnessed a thousand times in flashbacks, burned into memory, replayed during his teenage years in dreams and nightmares for weeks and months, a scene which he'd first witnessed on the nightly news—a Vietnamese girl, horribly napalmed, screaming in terror, running naked with arms outstretched trailing tatters of burning skin and flesh. And now, as in his dreams, the screaming, mutilated figures multiplied and stretched into infinity, never ending, like the war itself— never ending until his father's plane was shot down, until his father was dead and gone, out of his life forever.

He closed his eyes to endure the retching and sobbing that tore into his ribs and guts and sobbed until the horror went away into the past that he wanted to forget. When he finally looked up, Ms. Hung had vanished. When he looked down, the condom was still intact.

The three of them were scheduled to return to Ms. Hung's school the following day for another session of teaching English. They'd apparently hit it off with the kids and teachers, even though they'd bombed with the bureaucrats. He had to go, of course, if only to see the real Ms. Hung again.

When they arrived, students were milling around the statue of Ho Chi Minh in the large center quad. Many of them were crying; others were whispering quietly or simply standing in small groups. The headmaster waved his hand and motioned them to come his way.

"I don't suppose you've heard the tragic news," he said. "The English teacher, Ms. Hung, was struck by a taxi and killed on her way home from school yesterday."

"What time?" Steve asked.

"About 12:45," he said. "There are photos in my office."

There were several photographs taken by two students who lived near the accident site. Headmaster Khanh must have thought the detailed attention Steve gave to each photograph a bit unusual, if not macabre. But, of course, he was looking for a particular detail. He found it in a photo of Ms. Hung sprawled grotesquely, face down, with the *ao dai* torn from her shoulder. The ugly belt-like burn was clearly visible, with lumps of scar tissue like bullets in a bandoleer.

Steve returned to America and read *The Tale of Kieu* as Ms. Hung had suggested, as well as Le Ly Hayslip's richly detailed autobiography, *Between Heaven and Earth*, and Duong Thu Huong's tribute to women survivors in *Paradise of the Blind*. Only then did he begin to understand Ms. Hung's assertion, "It's all there, everything, even the story of my own life and that of other Vietnamese women."

To save her family from economic disaster and dishonor, the heroine Kieu sacrificed her personal dreams to marry a rich landlord who, with other evildoers, exploited Kieu as a prostitute. She endured as her fate a life of mostly abuse and betrayal without becoming bitter or vengeful. Only in death was she finally reunited with her family and first love as a reborn spirit.

It became clear that for Kieu and her Vietnamese sisters, even the strongest personalities had to bend before the demands of fate, of society, culture, circumstance and history; that the most truly virtuous woman may sacrifice herself for the sake of family survival; that reconciliation, not revenge, must be the ultimate closure to war and violence; that the world of reborn spirits is as real as the world of material existence.

Call it what you will—mystery, memory, myth—the spirit of Ms. Hung became as much a living, reconciling presence for Steve as the reborn spirit of Kieu was for her lover and family in the Vietnamese classic. Her offer of love, in whatever form, became for him an act of reconciliation. She enabled him to somehow transcend the bitter rejection of his father, to begin recovering the love and respect he felt for him before the terrors of war destroyed their family bonds.

Gradually, without being aware of the process, he transformed his encounter with Ms. Hung into a contemporary version of *The Tale of Kieu* with a platonic marriage of the spirit between himself and Ms. Hung eternally enshrined in memory, echoing Jim Burden's salvaged memories for his Antonia in Willa Cather's novel: "Whatever we had missed, we possessed together the precious, incommunicable past."

Steve returned to Vietnam the following year on a personal pilgrimage to find Ms. Hung's grave site and trace her family's whereabouts. He ran into a stone wall—several stone walls, in fact. It appeared that all official records of Ms. Hung's life and death had disappeared or were simply nonexistent. Neither she nor her family were from Hue and no one knew of their whereabouts. He could only curse the bureaucracy that could blank out her life and memory for what he assumed were politically tainted reasons and wonder what the bright and beautiful Ms. Hung had ever done to deserve such a fate. With no tomb to commemorate or family with whom to commiserate, he threw a dozen roses into the Perfume River, scattered some tears of rice wine into the wind and drank the nearly full bottle to drown his misery.

That evening he returned to his room at the Bac Man Hotel with a six-pack of Vietnamese beer and fell asleep listening to Chris Isaak's sweet, sad ballads on his Walkman. A persistent knocking that seemed to ricochet inside his earphones half-awakened him. By the time he pulled off the headset, someone bathed in garlic and sandalwood was giggling in the dark.

"You—are you a massage lady?" he mumbled.

"Okey-dokey," she laughed and jammed a set of steel fingers into his spine. She played his body up and down like it was a mariachi marimba all the way to his toes. Then she tickled his feet, turned him over and capped him with a condom. He did not turn on the light when she undressed and she did not leave, not until he had traveled the night in the burning labyrinth of her bandoleer scars, not until he pledged to come again and again into a future that, at the moment, stretched into infinity.

Replay

The first thing Vic Carlson thought of when the tour group started climbing the steep, rock-cut stairs of Marble Mountain was how many times he'd looked up at this massive, white-walled fortress while humping whores and fun girls on China Beach below. Then he had looked without seeing, without comprehending the complexities of either natural or human landscape.

He had paid the supreme masculine price for his singular concentration, for doing his tour of duty with an almost continuous erection. He hadn't really got it up since—not all the way up, anyway. Maybe getting it up enough to father four kids by three different wives was sufficient proof of his manhood, but, frankly, hitting one out of ten with his "Oldenberg softy" (his first wife's arty put-down) was a piss-poor batting average. He attributed his marital disasters to impotency (how he hated that word) and his impotency to his experiences in Vietnam— PTSD (Post Traumatic Stress Disorder) the vets' nut expert called it, a catch-all acronym for the ills of his generation. Well, he refused to be lumped with the psychos and freakouts and fuckups of his generation and hadn't returned for another session.

Now at almost fifty, Vic had at least wised up enough to avoid the so-called tender trap. He was putting all of his energies and precious bodily fluids (to quote *Dr. Strangelove*'s General Jack Ripper) into teaching and writing as if to convince himself that the pen is mightier than the penis. Not that he didn't think about sex. He did, so much so that he'd flown to Los Angeles to consort with a

Vietnamese karaoke bar hostess that a friend of his—a Vietnam vet who'd made a bundle in real estate—had set up. The girl was gorgeous, lubriciously lovely, but "it" hadn't worked. His once mighty Casey's bat had again struck out.

The more he thought about it, the more convinced Vic became that his problem could only be solved by returning to Vietnam where it all began. So when he heard about the friendship tour out of San Jose, he applied the same day. As a vet, a teacher and a searcher for a lost son, he was a shoo-in. To Vic's surprise and dismay, the persisting interest of the tour members in his colonialist offspring forced to the forefront of his consciousness what to him had always been a casual concern ("the random seed of his loins," he once joked).

The tour group reached the first rest stop after climbing 167 steps at a 43-degree incline (or so the cutest of the two-dozen teenage hawkers informed them). They were sweat-soaked, stinking and exhausted—and they had only begun! They cleaned out the soft drink vendor of every Coke and beat the air furiously and ineffectually with cheap bamboo fans. The vets were rolling the cold cans of Coke over their faces and around their necks, a cooling-off technique they'd learned as grunts in Vietnam. The others followed suit.

Tina Brown, the young journalist-seminarian, and the nurse, Kate Noonan, both hefties, were soaked with perspiration and breathing heavily. With asthma problems, Kate was gasping for air with lips pursed like a dry-docked fish.

"I didn't come to Vietnam to be a Sherpa," Kate huffed. She turned to Lily Okada and Sybil Patterson, the Vietnamese-American, who were quietly conversing under wide-brimmed sun hats as big as umbrellas. They were cooling themselves with large fold-out fans. Tina snorted, "Look at those slenderellas, cool as a couple of celery sticks. I can't believe it." She turned to Kate, who had recovered her breath, "Whenever you're ready girl, down the hill we go."

They were fifty feet down the steep trail when Neville sing-songed under his breath, "Jill and a jelly-roll down the hill."

Tina heard him. "There's a jackoff gonna tumble down the hill and break his crown if he don't shut his mouth."

Neville nearly choked himself laughing.

Phil, the tour co-leader, glared Neville into silence and then lifted his Coke. "Here's to the embargo," he said, "may it continue to provide us with cold Cokes."

Vinh laughed. "No problem. We get almost anything we want through Bangkok and Singapore. The embargo is more sieve than net."

Several vets sounded off. "Strikes me the embargo is like a defective condom. It doesn't work but somebody still gets screwed."

"Yeah, guess who, boo-hoo, good ol' Uncle Sam, boo-hoo."

"Shit, we always screw ourselves; everyone knows that."

"It's just like the goddamn war; half the stuff was getting ripped off at the docks and sold to the enemy."

"Hell, the same thing is happening in America. You could say we have an embargo on drugs, but Jesus!"

Until Danang they had adjusted fairly well to the heat, humidity and each other's quirks. Heavy rains with increased humidity seemed to melt the thin surface of civility. Betty went bananas first, completely losing her cool when the tour group was crushed by the army of teenage hustlers peddling tourist jee jaws. She exploded all over the guide-interpreter.

"Dammit, Vinh," she bellowed, "you'll never get tourists in Vietnam this way. You'll send them screaming out of the country!" She glared at him. "Tell them," she yelled in his face, "tell them to move their skinny little butts out of here right now!"

Betty's outburst backed the kids off temporarily, but Vinh was embarrassed—as if he'd been shamed and had lost face. Like most tourist guides, even government-sponsored, he survived by cutting a deal with tourist hustlers and entrepreneurs.

The teenage hawkers gave Betty some space but swept the rest of the group forward like a panicked herd of buffalo. In the clamor of pushing and shoving, Vic inadvertently placed his open hand on the breast of the step-counting vendor who had apparently picked him as her quarry. He froze for a moment until she smiled up at him.

"My name is Lanh," she said.

"Lanh," he repeated her name and removed his hand from her breast. He closed his fingers to hold the warmth of her.

Then, quite abruptly, the madding crowd pushed them into an opening where the marble rock had split apart to offer a view of the turquoise and emerald bay and China Beach below. With the girl's hand on his shoulder and the warmth of her breast still in his hand, he remembered with the clarity of longing his first encounter with another Lanh.

He was watching several GIs in swimsuits and bar girls in bikinis play an improbable game of tackle football while his own girl for the day changed clothes in a beach hooch nearby. There was the smell of hot dogs sizzling on the hibachis and the clatter of the guys pulling Miller High Lifes out of an ice tub between tackles. He reckoned it was a kind of athletic foreplay the way the guys were tackling the girls. The game play was so ludicrously funny he burst out laughing. Then a misthrown ball landed at his feet. When he stooped to pick it up, a bar girl chasing the ball knocked him on his butt and spread herself all over him as thick as jam. One of her breasts ended up in his hand.

"How you like, GI?" she asked, "pretty hot stuff?"

He started laughing and kept laughing until she turned angry and jumped off. She was stacked like a pint-sized version of Ann Margaret.

"Fuck you, GI," she said and kicked sand in his face.

He tracked her down to a sleaze bar called the Alamo Club to give her some hell. She became instead his permanent girl, his mama san. She was terrific—a good housekeeper, excellent cook, lover and conversationalist, smartass but smart. He loved it until she got too ambitious, wanting to take classes in English and nursing. Besides, she was taking care of her sister's squalling kid, and it was driving him nuts. He started drinking heavily, whacked her around and badmouthed the kid. She simply said, "Fuck off, GI." She was a survivor, tough as nails, as funny as Lucille Ball and one hell of a fuck. He missed that most of all.

The young vendor was jerking his shirttail. "Quick now, gotta catch up." She grabbed his hand and pulled him after her. He was skipping steps and stumbling to keep pace, a clumsy Peter Pan following a light-footed Tinkerbell. Every dozen or so steps, the vendor sang out, "Two hundra ninety . . . tree hundra tree . . ." in the senseless numbers game that seemed to obsess her. They joined the tour group to hear Vinh droning away like a bored schoolteacher.

"These five marble mountains that were once five islands represent five elements of the universe—earth, water, wood, fire and gold. When the Champas ruled this area, the caves were Hindu shrines. Over the centuries, with the infusion of Chinese culture, they were carved into Buddhist sanctuaries. Only one Champa cave still exists, a deep cavern too dangerous for us to explore."

In the dim, uncertain candlelight Vic and his self-appointed guide skirted the tour group like a couple of ghosts and descended into the largest cave. He tripped in the darkness but Lanh, holding a candle in one hand, turned and braced herself against him, so close he could feel her breasts and ribs and pelvic bones. She smiled up at him and then led him into the huge cathedral-like cave filled with magnificent Buddhist statuary that had once been the largest VC military hospital in Vietnam. The VC could, from their eagles' nest, observe the GIs frolicking and fornicating below. He wondered if the young soldiers had been jealous or repelled by what they'd seen.

Lanh pulled him into a small alcove sanctuary as the others trouped in with the herd of hustlers. "Come, quick," she urged. They were outside again and Lanh was reeling off the exact count of stairs: "Tree hundra twenty-four . . . tree hundra forty . . ." As they approached Thuy Son Mountain Shrine near the summit, Lanh took him climbing on a narrow ledge to the very peak.

Vic sucked in his breath. Far below him, stretching even beyond his vision lay the remains, the empty shell of what had once been the largest military base in Vietnam with the heaviest air traffic of any port in the world! It was now an immense ghost town with a few scattered barracks, the residue of America's military might conserved inside barbed wire fencing.

"Tree hundra sixty-four step. You finish one tour of duty, GI, maybe lucky you go home in one piece."

Dumbfounded, he glanced at Lanh, who was looking at him with such intensity, hope, expectation, or something, that he had to turn away. *Where in hell did she pick up the GI lingo? Was she Amerasian? How old was she, anyway?* She had pulled her hair back against the wind in a way that reminded him of the other Lanh. He could see the large building far below that must have been the PX where he encountered Lanh the second time.

She was slimmer, smartly dressed with newly-styled short hair. At the PX notions counter she playfully sprayed perfumes and colognes, drawing swarms of GIs to her like drones to a queen bee or, given their frenetic sniffing, like hounds to a bitch in heat. She was so gorgeous that his innards turned to mush.

He moved behind her, captivated by her charisma, impatient for the grunts to leave.

She tried to put him off, but he begged until she let him taxi her home. In the weeks following, they picnicked at China Beach a few times and then made love in a rented beach hut.

She let him move in with her again after impassioned pleading on the condition that she be allowed to keep her job at the PX and complete her nursing program. Her younger sister had moved in from the country to keep house and care for her baby.

The sister had a boyfriend who slipped in quietly late at night and left before dawn. He could hear them talking for hours, sometimes all night long. He figured the guy was VC, which really put him on edge.

He came off duty one day red-eyed drunk because he'd lost a close friend who was killed on patrol. He was feeling guilty and angry at himself for being an REMF and angry at the whole fucking country. He'd juiced himself on 45 Whiskey with Black Label beer chasers. He was furious as hell when he found Lanh gone.

"Goddamn whore is out fucking it up."

The sister who was trembling with fear at the gun he was waving around protested, "No, no, she go class, always go class."

"Class, my ass!" he shouted and slapped her across the room. "You goddamn VC whore, I know all about you." He tried to throw her on the bed, but she tore out of her blouse and ran outside.

When a furious Lanh threw him out again, he yelled from the street, "Your boyfriend's a fucking VC spy and both of you are VC whores!"

He returned in a week to make amends, but Lanh slammed the door in his face. He didn't know that she was pregnant with his child or that her sister's boyfriend was actually their younger brother or that he worked for the VC only because their village was VC-controlled, and that without the weekly remittance he collected from Lanh their parents would have been imprisoned or killed.

He held the vendor's hand as the two of them tightroped down the narrow, gravelly ledge. The voices of the tour group drifted up as thin as smoke from the parking area. They climbed down a series of ladders and wooden ramps placed by workmen repairing dozens of small shrines and temples carved into the marble mountain. Then quite suddenly they stood on the edge of a butte which offered a panorama of China Beach. Several new hotels were under construction, pastel colored beach cottages with "authentic" thatched roofs were connected by winding walkways and pools. China Beach was on its way to becoming a Waikiki.

"Wanna go Devil's Hole?"

"What? Where?" he asked. "I think we have to leave now."

"Come, I show you, Champa cave with lotta devils." She took his arm. "Only take a minute."

They backtracked twenty yards or so. The girl pointed to a small opening barely visible behind a large wall of rock.

"Very deep," she said. "You scare?"

He hesitated, wondering if he shouldn't rejoin the tour group, wondering what they'd be thinking. "Oh, what the hell," he said, "lead on, partner."

"You first, I follow," she said. She held the candle in the darkness while he descended somewhat unsteadily down a rope ladder. He missed the final rung and fell heavily, hurting his wrist. By the time he recovered, Lanh had slithered down and squeezed against him.

In the dim uncertain light he could see a huge cavern at least half as big as the Cathedral Cave with virtually every inch of its walls sculpted with bas-relief figures of demons and animals but with many more gods and goddesses joined in ecstasies of gymnastic sexuality. The nearest figures seemed to come alive, swaying to and fro in the flickering candle flame.

The spectacle so mesmerized Vic that he didn't see Lanh open her blouse until she pressed against him, placing his hands against her breasts. Her nipples were as firm as the fingers which opened his trousers and held his penis. He grew hard immediately. She knelt and took him into her mouth and made love to him.

He started crying then, not for the joy of sex or the easy erection he had long sought to achieve, but rather because the girl vendor's act of subordination replayed mental images of powerless fun girls kneeling in fellatio to please their GI masters. It was how he remembered the other Lanh the last time he'd seen her, begging on her knees with the country in chaos, when the Americans brutally abandoned their allies and dependents.

When he walked into the chaplain's office Lanh was bent forward on knees so bone-thin that her joints seemed enlarged or swollen. Her skin was blotched and bruised as if she'd been beaten. Lanh's once luminous eyes, hidden now by a curtain of stringy hair, were glazed by fear. She was holding a baby—their baby, she said.

"Please," she begged, "he's your son. You must take him with you to America. I ask nothing for myself, nothing. Only take him, please. I beg you, he's your son. I swear it."

He looked at the baby and wondered if the child was really his. That's what he told the chaplain, "How do I know if the baby is really mine? Lanh's a bar girl, a fun girl, a prostitute." The chaplain turned away from him. He must have listened to stories like Lanh's a hundred times and felt sick about them if he had a conscience.

At the time he'd felt sick, too. But he was just a kid and wanted to get the hell out like everybody else. So he made promises, told her not to worry, that he'd do everything he could to get her (their) child to America. But he was lying and he knew it. The rules of love and relationships were changing as fast as the horrendous events around them. No way was he going to be saddled with a gook kid in America.

The vendor was coughing and holding herself against him. "Twenty dollah?" she asked, "twenty dollah?" Her plea was more question than demand, or, given the context, begging really.

"Twenty dollars," he said, "sure, hell yes, twenty dollars. God, yes!"

When they arrived at the parking area most of the tour members were in the minibus or purchasing small religious carvings from the teenage entrepreneurs. Betty was fuming.

"I—we got sidetracked in Devil's Hole," he said, "an original Champa cavern filled with incredible Hindu religious art. You guys really missed it, no kidding."

Betty snorted and turned on her heel. Phil winked at him from the minibus. He glanced briefly at the Vietnamese-American woman, who was drilling holes through him.

"You not fo'get Lo-an?" The girl looked at him with eyes that asked for something more than the sale of sundries and sex, some human interaction that made him uneasy and defensive. He didn't want to be taken advantage of. Her name surprised him.

"Low-anh, your name is Low-anh?" He enunciated each syllable to get it right.

"Loan, yes, what you think?" she said and laughed.

"Low-anh," he repeated and laughed with the vendor. He was thankful for the misnomer that made her laugh, that had provoked his journey of remembrance and return to the only place he'd felt truly alive and complete as a man, maybe the only place he'd experienced real love.

He purchased several of the vendor's stone-carved Buddhas and one of the Hindu god Ganesha. He paid her twenty dollars, then laid another twenty on top of the first one. She smiled and waved as the minibus disappeared around the curve of Marble Mountain. She seemed as sweet and innocent and unpretentious as an American teenager waving her daddy off to work.

His encounter with the young vendor named Loan sent him reeling into his past and into the streets of Danang in search of the Lanh he'd once known and loved—yes loved—he admitted it now. He walked the waterfront at night by the big tourist hotels, staring into hundreds of faces until they became look-alike masks of Lanh, mocking his fruitless searching.

On their final day in Danang, the group met with the Municipal Women's Federation to study their rehabilitation program for ex-prostitutes, mostly middle-aged, whose fear of AIDS was driving them off the streets. A brief introduction by the director, Madame Truong, was followed by a tour of the retraining center.

During the tour he scanned the scarred and delicate faces, searched the classrooms and, with a guide, the dormitories. He didn't really expect to find Lanh. He realized she could have died in a dozen ways in the war's fiery finale, in postwar re-education camps, in prison or, most likely, of malnutrition or disease.

That same evening the tour group hosted ten of the ex-prostitutes in the hotel lobby over lemonade and ice cream. Betty and Phil, who believed in person-to-person contacts whenever possible (or impossible), had arranged the session. It was clear the women had no desire to relate their sordid life histories. But they were desperate for the promised contribution from the foreign visitors.

He didn't recognize her at first, not until he heard her voice and her excellent English. She could have been sixty, he thought. She was as wrinkled as crunched parchment; her hair was streaked with gray and half of her teeth were gone. She was nearly blind from glaucoma which relieved him immensely. So he closed his eyes, blinded himself to the present and listened to her youthful voice evoke the past.

She spoke of her early life as a village girl, the war's violence that broke her family into factions and drove her to Danang, her life as a bar girl and prostitute, and how she became the wife of an American soldier. The word "wife" startled him. What did she mean?

She told of the war's abrupt ending, of the horrifying traumas as so many Americans ripped themselves from the arms of wives and lovers, abandoning thousands of their children.

"But my son is safe, I hope, and living in America. I gave him to a family leaving by boat. I never hear from him, but I hope . . ."

Her voice suddenly came alive. "But my son had a twin sister, so I have a daughter who helps me now to replace the boy I lost. I know she's beautiful because I can feel her face and eyes and beautiful hands. Very beautiful. I have a picture . . ."

He held the picture until the eyes and nose and mouth and face became as palpable as the face of the young vendor, until his tears began to mar the picture. He held it until someone pulled it from his hand. He rushed then from the lobby into the street until he could no longer hear her voice, "but I don't know how long she'll still be with me . . ." Her voice broke and became inaudible.

Madame Truong completed the sentence matter-of-factly. "Like so many young women her age, she's tested HIV positive."

Tunnel Vision

The smile betrayed him.

His face was sensitive, handsome and expressive, but the smile made him monstrous. Tommy Neville had seen him before. The shock of recognition sucked him into a vortex of rage and violence he hadn't experienced for twenty-five years. He locked his fingers into iron fists, stifling the urge to cut the killer ear to ear, fixing him with a permanent smile, a grinning death mask.

The ex-Vietcong tunnel rat and sniper was telling Morley Safer on *60 Minutes* how a single kill had changed him forever. He'd killed dozens of Americans in the dark or at a distance but never at close range, not until this particular American soldier looked him in the eye and suddenly froze. The VC killed him face to face and realized for the first time he'd murdered a brother human and inflicted an endless chain of grief and suffering on the soldier's family.

Safer interjected, "Surely you must feel resentment, even hatred toward the Americans who destroyed your country and killed two to three million of your people."

"No," the VC replied, "I feel no resentment, I only grieve for the families of Vietnamese and Americans who suffered the loss of their children and loved ones."

In the late 1980s, when Tommy Neville saw the interview on *60 Minutes*, he was a paunchy middle-aged gay activist operating a coffee house and book shop called Iguana Dreams in San Francisco's Castro district. He'd even turned against the war in the early '70s. But when he recognized Bobby's killer, who had become a pacifist poet and tour guide at Cu Chi, watched him crying over the death of an American soldier, saw him express such genuine empathy for the people whose government had devastated his country, Tommy was not moved to tears of sympathy. He was filled with soundless fury. He was back in Vietnam, deep into the tunnels of Cu Chi, ready to avenge the death of Bobby McCafferty, the only man—the only person—he'd ever really loved. When the interview came to an end, he had to unwind his fists finger by finger to keep the bones from breaking.

From elementary school into high school, Tommy and Bobby were closer than blood brothers. They fought each other's fights, fished and surfed at Ocean Beach, skated and biked all over Golden Gate Park and teased the animals at Fleischacker Zoo. Summers they played Little League baseball and spent time at a Catholic boys camp on the Russian River. That's where some older kids taught them the joys of jacking each other off and the holy fathers warned them against the mortal sin of self-abuse. But like most of the other jackoffs, they pumped away like pistons in a gangster getaway car, hoping the combination of confession and abusing a friend instead of oneself would somehow salvage their souls.

During the testosterone rush of junior high, they hung out at Playland by Ocean Beach nearly every weekend just to jack each other off in the Tunnel of Love. Sometimes Tommy got carried away and gave Bobby more than a hand job. Bobby never returned the favor, but, hell, he was happy just to be with his closest friend. The Tunnel of Love became his ultimate trip, a journey that would never end, even when he and Bobby went their separate ways in high school and beyond.

In high school Bobby suddenly grew up as tall as John Wayne and twice as handsome. He made all-city basketball his junior year and started running around with jocks, cheerleaders and some hotshot kids from Pacific Heights. Tommy seemed to shrink by comparison; he hadn't grown one inch after junior high. His black frizzy hair, dark eyes and pug features gave him a bulldog look that sometimes put people off. Besides his size and feisty attitude, he got involved in school theater and drama classes which made him even more of an outsider. The jocks sweetened their insults by calling the drama kids dear queers or DQs, but it was no big thing for Tommy. He'd taken boxing lessons with Bobby at the Police Athletic League and could take care of himself. But he hated to see Bobby hanging out with a bunch of assholes and giving him the cold shoulder whenever his jock buddies smirked and pursed their lips with sibilant insults.

Funny thing, they always met at Sunday Mass and talked for an hour or two as if nothing had really changed. Sometimes they even rode their bikes into Marin or down the coast highway to Half Moon Bay and back. But neither of them suggested a trip through the Tunnel of Love. Something *had* changed.

Reflecting later, Tommy wondered how the heavy Vietnam protest passed him by, probably because he came from a conservative Catholic family. He remembered going with friends to a couple of peace rallies in Golden Gate Park just so he could listen to Joan Baez and Country Joe for free. He recalled being upset when Bobby and his jock friends ripped down some protest signs the DQs had posted and roughed up some of his buddies. That really cooled their friendship.

They parted company after high school. Bobby went to Saint Mary's on an athletic scholarship. Tommy went to City College on nothing, where he ran fast and loose (for him) with an arty theater group. He started smoking pot and stopped attending church, which really put him beyond redemption and into purgatory with his family. Eventually he moved out of the house and into a Tenderloin flat with some guys from school.

He was sure they'd never see each other again—just a feeling he had. He was wrong. A year and a half later they met again at Cu Chi, the monster base of the 25th Infantry located near the infamous Iron Triangle. They both got nailed by the draft for dropping out of college for a semester. Bobby lost his scholarship for getting busted on a DUI; Tommy needed a job to pay his bills.

The base at Cu Chi was sitting on top of a much larger enemy military complex. Beneath the American base and beyond, VC moles had rooted hundreds of miles of tunnels, three and four levels deep, with kitchens, clinics, schools, storage and supply depots where even artillery and tanks were hidden. The American brass (with its head up its ass) couldn't figure out what was happening until VC sappers had blown up half the base. Then they started training American tunnel rats to pursue the VC underground.

By the time Bobby arrived in country, Tommy had achieved a certain notoriety as a tunnel rat, one of the few Americans small enough and crazy enough to descend into the bowels of hell where every rat caught some kind of shit, usually lethal. His buddies called him Mighty Mouse after his picture appeared in *Stars and Stripes* with three dead VC he'd pulled out of a Cu Chi tunnel. He was the only medic in a narrowing elite defined by the motto "less than a few good men" because almost no one signed up for tunnel rat training at Cu Chi.

Tommy bumped into a half-drunk Bobby in a hooch bar for enlisted men a month after he'd arrived in country. He'd been assigned to a LURP unit after advanced jungle training in Guam. The first thing Bobby said was, "So, you're the fucking famous tunnel rat they call Mighty Mouse, the fearless crazy-ass medic everyone's talking about. Man, I'd shit in my pants and die before I'd stick my nose in one of those death traps."

Right off he knew Bobby was fresh in country, a macho greenhorn, an FNG, trying too hard to buffer the mud and death reality with Lifer bullshit they'd fed him in advanced training. Innocent abroad, Tommy said to himself, Bobby's in deep shit hanging out with Neanderthals who looked like they'd inhaled half the hash from Turkey. They wouldn't risk their lives for a gung-ho FNG oozing trouble. Bobby's recon platoon buddies were big and mean-looking, young men who had become old men. None of them smiled. They stared right through him and barely nodded when Bobby introduced him as the Frisco kid.

"Queertown USA," one of them said. They all laughed.

"Hell, Tommy's no queer, he's a goddamn hero, even made *Stars and Stripes.* Any of you John Wayne assholes want to apply for tunnel rat?"

They answered with ragged laughs, muted growls and a "Fuck you, Twinkie."

Tommy cracked two cold beers.

"It's not what you think, Bobby," he said. "It's just a dirty job in a dirty war."

"Hey, Tommy my boy, all I know is a lot of guys think you're a fuckin' hero."

Bobby was pretty sloshed, grinning his Alfred P. Neuman grin. "I'm buyin' you 'nother beer my man, my fuckin' hero."

Tommy was getting exasperated. "Bobby," he said, "you gotta stop this hero stuff. Shit, some days I save as many VC as I do Americans."

The VC comment shut Bobby up pretty fast. His recon mates gave Tommy deadly looks, as if they were sighting him in their M-16s. They knocked over their chairs and left.

"Assholes," Bobby muttered.

Better watch your backside, Bobby, those assholes will frag you the second you fuck up, if they even think you might fuck up.

Tommy got himself transferred to Bobby's recon company because they needed a medic and because he wanted to keep his best friend alive. His work as a tunnel rat seemed to be over. The tunnels in the Iron Triangle had been imploded, B-52s had carpet-bombed the area and Rome plows had finished the job, or so the experts said. They were fucked up, as usual. The VC simply dug deeper.

Less than a month later Bobby got wasted by a VC sniper. Half his face was blown away, and Tommy saw it happen. They were on patrol in the Iron Triangle. The elephant grass had grown back so thick and sharp it was like crawling through a field of bayonets. They were swimming in their uniforms from the heavy humidity and breathing like asthmatics. Their platoon was bypassing a burned-out wash, crawling through the bush on either side when a single burst from an AK-47 took out the point man. Bobby sprinted forward, stumbled and spread-eagled under a machine gun burst that cut the bush like a scythe. Tommy was fifteen yards behind Bobby in dirt up to his eyeballs with everything quiet as death except for the buzzing of crickets. They had walked into a trap.

The bush exploded in a firestorm of automatic weapons, mortars and grenades, of shouting, screaming and dying. A murderous crossfire trapped the two of them against the ground. Tommy hunkered down behind Bobby and heard himself recycling prayers he'd learned as a kid. Then off to the side behind Bobby, a sniper popped out of a tunnel hole as quick and alert as a gopher, then another and another. Tommy choked, his vocal chords froze. A sniper shot Bobby, looked at Tommy, grinned (taunting him, it seemed) and then disappeared as quickly as he had appeared. That's how Tommy remembered it. In the hail of bullets and shrapnel and screaming, he remembered the one sniper.

All he could do was pump morphine into Bobby, hold him in his arms and watch him die. Bobby didn't groan or scream or say one fucking word. He just looked at Tommy and kept dying. Then Tommy got creased by a round that knocked him into a large ditch where he eventually got medevacked out. The medics never found Bobby that day or the next day either. That really freaked him out because he'd heard all the horror stories about how the VC mutilated dead Americans.

From that day forward Tommy hated the enemy. Before Bobby died, he treated friend and enemy pretty much the same. After Bobby's death he said, "Fuck it, let the fucking wounded VC die." He even helped the little bastards along. He was also on a personal manhunt, tracking the smiling sniper who killed Bobby. He never found him, not until he saw him on *60 Minutes* twenty-five years later.

Four years after the *60 Minutes* program, he joined a tour group of veterans and teachers on a reconciliation mission to Vietnam. He was on a search and destroy mission, but he sure as hell didn't tell that to the tour leaders.

In Tommy's view their guided tour was a sham, carefully orchestrated by the Friendship Association to impress them with the goodwill of the Vietnamese people (no hard feelings over the war) and, at the same time, prick their consciences (Look what your bombers did to us!)—a two-pronged approach with both prongs aimed at their wallets.

Actually, the Viets' seductive style, emphasizing the new joint venture Renovation, reminded him of China in the 1980s, with its open-door trade policies serving as a facade for political repression *a la* Tienanmen. He wasn't buying the Vietnamese friendship hustle. It was all veneer.

Granted, the surface changes seemed impressive. Beginning with their Elvis Presley impersonator tour guide to the cowboy in Danang wearing boots and singing Hank Williams' classics, to the surfers at China Beach, to the woman who owned and managed five hotels in Saigon, the tour was a series of shocks and surprises. Betty called them reality checks. He told her to check the changes against reality.

Saigon *had* changed. Tommy felt at home with the choke of traffic and people, the squatting sidewalk vendors, aromatic markets and streetside restaurants, only now many of the vendors were selling Japanese motorbikes and techno equipment instead of American black market goodies. The moldering colonial hotels had been cleaned and renovated to bourgeois respectability for the new tourist trade. The sleaze bars and street girls had disappeared, reflecting Vietnam's new face on capitalist Renovation and tourist outreach more than strict communist rectitude.

Tommy was convinced the real Saigon was somewhere outside of the new sanitized tourist perimeter, in Cholon, maybe, where the Viets had moved in after the Chinese fled the ethnic cleansing of the late 1970s. Sure enough, he found dozens of junk and surplus shops along the narrow streets and alleyways with more visible street girls and occasionally the whiff of opium. He bought an eight-inch sheath knife from a skinny guy in baggy shorts and skivvie shirt who was busily converting war surplus bayonets into ten kinds of knives. The man was missing half a leg and worked with clawed hands.

"Russian?" the skeletal craftsman asked and fixed Tommy with yellowed eyes.

"American," he answered reluctantly.

"American," the man repeated and drew a finger across his throat. Black humor. Tommy could take it. He laughed and shook the man's twisted hand.

The taxi ride to Cu Chi was a time trip linking past and present. Turning off of Highway One, the tour group jolted over deeply rutted dirt roads, past rice fields with water buffalo, fish nets and cone-hatted peasants in black pajamas. The suffocating humidity and pungent stink of rotting mulch and shit made breathing difficult. When they drove by the old Michelin rubber plantation and Ho Bo woods with rusting hulks of M-48 tanks marking the violence of war, his stomach felt like a grenade, ready to explode.

They guzzled Cokes and beer at a crude, thatched-roof refreshment stand surrounded by a moonscape of bomb craters overgrown with weeds and American grass (seeded by American bombers to prevent the quick regrowth of Vietnamese jungle bush). For some reason he was offended by two young Frenchmen and their sleazy Vietnamese girlfriends. Like every grunt who humped in Vietnam he blamed the "fucking frogs" for sucking America into a shit-hole war.

A slender woman whose still-beautiful face was laced with napalm burn scars was selling souvenirs. He purchased a packet of postcards and a tiny kerosene tunnel lamp ingeniously crafted from an M-50 shell. She took his money with the only hand she had. The postcards were propaganda photos of VC medics giving aid to wounded Americans. He shuffled the photos like a deck of cards. Four Lilliputian VC were carting off an American Gulliver. He couldn't see the face, but he knew it was Bobby.

The photo pulled the pin of the grenade in his stomach, spewing fragments of breakfast noodles over everyone. The French kids splattered him with curses. He felt trapped in a tunnel of history with no way out. He wanted to escape. He knocked down three quick beers before a guide arrived to lecture them through a maze of *punji* stakes, tiger traps and tunnel holes landscaping the trail to the new Cu Chi Museum.

They were greeted by Mr. Nhu in a large lecture room inside the new museum. Tommy's nemesis smiled and looked directly at him just as he did two decades before. Using a large wall map and several pictorial models, Mr. Nhu spoke quietly and with pride pointed out that the Americans with all their bombs, defoliants and earth movers could not destroy the Cu Chi complex. He showed them the lethal artifacts of guerrilla war, the *punji* sticks, homemade mines and grenades made from American throwaways. A half-hour film followed, much of it wartime footage reinforcing the theme of the triumph of the spirit over technology. Tommy wanted to scream, "You forgot something, asshole, the AK-47 that you used to kill my best friend and all the tanks and heavy artillery and missiles received from your Soviet and Chinese allies!"

Five or six of them volunteered to negotiate the tunnel section reserved for tourists. Mr. Nhu took the lead, and Tommy chose the rear. He dropped through a small hole into darkness and immediately experienced severe breathing problems as if all of the air had suddenly been sucked from his chest. He dropped behind the others to avoid their panic and plan his strategy. He adjusted his breathing to the tunnel. He'd been here before. He clawed the sides of the tunnel with his bayonet knife until he scraped against wood. The branch tunnel, as he'd expected, was boarded up. He placed his back against the side opposite the intersecting tunnel and kicked at the boards until he forced it open.

He could hear the muffled cries for help and then the cheers, "We made it!" Mr. Nhu had apparently jammed his head down into the tunnel, because his voice carried clearly, "Mr. Neville, are you okay?" Tommy began crawling down the smaller side tunnel, blinded for a moment by a flurry of bats. He hoped to hell he could somehow avoid the snakes, scorpions and poisonous spiders. He was losing his breath. He lay flat on the cool ground until he recovered his breathing, an old tunnel rat technique. Mr. Nhu was honing in on him in the dark. Tommy could feel it, just as Nhu could sense where he was. He crawled around a sharp turn in the dark and waited, scarcely breathing. His heart was pounding like a pile driver. A light flickered. Nhu had made the first turn. He pulled the bayonet knife from its sheath. The light stopped flickering.

"Mr. Neville, are you there?"

Silence.

"Mr. Neville, please answer me."

He could barely breathe now. His arms and hands were becoming numb from the cramped position, but he had to survive long enough to avenge Bobby's death. He had to do it. The light flickered again. Mr. Nhu was crawling slowly, deliberately. He too was a time traveler back in the tunnels of a generation ago. Tommy was feeling dizzy, thirsty, weak, but he had to do it for Bobby.

Nhu's voice seemed to come from a great distance, as soft and articulate as the sappers who tried to penetrate their perimeters with their textbook English. "Mr. Neville, please, the war is over. I want to help you, please."

He blacked out for a moment and in that moment he saw a thousand Mr. Nhus like the thousand Buddhas he'd once seen in a Japanese temple, in perfect replicate, stretching into infinity. He ran from one to the other, desperate to find Bobby's killer. He couldn't. He wanted to kill them all, but he couldn't.

Every tunnel rat in Vietnam eventually reached a point of no return, a sudden and total realization that it's over, that you can never again face the terror, the darkness and the danger. Tommy got jolted twenty-five years too late while trapped in a time tunnel with the walls caving in. He threw down his knife and hugged the cool ground.

"Tommy, Tommy," the voice whispered from over his shoulder.

"Who?" he asked, knowing damn well who it was.

"It's me, Bobby. I knew you'd come back, old buddy. I've been waiting a long time."

"Mr. Neville, it's me, Mr. Nhu. Please answer me."

"Bobby," he whispered, "I don't think I can go through with this. I don't want to go through with it."

"Jesus Christ, Tommy, why did you bring the fucking knife? Why in hell did you return?" Bobby asked.

He couldn't answer. He didn't want to answer.

"Tommy, goddammit, answer me!"

"Mr. Neville, are you there? Say something. Please don't panic. I'm coming."

"Yeah, I hear you, Bobby."

"Tommy, you're the only one I've ever really loved. I never told you that but it's true, I swear to God."

He started crying and raised himself off the floor of the tunnel and reached for the bayonet blade. The hand with the flashlight appeared first and then, very slowly, the head of the VC killer. He lunged upward with all of the body muscle he could muster, torquing the knife, trying to stab upward through the mouth and into the brain. He lunged and then blacked out.

Bobby really did love him. They were deep inside the Tunnel of Love at Playland by Ocean Beach and Bobby was making love to him like he'd never done before and the aroma of garlic and sandalwood was new and sweet and wonderful . . .

Tommy regained consciousness with his head in Mr. Nhu's lap. Mr. Nhu's lips were pressed against his mouth, giving him mouth-to-mouth resuscitation. His breath tasted of garlic; a whiff of sandalwood drifted off his hair and clothing. When Tommy started breathing regularly, Mr. Nhu sat up and smiled. They were in a large dugout roofed with thatch barely above ground. It must have been used for a clinic or kitchen during the war. Mr. Nhu had dragged Tommy away from the suffocating tunnels so he could breathe freely.

Tommy tried to sit up but he was still too dizzy and weak. He fell back into Mr. Nhu's arms and heard a grunt of pain. He saw then that Mr. Nhu's right arm was wrapped with a bloodied shirt sleeve.

"I'm sorry," Tommy said. "I did it for Bobby. He's the American you and Morley Safer talked about, the one you killed. He was big and strong, as handsome as a movie star. I loved him."

Mr. Nhu seemed confused. "Don't worry about the wound," he said. "It's nothing, but after all these years, how can you remember who killed your friend?"

"I thought I remembered you," Tommy said. "I was sure I remembered you."

"I might have killed your friend," Mr. Nhu replied. "I was a sniper and sharpshooter. But whatever I did, whatever you did, it's time for us to end our war in Vietnam; it's important for both of us."

He paused, waiting for the American's response, but Tommy was too weak and confused to answer him. Mr. Nhu continued, "It wasn't your friend I was referring to in my conversation with Mr. Safer; it was someone like you, someone who had a cross on his helmet. I looked at him and he looked at me. He was small and strong and tender like a Vietnamese. That made me angry. So I shot him as he held the dying American soldier in his arms. I thought I had killed him. I have never escaped the horror of what I did that day."

Mr. Nhu was crying. He leaned forward and kissed Tommy on the lips. When Mr. Nhu smiled at him again, Tommy reached up, pulled his enemy's face to his own and followed his advice. He kissed him and kept kissing him until he saw light at the end of the tunnel. He kissed him until his war in Vietnam was over.

The Hustler

He was tanned and prematurely gray with a profile like Gregory Peck. He'd hustled the tour leaders like he'd hustled most of the other victims of his good looks and smooth tongue—with half-truths and persuasive fictions. The eye patch he wore with such aristocratic nonchalance resulted from a bar fight in Watsonville, California, not, as he claimed, from a mortar fragment in Vietnam.

Since his army days, Ben Hubbard had hustled everything from real estate to savings and loans and retirement scams. He had once romanced a Pacific Heights divorcee out of half a million dollars on an investment bilk and then, in a premier performance, had romanced her out of a lawsuit. After the S&L brouhaha, he'd been reduced to operating gambling-prostitution bars in shitty little backwaters like Soledad and Gonzales, skinning truck crop illegals of their slim pickings. At his best or worst, he was a slippery chameleon, a horned toad playing Prince Charming, a sleazy loan shark inside a sharkskin suit.

For Ben Hubbard, no scheme or scam could begin to compare with the star-spangled hustle of the Vietnam War where he'd been the ultimate REMF. As top supply sergeant at Bien Hoa Airbase, he controlled the continuous flow of American goodies—millions of dollars worth—that had turned the base into a kind of WalMart Club Med. "Ain't fucking nothin' I cain't get fur fucking nobody," he had twanged like Andy Griffith in the mangled syntax expected of the dumb-like-a-fox supply sergeants.

Hubbard and five supply sergeant buddies who'd made their first killing in Germany later connived to control supply for the giant military installations in Vietnam, where they received generous kickbacks from the Mafia contractor who served as supply broker for all the bases in Vietnam. The drug trade channeled from French Corsicans into military bases through corrupt ARVN officers provided even bigger rake-offs. Hubbard's mistress-partner, Mai Ly Chung, a classy Cholon Chinese, handled the stable of call girls and prostitutes in return for a skim of luxury items destined for the Bien Hoa PX.

The war's abrupt end exploded Hubbard's cozy setup so brutally he'd never fully recovered, partly because Mai Ly Chung, in retaliation for being summarily dumped (after he'd massaged her with promises of a honeymoon in America), had cleaned Hubbard's secret safe of fifty thousand American dollars. He still hadn't figured out how she'd stolen the combination.

So under the guise of reconciliation, he'd joined the tour determined to hack out his piece of the new capitalist Renovation, mainly in order to renovate his own shabby fortunes.

He carried all of his savings in a cashiers check for fifty thousand dollars as a down payment on his millionaire's dream. Maybe he could even exact a little revenge on the side since he firmly believed in what goes around comes around—for others, of course, not for himself. While other tour members extended their hands in friendship, Ben Hubbard was reaching for the fast buck, hustling joint venture possibilities and casing out the most energetic free-booters. Hubbard's freelance finagling became a pain in the ass for the tour leaders, but he finessed their whining with his facile Vietnamese and glib, gregarious style that the Vietnamese, at least, seemed to appreciate.

But all of Hubbard's scheming and schmoozing, however entertaining to the Vietnamese, brought him nothing tangible. "You very funny man," they would laugh, "but we can do nothing until the U.S. embargo is lifted."

"Fuck the embargo," Hubbard had growled to himself again and again. In Danang he persuaded the tour leaders to fire off an angry fax to the president with a dozen reasons for lifting the embargo. Two days later trade restrictions were partially relaxed. Hubbard naturally credited his fax as the persuader that broke the impasse and took it as a sign of his soon-to-rise fortunes. Vietnam had always been his oyster. Now he only had to find the pearl. And the pearl he knew was buried in the pearly parts of the whore called Miss Saigon, mistress to Ho Chi Minh City. If anyone could suck out the pearl, he was the man, even if he had to go down on his fucking knees, by God!

Hubbard ditched the tour his first day in Saigon in order to revisit his old haunts. All the girlie bars, gambling dens and opium houses, he discovered, had been obliterated during the massive re-education program following liberation. His former connections as antisocial elements he assumed had also been obliterated, or were still doing time in the rural boonies.

He returned to the hotel in a funk, exhausted and stinking with sweat, where he was met by Betty Volsted, his petite and energetic tour leader. He expected a chiding, but she only pinched his fat ring and laughed. "Ben, whatever you do this afternoon, don't miss this evening's session. We're meeting with the woman who owns this hotel and several others. She's one of the new entrepreneurs behind Renovation, a real mover and shaker in more ways than one." Betty winked at him and did a quick hip twist. "I've met her; she's elegance personified. She must come from some old wealthy Chinese family."

Ben winked in return and grinned, "Wouldn't miss it, sweetheart. Now I gotta get out of these stinking clothes. This heat is killing me."

He spent the afternoon at the Hotel Continental bar listening to Japanese and Scandinavian businessmen trying to converse with each other and their Vietnamese hosts in English. It was a fucking scream. Eventually he was joined by a young American in his early thirties who represented several California developers. David King had arrived with power of attorney agreements for a dozen American-Vietnamese families willing to part with former properties they had long ago kissed good-bye. Convinced that normalization would include compensation for confiscated properties, King and his corporate clients determined to move quickly in a buyer's market.

"Jesus, man, aren't you jumping the gun?" Hubbard was astonished.

"Not really," King replied, "at this point both governments are eager to facilitate good relations and smooth out all the kinks. Hell, there are at least a dozen MIA-POW groups from the U.S. digging up the jungles for American bones."

"Yeah," Hubbard mused, "but your enterprise still strikes me as pretty damn iffy, as one hell of a risk."

"No way," King said. "Six months from now, if this Renovation thing flies, my clients would be paying ten, twenty, maybe thirty times as much. Prices are gonna go through the fucking ceiling."

After King left, Hubbard cursed himself for a fool. He lived near the largest Vietnamese community in America and missed the chance to make his fortune. He started drinking seriously, chasing every beer with a jigger of whiskey.

In the late afternoon he wandered half-crocked past the big hotels and new tourist boutiques to the Saigon River waterfront. Purely by accident or stumbling fortune, he chanced on the pearl of his dreams, a ramshackle double-decker ferry with small shops on the ground floor and a restaurant on the second level. What Hubbard saw through his mental haze and visionary stupor was not a peeling junk heap but a beautifully accoutered gambling casino and restaurant bar bathed in the golden glow of circling lights. He envisioned a mecca for wealthy Asian businessmen, flying in for weekend R&R where they could be fleeced and fucked by lubricious, leggy hostesses and go home happy. He startled passersby by shouting with drunken enthusiasm, "Mai Ly Chung, you beautiful bitch, where are you now that I fucking need you?"

So captivated was Hubbard by the pot of gold vision culminating his rainbow dreams that he plopped on a rickety bench, taking nips from a fifth of Suntory. He stayed until the sunset glow turned to grimy dusk and the wetness in his crotch where he'd dribbled a bit began to rub him raw. Then he remembered the evening program.

"Jesus," he laughed, "I'll have to change these pants. Can't let the elegant Chinese lady see that I've got a leaky faucet. No shiree, wouldn't do 'tall, no shiree."

He laughed again at the improbability of a Vietnamese woman, even Chinese, owning several hotels. Impossible. "Jus' don't fuckin' believe it," he said out loud and signaled for a cab.

He didn't laugh when he first saw the elegant hotelier-businesswoman. She was celery slim, except for curvaceous hips and a bust that strained against her clinging *ao dai*. Her hair was cut short in the chic 1940s film noir style—*a la* Anna Mae Wong. With her sculpted cheeks and exuberant lips she was a knockout, striking and mysterious. Hubbard closed his eyes to imagine her ungirdled body parts. *Dark obsidian eyes lasered into his naked fantasies; a reptilian tongue flickered out of a ripe mouth and stung him on the lips; razor-sharp geisha teeth caressed his throat.* Christ! He awakened with a jerk that snapped his neck. He cursed his stupidity for getting sloshed. The cold shower helped, but after popping several uppers his face was still on fire, and the veins in his nose were flashing like neon lights. Goddamn, if the woman didn't seem as confident and tough as Madame Nhu herself. "We'll see," he muttered to himself. "I've dealt with tough tomatoes all my life. Beneath the peel they're sauce for the spreading."

"Good evening," she said and held out her hand with the index finger missing. The shock of recognition almost sent him spinning into cardiac arrest. He was still trying to catch his breath when she smiled ever so slightly. Her hint of recognition—if it was that—was barely a flicker. As she turned away, the hairball in his throat was drowned in a rush of angry bile spewing into his throat and mouth. He ran to the bathroom, spat the bitter bungee strings of yellow phlegm and rinsed his mouth. When he returned, Mai Ly Chung, ex-hustler and whore, was speaking quietly in elegant English.

"I want to be frank," she said. "My story is not very pretty. It may not be very interesting to media hype Americans."

Oh yeah, it's gonna be more than interesting for me, Pimples (he remembered his pet name for her). *It's gonna be as fascinating as hell. Tell it straight, baby, like it was, 'cause your daddy* Doppelganger *is looking up your crack into your black double-crossing heart.*

"I was not a poor country girl forced into Saigon by family poverty or the destructive bombing, nor was I forced into being a bar girl, a boom-boom girl servicing the animal needs of young Americans in heat."

Spare me, Pimples. I'm gonna cry. You gonna say you never played the Star Spangled Banner *on your boom-boom box, never fucked Americans?*

"My father, long since dead, was a successful businessman. He had a clothing factory and rice processing plant in Ho Chi Minh City-Saigon. I had been sent to secondary school in Hue and later to a Lycee in Lyon, France. When I returned in the mid-'60s, the Americans were here in force. They seemed to be everywhere, spreading like a disease."

Oh yeah, baby, tell them about disease. You're the expert. Tell them about the dose of clap you fucking laid on me. Tell them.

"While I was studying in France, my father's business collapsed—went down the tubes as you Americans say. Everywhere the rice fields were being destroyed by the bombing and toxic poisons. Cheap clothing was being imported with the rice so both businesses collapsed simultaneously. Our family had lost both legs, so to speak. My education and language skills helped to get me hired as a pool secretary for MACV headquarters. Eventually I became private secretary to Colonel Tanner, who was in charge of intelligence for MACV."

Beautiful, baby, fucking beautiful. You went vertical by going horizontal. You slept with every fucking officer at MACV except the general himself, because rumor was he could only raise the flag to half-mast. Tell it like it was, baby.

"To make a long story short, I became my boss' mistress. It was simply expected, no questions asked. That simple. He did set me up in a beautiful apartment and made me his Asian doll. Bottom line, I was the main support for my family. They depended on me. I couldn't afford to offend my powerful master."

I'm crying, baby, such a touching story. You had it so rough being set up in your luxury apartment. Compared with most Vietnamese girls, yours was a Cinderella story. And just who is the Prince Charming who put the slipper on your footsie? I can't wait.

"Eventually, of course, my colonel started seeing other younger women, girls even, teenagers. And he was in his forties. When I complained, he beat me up, kicked me out of the apartment and out of my job. I was blackballed at MACV permanently."

Yeah, sweetheart, and the ruckus you caused got the most competent officer in Vietnam a reprimand that ruined his career and eventually his marriage. But, hey baby, what happened to Prince Charming, yours truly, the guy with the golden slipper?

"Fortunately, I guess, a sergeant in charge of supplies at Bien Hoa rescued me. The enlisted men, you see, get the officers' castaways. To my surprise, the sergeant had more clout, influence and power than any officer. I supplied girls for the base in return for a cut of PX goodies destined for the black market. He also gave me a case of VD that left me permanently sterile, but, as you Americans say, it comes with the territory."

You fucking bitch! After all I did for you and now you turn everything around. I always suspected you were a commie VC, a fucking traitor. I knew it. I fucking knew it!

"Like most of the other American saviors in Vietnam, my sergeant hero abandoned me in spite of sworn promises of marriage and returning with him to America. He made no provision for my survival in Vietnam, so I had to look out for myself."

Beautiful. She looked out for herself. I wanna cry my eyes out. The fifty thou must have bought you a few spring rolls, some bowls of Pho. *Jesus! With that kind of money, you could have bought the whole fucking country in 1975!*

"I went through a painful re-education which, if nothing else, gave me pause to reevaluate my life. Who I was and where I was going. Eventually, it seemed like a lifetime, I used the money I'd saved and set aside to invest in some rundown hotels which I renovated just before the tourist boom. My five hotels are doing very well and I think I am too. Any questions?"

Any questions? Jesus, bitch. I've got fifty thousand questions, but let me ask just one, only one: What the fuck happened to my money?

Ben Hubbard swallowed the bitter bile that roiled up in his gut. Mai Ly Chung, he realized, was the one person in Vietnam who could turn his fantasy into reality. She was the Miss Saigon whose pearly parts held the pearl of his dreams.

A day later, after he'd slept off and sweated out his delirious inner demons, Hubbard took a taxi to one of Mai Ly Chung's larger hotels which catered exclusively to businessmen. "Madame Chung isn't in," the secretary said.

"I'll wait," he said.

"She's not coming in today," the secretary said.

"I'll come back tomorrow," he said, and so on. He called a dozen times the following day and got stonewalled each time. He couldn't believe the whore who sucked his dick on cue was putting him down. In a final fury of frustration he yelled, "Fuck you, bitch!" into the buzzing phone.

The tour was winding down to its last twenty-four hours. He went to the Hotel Continental bar as he had every evening to schmooze with foreigners and suck up to the Vietnamese. Only now he knew he'd missed the main chance. The game was over. Fuck it. He took an obscure corner and simply drank.

He was on his third whiskey sour when a Vietnamese with a briefcase smiled and walked his way. (The man, in fact, was one of several dozen operatives who cruised Saigon's big hotel bars looking for prime entrepreneurial suspects.)

"May I please sit down?"

Jesus! The man's scabby red face looked like he'd fallen into a fucking fire. War-related, probably.

"Sure, what the hell; it's a free fucking country now, isn't it?" The man laughed politely. Hubbard thrust out his hand. "Ben Hubbard, glad to meetcha."

"Bao Duc Binh; my pleasure." The man's hand felt as cold as a fish on ice.

The Vietnamese ordered a soft drink for himself and another whiskey sour for Hubbard. "Tell me, Mr. Hubbard," Binh said, "are you in Vietnam to give or to take?"

Hubbard, always quick on the uptake, replied, "Everyone's on the take. How's about give *and* take, trade, investment, joint venture or whatever is always a two-way street, right?"

Mr. Binh laughed again, less forced this time. "Okay, fair enough. Tell me what you have to give and I'll tell you what I can take and give in return."

Ben Hubbard was as eloquent as he'd ever been. He chortled silently at what an easy mark the guy was. They talked and drank for three hours, enjoyed a late dinner together and agreed to meet in Mr. Binh's office the next morning.

Mr. Binh had everything laid out. He was authorized by the Department of Commerce and Trade to negotiate joint venture contracts as a representative of the 333 Corporation, duly incorporated with the Democratic Republic of Vietnam. Hubbard was not surprised at how smoothly the deal was consummated. His salesmanship had, after all, been irresistible. For an initial good faith investment of fifty thousand dollars followed by five hundred thousand more in three months, Ben Hubbard was guaranteed forty-five percent of a restaurant-entertainment venture to open in six months, dependent on the United States lifting the embargo.

The only glitch—a minor one, in Hubbard's view—was that if he did not come up with the half-mil in six months the deal was off; he'd lose his fifty thousand. Hubbard figured to raise the half-mil in a month, less than a month—Jesus—in a fucking week! What he couldn't tell Mr. Binh, of course, was the thing that made him supremely happy. He knew that with his foot in the door he would soon enough have it up one elegant lady's ass, the bitch-goddess entrepreneur who'd stolen his money. He would have her hotels in a year at the outside and have her begging on her knees, sucking his dick, if you please.

He signed the cashiers check with a flourish and gave it to Mr. Binh with a smile and a handshake.

"By the way, Mr. Binh," he inquired, "333 is also the name of my favorite Vietnamese beer. Is your corporation also into beer making?"

"Yes, we are the beer makers. That's our main enterprise; hotels are only a sideline."

"Does your corporation have someone like a CEO, a person who really runs the show?"

Mr. Binh laughed. "Oh yes, very much so, believe me, a real tiger lady as you Americans might say. She's also the major stockholder." Mr. Binh leaned forward to whisper behind his cupped hand, "Some people even claim she has brass balls. Ha! Ha! Ha!"

"Really," said Hubbard. "Does this wonder woman have a name?"

Mr. Binh put the cashiers check in his briefcase, locked it and rose slowly to his feet. "Her name is Madame Mai Ly Chung, but we call her Chairman Mao because she runs the corporation like a Chinese dictator."

The Wall

From where he sat some fifty yards up the slope, the long black slab of granite stuck in the gash of earth between America's most sacred icons reminded him of an unhealed wound, a wound that stretched all the way to Vietnam, a wound that left a hole in the jungle wall of his unconscious big enough for the ghosts of his old recon squad to return on a mind-fucking search and destroy mission.

So he'd come to the Wall, finally, to make peace with himself and his recon mates, to heal, if he could, the wound that lay between them. If his mission failed, well, hell, he'd put a fucking gun to his head. He'd screamed at the motherfuckers every night for weeks and months until he lost his fucking voice, lost his family and lost his fucking business to the fucking banks.

I DID NOT TURN MY BACK AND LET YOU MOTHERFUCKERS DIE!

He sucked the fifth of Johnny Walker dry, tossed the bottle down the slope and watched it sink into one of the muddy rivulets bleeding from the soggy turf as if the earth itself were wounded. Then he spread himself on his raincoat in a crucifix and stared through naked limbs still defoliated from the winter's freeze. He stared into space and remembered.

He remembered the shock of arriving in country as a clean, green cherry in new fatigues and battle gear and getting totally whacked by the humid heat and burning shit (the military's sewage solution). Some god-awful grungy grunts, stripped to the waist, were stirring gasoline into half-drums of latrine shit and firing the devil's brew into an inferno of flaming black smoke. He watched, in disbelief, a minstrel show from hell; marines in black face were cursing and prancing in circles to ribald marching chants, howling insults at each other, fighting and laughing, coughing and puking, stoned cloud cuckoo crazy. When the wind shifted suddenly his way he gagged and puked all over himself.

Five marines just in from patrol, sitting on packs and swilling beer, started laughing. They were lathered in mud and sweat and caked with ten kinds of shit. They inhaled the sickening smoke like it was a Saigon whore's perfume and laughed as crazily as the shit-burners.

"Better get used to it, son," a sergeant said, "this stinking shit is like the whole dirty, fucking war. You ain't never gonna get clean again, not as long as you fucking live."

Laughter and shouts of "Fucking A" arose from the group.

"Man, we so buried in shit we cain't burn it off."

"Yeah man, but we keep risin' from the shit jus' like old Lazarus."

More laughter was followed by several amens and "Preach it, Brother Belcher."

"Some of us even—" the tall black marine interrupted himself to walk over and shake hands. "What ol' Sarge means, man, is even if you survive, you ain't nevah gonna wash this shit off. But don't sweat it, man, we all in this shit together. Fact is this shit is the fuckin' glue, man, that keep us together, you dig?"

"Man, you are full of shit," added a wiry little Mexican, who would later be called la Bamba.

When the big black man turned around and yelled, "No shit?" they rolled in the dirt.

Someone said, "Take a load off, brother," and passed him a lukewarm beer and a roach.

The LURP patrol had all been in country six months or more. He reckoned they had chosen him as a mascot on a drunken whim or because he was the sorriest looking FNG (Fucking New Guy) they'd ever seen. Whatever their reasons, one fact stood clear to him, without them he'd have been wasted a dozen times over, sent home in a zippered bag or blown to scattered shit. He wasn't aware at the time that he'd been accepted by the most elite unit in Vietnam, four of the half-dozen survivors of the A Shau ambush that wiped out an entire company. Hence their moniker and motto, "the Meanest Motherfuckers from the A Shau Valley of Death who feared no evil but Victor Charlie because he was also one mean motherfucker." Their respect for the fighting qualities of Sir Charles had saved their asses more than once.

As a wild bunch, they put the Dirty Dozen next to Victorian ladies at high tea—not on patrol where every move, every breath was disciplined by a finely tuned fear, but when they returned to the fire base and cut loose like Viking berserkers in Valhalla. He remembered coming off his first search and destroy, utterly exhausted and ready to die from the heat and hell of it all. The new CO, appalled by their draggle-ass appearance, stupidly called them to inspection. "Fuck you, captain, sir!" the mothers yelled and stampeded the entire company over the hapless Lifer, shedding packs and rifles and clothing on a wild race to hot showers and cold beer.

When that same captain retaliated by sending the MPs to close down the Mothers' private clubhouse, a bunker stocked with the best booze and grass and sweetest whores (smuggled with recon expertise through a mass of razor wire) on base, the Mothers fought them off in a furious battle known as "The Night They Tried to Tear Old Dixie Down." Nobody, not even the captain, gave the Mothers shit after the MPs bugled retreat.

They were closer than husbands and wives and families because they had experienced the ultimate communion, the intimacy of death, in which the giving and taking of life, the sacrifice of oneself for others, was a daily ritual. Before every patrol they'd link arms in a tight circle and recite the Motherfuckers Creed—Cal Belcher, the "preacher" from Indiana, Hector Rojas from Texas known as la Bamba, Bad Ass Albert Johnson, the black dude from Tennessee, Ken Chisholm the Arkansas razorback and the half-assed cherry from California, Andy Fetzer. Preacher took the lead, the others responded in rhythmic chants:

"Tell me, brothers, tell me, who's gonna die for the sins of Amereekay?

No way, no way, we gonna die for the sins of Amereekay.

Tell me, brothers, tell me, who's gonna die for the sins of Amereekay?

Tell the NVA and the VCA, they gonna die for the sins of Amereekay?

No way we gonna die for the sins of Amereekay! No way!"

As a finale they'd raise their canteen cups full of whiskey piss and drink to the Meanest Motherfuckers from the A Shau Valley of Death. Then they'd slap each other through a soul brother dap led by brother Albert Johnson, hoist their packs and hump into hell.

Neither prayers nor curses uttered in religious ribaldry had saved them. His recon mates died for America's sins and for their own. They fucked up and they died. He did not fuck up and he lived. That's what he had to tell himself, as simple as that. But he knew he had survived by turning his back on his recon group. The pain of that wound and separation almost put him under.

He survived by crawling inside the hard core of himself. By numbing himself to the compassion and vulnerability that brings death in its wake, he was able to walk the razor's edge of sanity. Otherwise he'd have sucked his M-16 on full rock and roll, OD'd on smack or fragged a Lifer into hell and himself into Leavenworth.

He survived after the war as he had during the war by building a thick callous around his feelings. That's how he freed himself of the demons that crippled or destroyed so many fellow vets. He figured a lot of them had been fuckups in the service. That's what he told himself.

Maybe he was taking too much credit. He reckoned the key to his success was his work in carpentry and construction. By building houses he'd rebuilt his life. That and Sally—Sally for sure. Hell, he'd veered off track for a time, during his years at City College especially, playing Mr. Goodbar, getting in bar fights, busting up war protesters, racing cops on 280 in his souped-up Trans Am and getting zonkered on grass and Johnny Walker. Sally, yeah Sally, the cute little dishwater blonde in his psych class, had finally straightened him out, thank the Lord.

Thank the Lord. He never thought he'd say those words with a straight face, or get religion, or get baptized. But God Almighty, when he came out of the water he felt so clean, like he'd finally got all the shit washed off, "washed in the blood of the lamb" as they liked to say in Sally's little Baptist church.

Their marriage had survived, he supposed, because they'd both kept so busy—he with his own construction business, finally; Sally with the girls and teaching school. Sally was one hell of a woman—all woman—in bed and out. So he'd kept his nose pretty clean. Enough said.

He laughed. Sally had been his teenage sweetheart and now he had teenage daughters of his own attending City College. Good girls and good students. For that he gave Sally most of the credit. She'd raised them, really, guiding them through the middle school terrors of sex and drugs, through the pains of growing up in a society without clear-cut standards and values where anything goes. He supposed they'd experimented with sex and drugs. He really didn't know, because he'd always kept his distance; it was his way of surviving.

Sally had once told him, laughing with a cutting edge, how Julie had responded to a counselor's query regarding his role in family crises. "Well, Dad is kind of like the Goodyear blimp I see on Monday night football. He's always floating at a distance, never really involved."

He knew that Sally told him the story as an invitation to change his behavior, to participate in family problems, but he couldn't survive that way. He survived by keeping his distance, by avoiding counselors, therapy groups, vet organizations, or anything that might recall Vietnam and get him buried in shit again.

Then, out of nowhere, came the nightmares once or twice a month, then weekly, then several nights a week, encounters with his old platoon mates, just as he'd seen them that terrifying day in An Khe—filthy, caked with mud and shit, faces lined like old men's faces with eyes sunk in caverns, eyes that held an inflammable mixture of anger, hate, terror and utter cynicism, eyes devoid of human sympathy, eyes which had witnessed such horror they had become blinded to horror. Now they were circling him, closer and closer with flat, hard eyes as accusatory as demented holocaust victims staring through barbed wire.

I DID NOT TURN MY BACK AND LET YOU MOTHERFUCKERS DIE!

He knew, finally, that he would have to go to the Wall because they came at him through the Wall, crawling through cracks oozing shit and slush, snakes and leeches and rivers of blood. He knew it was the Wall, because he could see all the neatly chiseled names under the blood-smeared graffiti.

Sally had cried and begged to come with him, but he insisted on going alone. "I've always wanted to see the Vietnam Memorial," she said. "I don't care about the others, Washington, Lincoln whatever. Mostly though, I want to do it with you."

"What about the girls?" he asked.

"Maybe you hadn't noticed," she said, "but they've grown up. They're young women."

"Maybe you need to grow up," he said without thinking.

She started crying. "You bastard, how can you say a stupid thing like that? You're the one who's never grown up. You've never left Vietnam. You've never really come home!"

"Look," he said, "I don't want to argue about it. I guarantee the Wall is not going to walk off; believe me, it'll still be there. We'll see it together later, I promise."

"Fat chance," she said, "but will I be here, later?" The bitterness in her voice surprised him.

"What in hell do you mean by that?" he asked. He could almost feel the ground beneath him breaking apart.

She tried to gain control, biting her lip until it bled. "It's just that I'm always here like some fixture, a faucet to be turned on and off. You simply take me for granted."

"No," he said, "I don't. Not really. I just don't know how to show my feelings."

"Well you can show your feelings by taking me with you," she insisted.

"You don't understand," he said. "You just don't fucking understand." He turned and walked out the door.

He moved out of the house because he wanted to be in control. The LURPs from hell were crawling through the cracks in his cranial wall several nights a week and he didn't want anyone to get hurt, least of all Sally. But moving out only made things worse. With a downturn in construction, he started drinking heavily and popping pills. He got ambushed by the banks on his loans, and wouldn't answer Sally's calls. When she came with Susan and Julie, he drove them off. Then he punched the Baptist minister. Sally stopped calling after that.

Well, he got what he wanted—to sit alone on a lonely slope feeling lonely as hell. Jesus, how he missed Sally and the girls. She was right, of course; he hardly knew his daughters. But hell, he'd busted his ass twelve, fourteen hours a day for his family. And what did Sally mean by saying, "Will I be here?" She'd never talked that way. God, how it rankled. That's what really pissed him off, that she had talked to him that way.

He sat and watched the pilgrimage below him: veterans of every description, whole and handicapped, bearded and clean-shaven, in suits and old fatigues. How many of them, he wondered, had fucked up their personal lives? Some could have passed for homeless, and maybe they were. The vets were mixed with family groups, seniors, teenagers and others, most of whom stopped along the way to trace their fingers over names, leave flowers, medals, pictures and other mementos. Mostly they walked silently, wept silently and left silently.

He'd been sitting here for three days. He kept telling himself there were too many people. He didn't like crowds. The real reason, of course, was that he couldn't face "them." So he spent his mornings on the slope above the Wall and his afternoons visiting museums.

On his third visit to the Smithsonian he met a black man, his Vietnamese wife and teenage kids, two daughters and a sullen-faced boy with a Mets cap worn flipside. They were looking at Lindbergh's *Spirit of Saint Louis*.

"*Chao* (hello)," he said. The wife smiled and whispered to the kids, who mumbled an obligatory "hi." The husband looked him over carefully before saying, "What's doin', man?"

The two of them had a guarded conversation, mostly marine talk, while the wife and kids wandered off to look at other exhibits. Ishmael Breedlove had been with a river patrol in the Delta in 1967 and 1968. He'd re-enlisted to eventually become a topkick at Pendleton and Paris Island before returning to Vietnam for a second tour when he got scalped by a razored chunk of hot shrapnel.

"You retired now?"

"Yeah, partial disability. Fucking headaches drive me crazy sometimes." Breedlove looked at his wife. "She's the one who catches hell."

"Yeah, I know, I've had some problems myself; wife and I are separated."

Breedlove grunted and laughed, "Can't afford that," he said. "Need the wife's income. She makes top salary as a translator. If it wasn't for her income . . ." When his wife looked at him, Breedlove motioned her away. "She sends half her salary to her family in Vietnam. Most of it goes down a government rat hole or into some bureaucrat's pocket, I'm sure. Shit. We go around and around on this but, hell, you marry a Vietnamese, you marry the whole fucking family. Careful where you dip your dick, man. They got muscles you wouldn't believe."

He laughed because it was the farthest thing from his mind. When he saw Breedlove's wife frowning their way, he changed the subject. "You said you were out of the service?"

"Yeah, well, not really," Breedlove said.

"I guess a marine never retires, at least not mentally."

"Well, that's just it," the man said, "I've been counseling, working with vets, mostly with stressed-out brothers."

"I guess we've still got a lot of fucked-up vets around."

"Yeah, only they got a fancy name for it now, call it Post Traumatic Stress Disorder. How you doin'?"

"Okay, man, I'm doing okay." But he put a quick freeze on the conversation, shook hands and left quickly. Despite his awkwardness, he felt the encounter with the vet and his Vietnamese wife and family had somehow liberated him. He believed he could now face his recon mates at the Wall and reunite with his own family.

On the following day, clouds rolled in with flurries of rain. He left the hotel early to beat the crowd. He had the taxi driver drop him by the Lincoln Memorial and handed him the fee with a nice tip. The driver returned it, smiling.

"Semper fi," the driver said and turned around with a thumb upturned. "No pay marine, okay?" He was Vietnamese.

"Yeah, thanks," he smiled and returned the thumbs-up salute. He walked around the Lincoln rotunda to escape the rain and thought about the earlier war that had been so divisive and unpopular, if his history books had been correct. How many had died, over half a million? He wondered how far the Wall would stretch if the two million dead Vietnamese were added. He read the chiseled words of the Gettysburg Address: "that these dead shall not have died in vain." Neither Nixon nor Johnson had said anything meaningful about the Vietnam War. Maybe some future president would make sense of the tragedy. Maybe, but he had his doubts.

The rain had reduced the visitors to a trickle. Several older ladies were placing flowers at the base of the Wall near the entrance. He nodded to a man his age in a wheelchair who was wearing dark glasses. The young woman who was pushing him smiled. He passed several people who were reaching up to touch the names of brothers or sons or husbands.

He stopped because he felt their living presence, not because he knew where the names, Kenneth Chisholm, Hector Rojas, Albert Johnson and Calvin Belcher, were chiseled in granite. He knew they would be at eye level and they were, not just the names but the faces, just as he'd seen them in his dreams, smeared with shit and mud and staring with eyes gone dead. He felt dizzy and fell forward, bracing his hands against the Wall. When he regained his balance he saw that his hands were covered with blood. "Jesus Christ. No!" he yelled and wiped his hands against his coat.

I DID NOT TURN MY BACK AND LET YOU MOTHERFUCKERS DIE!

He was still wiping his hands when he heard the whop-whop-whopping of the helicopter gunship. The death machine always sucked his breath away and loosened his bowels. He felt the heat envelop him as it had the day they torched the hamlet near Khe Sanh. Their company had been on search and destroy for three days. Three men had been lost to a VC ambush with five more wounded. They'd killed three of the enemy. They were as filthy, exhausted, angry and hungry for revenge as grunts could be. He knew something bad was happening when Hector knifed a wounded VC, cut off his balls and jammed them down the boy's throat. Ken and Albert cut the ears and strung them on their belts for the first time ever.

They received sporadic fire from the ville, which was all the captain needed or maybe wanted. The Cobra gunships swooped in with napalm and M-50s and turned the ville into a firestorm. The grunts walked in for the cleanup, machine-gunning leftover hooches, throwing grenades into tunnels and storage holes, torching the leftovers. It was stupid, really. The VC would always be long gone; the women, oldsters and kids would be cowering in the woods or rice paddies.

Albert had shredded one of the burned-over hooches with his M-16 on rock and roll and was about to torch the leftovers when Cal Belcher yelled, "Hold it, Bad Ass, I think we got some gook leftovers for the captain's body count."

By the time he arrived, Cal, Albert, Hector, Ken and another grunt were in the hooch looking at the carnage, at the blood, brains and dismembered body parts splattered among the splintered household items.

Ken Chisholm gagged, "Jesus Christ, what a fucking mess. Somebody's shit really got scattered."

Hector looked at Ken and sneered, "Yeah, they picked the wrong fucking side, didn't they?"

Hector must have seen the girl when he turned because he had his M-16 on her before her head was out of the hole. She was young, maybe fourteen, and badly burned. She was holding her busted eardrums, crying and shaking uncontrollably. She'd messed her pants and streams were running from her eyes and nose and mouth. She fell to her knees and tried to cover her breasts.

"Well goddamn, lookee what we got here," said Cal. "Looks like we got some free VC pussy."

He unbuckled his belt and pack. The other guys followed suit. All he could hear was heavy breathing and the girl's crying. He couldn't look at the girl, and he couldn't look at them. He started to walk out. Cal stopped him.

"Hey, man, where the fuck you goin'? Are you one of us or not?"

"Maybe he's too good for VC pussy."

"Thinks he'll get the commie clap."

"Betcha Andy never fucked a gook."

They surrounded him in a tight circle cutting him with their taunts like they were slicing him with knives.

"You guys are fucked." He shouted it several times and busted out of the hooch. Cal's command followed him out the door, "You damn well better cover our asses, man."

Between shouts and laughter, he heard the girl's whimpering, then screams between shouts of "Fuck her, man, fuck her!" He turned his back and walked away from the hooch so he wouldn't hear the girl's screams and so he wouldn't bear witness.

The explosion kicked him twenty feet into a paddy field, filled his back with shrapnel and knocked him unconscious. VC sappers had closed in with a murderous mortar attack and scored a direct hit on the hut behind him.

He was conscious of being dazed and disoriented, of staring into a dark mirror that extended right and left into an endless wall. Refracted images appeared and disappeared like reflections in undulating water, the still burning ville, a Vietnamese family miraculously alive and milling around their smoking hooch, a helicopter gunship circling with lethal intent. He turned slowly and saw the Vietnamese family exposed on the slope behind him. The helicopter was angling around to give the gunner a clear field of fire.

"No! No! No! Jesus Christ!" he yelled. "Take cover, goddamn it. Don't run, take cover!" The Vietnamese looked puzzled and dumbfounded.

"Dumb fucking gooks!" he shouted and sprinted up the slope. The whop-whop-whopping of the gunship was deafening. "Get down! Get down!" he yelled. He threw the kids into the bushes and flattened himself over the mother.

The kick caught him from behind and hurt his ribs. He rolled away quickly, instinctively, but the pain kept him grounded. He looked up into the angry eyes of a large black man who wanted to kill him. "What the hell you doin' with my family?" the black man yelled in his face. "Who the fuck you think you are?" A shock of recognition crossed the black man's face. "Oh, it's you. What the fuck's goin' on, man?"

He watched the helicopter land and disgorge several smartly dressed military officers with two civilians in rumpled suits. Now the black man would understand. "All clear," he told the Vietnamese woman. "It's safe to come out now, it's okay."

He tried to get to his feet, but the stabbing pain in his ribs forced him to his hands and knees. He began crawling down the slope. The sun suddenly pierced through the clouds like a bright sword. Reflecting off the mirrored granite, the Wall appeared as a mirage, first coming closer and then receding into the distance. He moved forward desperately, almost in a panic, like a man lost in the desert seeking water.

Ken . . . Albert . . . Cal . . . Hector . . . He needed to tell them how it happened, that it wasn't his fault. He had to tell them they died for their own sins, not America's or anybody else's. He needed to tell them . . .

He felt strong hands heave him up and brace a muscular shoulder under his own.

"Easy does it, brother," Breedlove said, "easy does it!"

"I have to talk to my old recon team," he said. "I have to make my peace with them."

"I hear you," said Breedlove. "I'm right with you all the way. Together we can take care of business. I've been there before. I've seen those motherfuckers, too."

"That's what we called ourselves," he laughed, "the Meanest Motherfuckers from the A Shau Valley of Death." He laughed again. "Some stupid, fucking moniker," he said, "a real dumb-ass macho name."

He tried to walk alone and fell. Breedlove shouldered him again. "Relax, man," his friend said, "take it nice and easy; we'll make it together."

"I'm sorry," he said, "I wanted to see if I could go it alone."

"You don't have to walk alone," the black man said. "None of us has to walk alone."

He remembered then the phrases he'd read that very morning, the phrases that had defined the meaning of another divisive war, phrases that had recurred to him throughout the day: "It is for us the living . . . that from these honored dead . . . shall not have died in vain . . ." We the living . . . we the living . . . we the living . . .

When he raised his head to face his unforgiving accusers at the implacable black granite wall, he saw instead his wife and daughters. They were standing in the mirror of the Wall, smiling and waiting for him to join their world. He pulled at the arm of his friend.

"Don't you see them?" he asked.

"Who, where?" Breedlove asked.

"My family, they're just ahead of us, standing by the Wall."

When he turned to face the memorial, they were gone. He ran forward, tripped and fell and rose to his feet slowly. He stood before the mirrored granite memorial waiting for the ghosts of his recon squad to return. But the Wall remained as it was, a long black slab of granite with the names of the Vietnam War dead chiseled into its surface.

He tried to say, finally, what he'd come to say: "I did not turn my back and let you motherfuckers die." But he choked on the words, silenced by the implacable wall. He stood in mute contrition before he was able to confess his complicity in the atrocity, the complicity he had for so long denied: "I could have saved the girl and your lives as well. I could have tried, but I didn't."

And the grief he felt was not so much for his recon squad as for all of those who died in the war, for those inscribed on the visible American wall and for the larger, invisible wall of Vietnamese, including the girl he'd turned his back on, the girl he'd abandoned to violence and death.

Breedlove took his arm. "How about a beer?" his friend asked. "My wife and kids have gone home. Maybe we can talk awhile."

"Yeah, sure," he said. "I could use a beer, one beer for every name on the Wall."

His friend laughed. "Man," he said, "you are in a hell of a lot better shape than I thought you were. C'mon, I'm buyin' the first two rounds; the rest is up to you."

Turncoat

The PBR (River Patrol Boat) idled noiselessly into the dank canal under a tangled canopy of mangrove trees. The stink of rotting vegetation, thick humidity and silent terror which held him prisoner made him breathe in short gasps—chug-a-chug, chug-a-chug—in rhythm with the PBR motor. Then, with a sudden opening in the canopy, five VC leaped like startled animals into the shadowy bush. A slender beauty, trapped in a motorized sampan maneuvered expertly to avoid their grappling hooks. He held her in the sights of his M-50. "Fuckee, Yankee bastid," she screamed and exposed her breasts. "Shoot me, shoot me, Yankee bastid." But he couldn't—or wouldn't—shoot her as his mates yelled, "Kill her, kill her, shoot the fucking bitch." Then, unbelievably, she leaped ashore and disappeared. The Navy Seals were after her instantly, scrambling up the bank and crashing through the underbrush—and he with them, following the Seals into a VC ambush, into a mine field of exploding body parts. He regained consciousness looking into the killer eyes of two VC with AK-47s, one of them the beautiful sampan girl. The man laughed and raised his rifle. The girl pushed it aside and shook her head. "Thua Khong! Thua Khong! No! No!" The man cursed and backhanded her viciously. A burst from the girl's AK-47 sent the VC reeling stiffly backwards, a robot in reverse, firing wildly into the overhead canopy. Then the girl turned her rifle on him, the American.

Andy Fetzer rolled off the bed, hit the floor and kept rolling until he smacked into the wall of his hotel room. He was sweating profusely. The fan was off again. Generator problems. His dream, he realized, was a replay of Ishmael Breedlove's story—the friend he'd met at the Vietnam Memorial, the friend who'd helped him regain his sanity. In Breedlove's version, the VC girl had rescued him, turned *chieu hoi* (turncoat) and later became his wife. He had abandoned a woman and child in the U.S. to marry and save the VC girl. For that he carried a shitload of guilt—and grief—mainly because his own deeply religious family had turned against him. Discovering that Ishmael Breedlove experienced dark valleys of depression and self-accusation had given Andy a strong bond with his friend. He wondered if that was why he kept dreaming Breedlove's story, or was it because he planned to meet with Ishmael and his wife in Ho Chi Minh City? To be honest, he'd never forgotten the feeling of his foolhardy flop on Breedlove's wife during his flashback theatrics at the Wall. He remembered the steel spring of her body and the soft succumbing and the smile. He remembered her smile in a perfectly oval face just before Ishmael kicked in his ribs. It was hard to believe the slender beauty had once been a VC guerrilla. He looked at his luminous watch—2300 hours. He dressed quickly and took the stairs to the third-floor deck to cool off.

He smoked one of the twenty panatelas he'd carefully packed to enjoy on an evening like this—sitting on the third-floor deck of the Huong Giang Hotel in Hue, catching breezes off of the Perfume River below him. Because of the nearly full moon he could see the Trong Tien bridge destroyed by VC sappers during the battle of Hue, and beyond the bridge, a flotilla of silent sampans stretching as far as the Thien Mu pagoda. From the banquet hall below, he could hear the clashing cymbals and sing-song voices of performers mixed with the laughter of French tourists (after the film *Indochine*, they'd been coming in droves, the hotel clerk told him).

Six months ago, he realized, this scene would have been a total fantasy. It still seemed unreal. He had never wanted to see the hellhole sewer of Vietnam again—ever. His life in America seemed to be completely on track—marriage, job, family, future. Then, out of nowhere, like a fucking freight train from hell, came the nightmares of his old recon team, accusing him with images of death, torturing him until he started coming apart emotionally, until he unraveled and lost his business, wife, family and future all in a matter of weeks.

But he'd faced the ghosts of his recon squad at the Wall with the help of a new friend, Ishmael Breedlove, and achieved a measure of reconciliation—at least enough to stop the nightmares. When he returned to California hoping to find his wife Sally with open arms, he found her instead in the arms of a churchgoing friend who was able, she said, to offer her the Christian comfort she so desperately needed. Like he, Andy Fetzer, was a fucking heathen! His daughters had moved out, too, and were pretty cool to him, even resentful. Things had changed. So he moved to the Peninsula near the veterans hospital for counseling and started carpentering—rebuilding his life a second time.

Then a buddy at the veterans hospital told him about the ex-NVA who was speaking at the Palo Alto Community Church. He was on a mission of reconciliation sponsored by Vietnam Veterans for Peace and Justice. "Shit!" he'd said to himself, "another fucking peacenik. Maybe I can give the slope some grief and knock a little sense into the fuzzy-headed vets." Instead he ended up drinking beer with Tran and the vets at a local pub, not because he agreed with the dink but because the vets wanted to thank him for shutting up a crowd of Vietnamese students from Stanford, yuppie offspring of ARVN expatriates who'd come to shout down the speaker.

"Shut the fuck up and let the man speak, assholes!" he'd shouted, and they did shut the fuck up, even if the church crowd glared bullets at him.

Tran was a slight, flat-faced man with a perpetual smile and dancing eyes, one of which winked involuntarily. Only his brush cut and muscular arms gave evidence of his soldiering past. Tran said he had not come to defend or condemn; his talk was mostly personal, about how the hatred and violence of war had turned him into a reconciler and peacemaker. Andy remembered Tran's finale because he praised a character type Andy despised—the rallier or turncoat who switched sides. "So I think until we all become *chieu hoi*, willing to journey to the other side, walk in someone else's moccasins as your native people say, we cannot be truly reconciled."

Andy had wanted to talk about the *chieu hoi* thing, but then he discovered he and Tran had both fought in and around Khe Sanh in 1968. That was a bridge that kept them talking for two hours. "Old soldiers never die," one of the vets laughed, "we just keep talking."

"When you come to Vietnam, Andy," Tran insisted with a hand on his arm, "we must visit the old battle sites together. I'll be your guide, I promise." Tran handed him a bilingual card with phone and fax numbers that read "Teacher and Consultant in English." Andy clinked glasses with the *chieu hoi*, figuring he'd never see him again.

But, as he'd already learned, life was full of unexpected reversals. Andy received notice of divorce proceedings from his wife's lawyer a day or two before he heard about the Vietnam tour out of San Jose. He walked into a class of mostly buzz-saw vets engaged in verbal firefights and felt like he'd come home. He joined the combative vets for the tour and experienced a rush of exhilaration and fear he hadn't felt since re-upping for a second tour in country.

He sent a fax to Tran wondering if he'd even get a reply. He received an immediate response: "Good to hear from you. Great you could come. Call me in Hanoi. Tran." With Tran's response Andy really wanted to go and couldn't wait to leave. Crazy how quickly one's head could get screwed around when circumstances changed—fate, karma, whatever. He was still going to play it close to the vest. He was no fucking *chieu hoi*.

He met with Tran at the Foreign Language Institute in Hanoi. Everything clicked. They would meet in Dong Ha, where a friend of Tran's, a former comrade in arms who ran a transport service, would drive them out to Khe Sanh.

The week in Hanoi passed quickly. He was dizzied by the whirl of activities with so much to absorb. Then came the long train ride from Hanoi to Hue. While some of his colleagues squabbled over the accommodations, he stared at endless green and yellow fields of rice stretching into infinity—with the same cast of characters—water buffalo and miniature people in conical hats—he'd seen a generation earlier.

After a day in Hue, Andy took a local bus to Dong Ha on the stretch of Highway One called the Street without Joy by the French and the Avenue of Horrors by American drivers dodging land mines in the 1960s. Andy Fetzer found little joy traversing the gouged and rutted highway in a rattletrap bus filled with peasants, pigs and produce in the 1990s. Outside, the mass of people on bicycles, motorbikes and foot seemed as stunted as the roadside trees and shrubs struggling against years of toxic defoliation.

The bus rattled through the ghost town of Quang Tri City, still piled with rubble from having been bombed like Dresden during World War II. Dong Ha, the new capital, boasted a string of pastel-painted tourist hotels, of which the Trang Son, modeled on Hanoi's French Colonial style, was the most impressive.

He walked through tinted glass doors into an empty foyer. Through cracks in swinging doors to the dining room, waves of laughter tumbled out. Inside, a dozen beauties with gold filling grins, half in slinky blue *ao dais* and half in blue hotel maid uniforms, were plastering each other with makeup and watching Western videos. The maids surrounded him like chattering monkeys, grabbing his bag and pushing him upstairs to his room. Later, when he asked about the gobs of lipstick and mascara, Tran laughed, "They're not prostitutes. Makeup for the masses is something new in Vietnam. They've gone, as you Americans say, slightly bonkers."

After a cold shower and nap, Andy stumbled down the stairs for dinner. Karaoke songbirds were warbling love ballads from the TV screen, while waitresses in blue *ao dais* were serving three or four tables of foreign businessmen who were laughing loudly and salivating over the waitresses instead of their food. Andy dined on the house specialty, a ring of crisp fried birds on a bed of rice. A pretty waitress showed him how to twist off the head and take the bird in a single bite. He tried it, gagged, and then washed the morsel down with cold beer. "Delicious," he lied. Some fat Asian businessmen looked his way and grinned drunkenly. "Delicious! Delicious!" they said and ogled the waitresses.

He took three quarts of beer to his room and put himself to bed in the dark. With all of the exposed electrical wires and naked outlets, he was afraid to play with the switches. He drank the beer with a terrible thirst from eating the salty birds and immediately fell asleep.

ARVN rangers, their thin, cruel faces bloated with anticipation, threw the guerrilla girl into the interrogation room. Her arms were tied tightly at the elbows, pushing her breasts against her blouse. When the lieutenant cupped a hand over one of her breasts and squeezed, she bit down savagely into his hand. He slapped her, brutally, back and forth until blood and froth ran from her mouth. The pack of soldiers surrounded their panting victim like hyenas circling a crippled gazelle, eyes glinting, lips pulled back in toothy grins, waiting, watching the lieutenant spit questions into the girl's face: Name (slap!)? Unit (slap!)? Village (slap!)? Commander (slap!)?

The guerrilla girl cleared the mucus and blood in her throat, coughed and spat the mess into the lieutenant's face. He struck her with a closed fist. When she fell, ARVN soldiers lifted her upright again and doused her with cold water. The lieutenant stripped her naked with his K-bar knife and then held the knife between her legs while ARVN hyenas laughed and burned her front and back with cigarettes. When she spat again and cursed him, the lieutenant reached behind him, grabbed a flare and thrust it brutally into her vagina. She started screaming—scream after scream—as he asked for a lighter. Then Andy burst into the room just as Ishmael had done, cracking the grinning ARVN skulls with the butt of his M-16, covering the girl with his body and smothering the flames, protecting her as he had the Vietnamese woman at the Wall, holding the squirming naked body beneath him until the orgasm burned like fire between his legs. When he finally lifted himself up, he was looking into the face of the girl in the hooch, the girl he too had wanted to rape, the girl he'd failed to save. He was conscious of a terrible burning in his chest, of captive voices crying to be heard. He realized with a horror that he was hearing something deep inside himself . . .

He met a smiling Tran and his unsmiling friend and driver outside of the hotel entry. "Please meet my old comrade in arms, Bat," Tran smiled. "I stayed with him and his family last night. We wanted to reminisce about the past." Andy extended his hand. Bat removed his glove to show him a prosthesis. Bat's eyes, staring through a face mask of keloid scars, were expressionless. One side of his face, because of the scars, was pulled up into a perpetual grimace.

"Don't worry," Tran said, "Bat drives expertly with one hand."

Their transport vehicle was an old Chinese model jeep, a relic from the war that would, according to Tran, carry them to hell and back. "Like Audie Murphy," he added and laughed.

Highway Nine branched off of Highway One and snaked eastward all the way into Laos. Green conical hills, shaped like peasants' hats, were lushly carpeted, looking as if the war had never happened. Some of the farmers were wearing tattered army jackets and faded green pith helmets, while others hobbled on homemade crutches. The kids, as during the war, were running around half-naked. The trio stopped briefly at the sites of the former U.S. Marine Camp Carrol—bare, except for rusted shell casings and barbed wire—and the nearby Rockpile, a flattened butte where American artillery had pounded NVA bunkers surrounding Khe Sanh.

Twenty-five years after the war, Khe Sanh was a horrifying wound in the red earth—bare, gouged and still bleeding. Nothing had grown back. "The Americans poisoned the earth with Agent Orange," Tran commented. "Locals believe the hills are red and naked of vegetation because the ghosts of unburied soldiers constantly sprinkle the earth with the blood of slaughtered Vietnamese." Images of the past filtered and flashed in kaleidoscopic disarray—C-130s and helicopters crashing and burning, exploding on runways, the constant shelling back and forth that crushed the skull in a vise that never let up, the drinking and drugs, the trash and mud and blood and shit, the insanity of it all as the Animals screamed from a dozen bunker boom boxes, "We gotta get outta this place . . . If it's the last thing we do . . . We gotta get outta this place. . ."

When he lifted his head from his hands, he saw Tran and Bat pointing to different hills, trying to locate where they'd fought with American patrols or hunkered down to escape the horrific bombing of the Phantom jets and B-52s. "Over there, Hill 881, is where Bat got burned by napalm." Tran said. Andy didn't know what to say in reply.

They stopped for lunch in Khe Sanh City at a sidewalk cafe filled with shady-looking characters, hard bitten with scarred faces, speaking a different language. "Laotian smugglers," Tran said quietly, "probably drug dealers. During the war we exploited their country; now they're getting back at us."

Shortly after leaving Khe Sanh City, Bat turned south on a narrow, rutted, dirt road that was hardly wider than a path. "We're on the truckers' Ho Chi Minh Trail now," Tran said. "Once we could have followed it south into the A Shau Valley, the Central Highlands and nearly to Saigon." Andy looked east to the Truong Son mountains and the razor-like ridges where triple canopy forests and tangled bush hid the central supply base of the NVA that their recon squad had been ordered to find. "We gonna track down their stash so the goddamn B-52s can bomb the fucker back to the Stone Age," their Texas captain had snarled (quoting General Le May). "Not, I repeat, not so any of you gung-ho John Wayne assholes can play hero." Actually, there were several, maybe dozens, of mobile bases concealed in a labyrinth of crisscrossing trails in a multilayered jungle that turned day into the dark of night and virtually assured they would engage the enemy.

The new CO, Captain Donald, brought the Kit Carson scout, a *chieu hoi* nicknamed PC, with him from his old unit. He'd used him before and trusted him. There was no way in hell Americans could negotiate the convoluted maze of trails without a Kit Carson guide. PC had been running infiltrators south for several years. "He knows the trails like you men know the shortest paths to the whorehouses in Danang or Quang Tri," the captain said, and everyone laughed. "Furthermore, let me tell you why PC turned *chieu hoi*. His thirteen-year-old sister who was a courier for the VC got raped by the bastards. You think he doesn't hate the fuckers? Think about it."

The captain's talk didn't stop the grumbling, resentment and distrust of the Motherfuckers. They'd seen their entire company, close buddies, wiped out by the NVA in the A Shau Valley. So they pilloried PC's pedigree with unspeakable insults, cursed and groused. "The goddamn gook is taking us in circles just to fucking confuse us." But the *chieu hoi* saved their asses more than once by circling NVA battalions moving south in the night on silent, calloused feet, whole fucking battalions. So the mothers sucked in their assholes and kept humping.

From across the river the village looked about the same as it had a quarter century before—thatch roofs, pigs and chickens, naked kids. Some of the houses were elongated and set on stilts, and fields of rice had been replaced by manioc. What looked like piles of manure between the houses were stacks of bomb and shell casings. Bat refused to drive his jeep onto the ferry, so Andy and Tran left him to fry in the sun. "He says they're Montagnards. He doesn't trust them." They hand-pulled themselves across the river, letting the old ferryman smoke his pipe and engage Tran in conversation. "His son was killed during the war and his wife also. He says he's the only Vietnamese left here."

As they approached the village, Andy pointed to a ridge of serrated hills. "We came out of those mountains, crossed the river during the night, and entered the village at mid-morning. There were sniper shots, or we might have passed it by."

The sniping followed an ambush for which the chieu hoi *was blamed. He'd led them to a large NVA supply base, only to find it abandoned. It was a trap. In the bloody retreat, the RTO Linstrom and the machine gunner Dotson were killed and several others were wounded. Three NVA were killed. Then someone discovered the point, Workman, horribly mutilated. PC had abandoned him to warn the others. The Motherfuckers went berserk, cutting off NVA noses, ears and genitals in a frenzy of retribution. Belcher and the others were cursing and slapping the* chieu hoi, *forcing the grisly trophies in his face, when the captain intervened and led him away. "Fucking double-crossing gook; you got us into this!" Belcher yelled. The captain played it cool, nice and easy; he knew his ass was close to being fragged. During the night the squad tripped and stumbled down a razorback ridge into the valley where they got the dead and wounded dusted out. Just when they were stretched thin and ready to explode, the patrol took incoming from the ville. Two shots. That was enough to call in the Cobras and a killer Puff.*

They were greeted by a squad of naked children and a half-dozen scroungy dogs. Several of the children were badly scarred; two of them were missing limbs and hobbled on makeshift crutches. "Mines," Tran commented and tousled the scabied scalps, "thousands of mines and bombs are still buried here; generations more will suffer crippling and death. This is one way your country could reconcile, by clearing out these lethal toys."

Behind the kids and dogs came the village head man with several elder companions. Their toothless grins were bleeding with betel juice. They were dark-skinned and wore the headbands and loincloths of Bru Montagnards. Women in colorful wraparound skirts hovered in shadowed doorways, smoking pipes.

Andy had never met a Montagnard during the war, but he and every American knew of their reputation as scouts and fearless fighters. "We were grateful for your help during the war," Andy said. "Your people saved many American lives."

Tran translated his words for the head man and then returned the old Bru's response. "He says they helped the VC and NVA even more. With the help of the Montagnards, Vietnamese were able to defeat the Americans."

Andy figured he was being fed the official line. He decided to take a different tack. "How can they make a living off of old scrap metal?" he asked Tran.

Tran held an animated discussion with the old man. "He says they make a better living now than before. The metal from dismantled bombs is sold to Japanese who make it into cars for Americans."

While the head man laughed, Andy recalled the story of American scrap metal sold to Japan in the 1930s, how it was returned as bombs at Pearl Harbor. Better this way, he said to himself.

"What happened to the Vietnamese who once lived here?" he asked, as if he didn't know. Tran repeated the question for the head man. "He says the Americans destroyed the village. The leftover Vietnamese were removed to the coast. He doubts they would want to farm here now. It is good for the mountain people because they can no longer live by slash and burn in the forests. They are restricted by law."

Andy wanted to leave, but the head man insisted they see his pet project, an excavated line of old petroleum pipes, cleaned and reconnected to bring fresh water from the mountains. During drought times the piped water insured the fish ponds in old bomb craters would survive. A slender girl packing spring water in one of the bomb canisters offered him refreshment from her cupped hands. For a brief and terrible moment he flashed on the burned and bleeding girl from the hooch. Then she was gone and he drank handful after handful of the sweet, cool water.

They recrossed the river, pulling on the ropes with the old ferryman. Bat and the jeep had disappeared.

"I should have known," Andy said, "the bastard hated my guts." He turned to Tran who was spreading his hands in bafflement. "What do we do now?" Andy asked.

Less than fifty yards away, several bushes suddenly moved and fell away from the jeep. Bat was grinning wickedly.

"He was a driver once on the Ho Chi Minh Trail," Tran laughed. "He's showing off, showing how he fooled the Americans."

They returned to Dong Ha as night was settling in. The stench of sewage, his most familiar remembrance of the war, turned his stomach. "You okay?" Tran asked. "I'm staying with Bat again, but I'll see you off in the morning." As they wheeled off, Bat surprised him with a grin and a wave. Then, through a sheet of dust in the distance, Bat raised his middle finger in a "fuck you" salute.

Bat's finger pulled a trigger to his emotions. Andy Fetzer laughed as he hadn't laughed in Vietnam or anywhere else in a long, long time. He purchased a bottle of Suntory scotch at the hotel bar, still laughing, and went up to his room without supper. He laughed without reason or knowing why during his shower, and he laughed as he lay naked under the fan tossing down successive jiggers of scotch, laughing until a mood of darkness embraced him. Then he thought of the *chieu hoi*, PC, who was as slender and pretty as a girl, and of his sister who'd been raped, and of the girl in the hooch that he, too, had wanted to rape. And he cried out in the darkness, masturbating himself to sleep.

In his dream they came out of night and fog—monstrous shadows, ghosts risen from graves like the walking dead. He'd seen them before in his dreams, covered with shit and blood and brains, staring out of cavernous skulls, his recon mates coming through the wall again and again.

Only now they walked into a blackened, burning village of the damned, baptized by napalm in the name of the founding fathers, native sons and the holy ghosts of America's holy wars, making sure these heathen better dead than red would never rise again. When the burned and bleeding girl, shitting in fear, dared to rise from the grave, the holy warriors unbuckled their loins in fury while he, the coward, fled from their violence and his own. With a third eye, he saw the slender shadow slip behind him into the hooch, the boy as slim as a girl, his body taped with grenades, an avenging angel. Now he knew why his comrades had to die. In raping the girl they raped themselves of their last few shreds of humanity. They had to die. They deserved to die. The chieu hoi *was their appointed death angel.*

After his trip to Khe Sanh, Andy Fetzer crawled inside of an emotional cocoon as he had during and after his military tour. It was his way of dealing with emotional trauma. So many of the places they visited gave him nightmares—the rehab center for ex-whores, Le Ly Hayslip's prosthetics clinic, the Tu Da hospital for kids malformed by Agent Orange, besides which he couldn't relate to his fellow vets, most of whom were REMFs. And the one genuine grunt turned out to be a fucking fairy! Jesus, the women were even worse: a freaked-out vet nurse, two weird Asian chicks and a wild black woman who was out to break the cherry of their guide, who was himself a grotesque reincarnation of Elvis Presley. He couldn't wait to hook up with his old buddy, Ishmael, and enjoy a sane conversation. He'd received a call from Ishmael just before he left telling Andy when to meet him at the Caravelle Hotel bar in Saigon. He intended to hang out at his former favorite watering hole while his wife reunited with relatives. "This whole trip is going to be a fucking lick on me, worse than the fucking war," Ishmael said.

Finally the tour arrived in the whorehouse city where Andy had taken all of his R&Rs, where he had savagely sinned himself into exhaustion trying to ejaculate the demons of war. He took a taxi to the Caravelle Hotel and walked into the bar ready to bust his cheeks with a grin. Shit! He scanned the room in circles until he was dizzy; no Ishmael Breedlove. Instead, a small Vietnamese woman jerked at his sleeve. A panhandler? Prostitute? No, Ishmael's wife, Hoa.

"Where's Ishmael?" he said.

Hoa, distraught and crying, kept pulling on his arm. "Come, you come. Please, you come now. Ishmael, he—he—" She sliced a hand across each wrist.

"He cut his wrists?"

"Yes, yes, cut wrists. He go crazy."

Andy calmed her down in the cab and pulled the story out in jerks and fits like pulling shards from an old wound. Hoa's homecoming, it turned out, had been far more traumatic for Ishmael than for his Vietnamese wife, mainly because she insisted on staying on for several months.

"I tell Ishmael I join him laytah but he not undastan. He think I leave him— go crazy—cut his ahms. Now he callin' fo you—all da time callin'."

The hospital was housed in the old 4th Evac in Bien Hoa. Everything looked gray and grainy, like nothing had been done since the war. The walls were faded, the linoleum was peeling, and the sheets were dirty. Doctors and nurses were dressed in blood-stained whites (grays). The stink of disinfectant was everywhere.

He talked briefly with a Dr. Nung. "We think it's an old head injury acting up, maybe a tumor; we can't tell yet. His wife says he has lapses where he can't remember a thing. Could be an aneurysm; he's been having convulsions. We'll do further tests next week when our brain specialist returns from a conference in Helsinki."

Ishmael looked like a great black whale beached somewhere he didn't belong. He'd kicked off most of the sheets and lay there naked, panting for breath. He knew they were there. He didn't want to recognize Hoa.

"Howzit, man, thanks for coming," he greeted Andy. Then he glared at Hoa. "Go!" he roared, "*Di di mau!* Go! Go! Get the fuck out!"

Hoa scurried out with a frightened nurse. When the nurse peeked in again Andy waved her off.

"Hey man, slow down. You gotta slow down, okay? They tell me your ticker is in bad shape."

"Naw, I'm okay; it's her. I knew things would go to hell if I took her back to this shitty goddamn country. I've been fighting this all my married life. Bitch never left Vietnam; can't even speak half-assed English."

"You know she's got family here, and hasn't seen her people in twenty-five years. That's a long time."

Ishmael sat straight up. "Goddammit man, I never figured you'd be against me. Can't I trust you motherfucker? Can't I fucking trust you?"

Blood was seeping from his bandaged wrists. The little Vietnamese doctors must have had a hell of a time trying to stitch Ishmael together. And he was having a hell of a time trying to stitch together the severed threads of Ishmael's emotional network. He'd been through some heavy emotional shit himself, but he was not equipped to deal with Ishmael's mental disintegration; he was no psychotherapist. The two of them simply recycled the same conversation.

"You gotta loosen up, man," Andy said. "Hoa doesn't want to stay in Vietnam. Her old mama's still alive and needs some help. Hoa's got family here like you've got family in the States. You gotta loosen up, man. I know she loves you."

"I don't have no fucking family," Ishmael sobbed. "I abandoned my family." Then he glared into space. "She'll always be a fucking gook, cain't help it. Never trust a gook, man, never marry a fucking gook."

Then Ishmael collapsed. Boom—out like a used light bulb into sleep or unconsciousness. Andy called Hoa, who came running with the nurse. Once they got Ishmael on a respirator Andy said good-bye and promised to return early. He had to peel Hoa's fingers off his arm.

Andy didn't want to spend the evening alone. Sharing Ishmael's trauma had brought his own walls closing in. So he commandeered Cole Parker for an evening of beer and buddy talk. That's how he learned about Tina Brown's father who had divorced her mother to marry a Vietnamese.

"We'd better see Tina right away," Cole said. "It's a long shot, hundred to one, but, hell, anything's possible. We'll taxi her to Bien Hoa first thing in the morning."

When Andy returned in the morning with Cole and Tina, Ishmael was dead. An artery feeding the brain had burst, killing him instantly. Tina seemed to go into shock momentarily. She stiffened, almost like she was having a seizure. Then she relaxed and spoke so softly they could barely hear her. "It could have been my father, but it isn't. My father lost an arm in Vietnam."

During the following week, Andy helped arrange Ishmael's final journey home. He knew the military rigmarole, which helped immensely. Because of his medals, Ishmael would be buried with honors in an adjunct cemetery of Arlington. Hoa was with Andy constantly, hanging on his arm like a wartime street urchin. Her slim face, drained of color, and always looking up at him with large, luminous eyes, reminded him of a William Keane painting. She grew more beautiful every day. He met Hoa's family, ate with them, marveled at how Hoa blossomed in their presence in spite of her tragedy. This was where she belonged. In the U.S. she was a stranger in a strange land.

In the process of helping Hoa arrange Ishmael's insurance, pension and dozens of nit-picking legalities, Andy found himself changing and transforming, so palpably it was almost physical. It frightened him. Was he becoming a *chieu hoi*? He began to see the Vietnamese as human beings, as gentle people with iron wills and strong survival qualities. Sometimes he would say things to Hoa he hadn't anticipated: "You can stay with your family for however long you need. I'll take care of the funeral and your family. The kids will be okay. Don't worry."

Hoa stood there looking up at him like she didn't know what to do or say. So he reached out and took her hand in his and said something really unexpected. He couldn't believe himself what he was saying. "Once this is over, I'd like to take care of things—I mean, of you and your kids. More for my sake than yours, if you understand."

Hoa didn't seem to understand anymore than he understood what was happening. She looked at him as she would a fool or a crazy man, the second one she'd had to deal with in a single week. She turned and walked away. Then she stopped abruptly and said without turning around, in perfectly articulate English, "I want to come home with you; my children need me and I need them—and you. I can return to Vietnam later, sometime. I think they will understand."

She turned and came so close to him that he could taste her breath. She smiled the loveliest smile he'd ever seen and said, "You sure you wanna be *chieu hoi*?"

"Yeah, I'm sure," he said. And that was all that needed to be said.

MIA

Nurse Kate Noonan was one of the most self-contained and unemotional members of the tour group, but she cried, privately and silently, for virtually the entire first week. Then she dried up completely.

Tour members thought she was reliving the horrors and pain of her two years in Vietnam, when she had, in fact, experienced the sudden and unexpected joy and relief of finally coming home. The only pain and horror she might have relived was the memory of coming home to the United States twenty years before. Kate had been dumped at Travis Air Force Base near Sacramento, California, with a hundred other returnees and needed to catch a flight east from San Francisco. Unwilling to wait several hours for a military bus, she hitched a series of rides, mostly from older men who wanted to know about the sex life of women in the military. Upon arriving on the outskirts of Oakland, she had immediately caught accusatory stares, silent curses and people turning their backs when she asked for directions. When she finally found the highway to San Francisco and tried to hitch a ride, people spat at her from car windows, threw cans and bottles and screamed "Whore," "Bitch," "Baby killer," and worse. The nicest greeting she got was "Welcome back, asshole."

She arrived in Indianapolis a basket case, unable to converse or connect with anyone. Even her parents seemed to be infected with the pervasive antiwar, forget-the-war syndrome. Her old friends avoided her like the plague. She was tainted with the leprosy of having served in Vietnam. She felt like dressing herself in sackcloth and ashes and crying through the streets, "Unclean! Unclean! Unclean!"

Stepping on Vietnamese soil was also coming home to Charlie (Warrant Officer Charles Leppart), popularly known as Doctor Hawk because of his fearless daring as a Medevac chopper pilot. Kate's brief affair with Charlie had been the most intense and lasting experience of her life. When Charlie was listed as an MIA, her life for all intents and purposes ended. She survived by working all of the extra hours she could until she dropped from fatigue. Off duty she relied on straight Jack Daniels to numb the pain of memory. She lived only for word of Charlie, the word that never came.

When she unraveled emotionally in the States, she eventually survived as a workaholic. She'd had a series of affairs that kept eroding her life further until she had the child that stopped the affairs and put her on track again. On track was working intensive care at Cameron General and working even more intensively for the National Veterans Coalition Committee on POWs and MIAs and its civilian complement, the Telephone Tree, organizing, writing letters, speaking, phoning Congressmen and trying to protect citizens from their own government! That was the shocker: realizing the government's strong public posture on MIAs was a phony front. Behind the scenes they worked to subvert the coalition. There were too many skeletons in the closets of the CIA and other agencies. Kate was more than once referred to as hysterical.

She had returned to Vietnam for the sole purpose of tracing Charlie. At every meeting with civic groups, government officials, unions, it didn't matter who, she raised the same question: "What are you doing about the MIAs?" Always polite, the Vietnamese answered, "Ten separate groups of Americans are in Vietnam at this very time working on the MIA situation," or "Please ask your own government officials," or "The POW question was settled by agreement in 1974," or "The Vietnamese are searching for two hundred thousand of their own MIAs." Always there were Vietnamese as persistent as she was asking her about missing or lost relatives and friends in America, loved ones they hadn't heard from in nearly twenty years. Kate was offended that the Vietnamese felt as deeply as she did about losing sons and lovers, as if their losses were as legitimate as her own.

Kate persisted in her mission even when she became an embarrassment to the tour group, even when they begged her to cool it. She held her ground until the evening she went to the Hotel Rex bar for the reunion with Charlie. It had been their favorite watering hole whenever they were in Saigon together. She wanted to share at least one drink with Charlie's ghost.

The bar was filled with foreign businessmen, mainly Asian, who were in for the joint venture adventure. They reminded Kate of a school of sharks. She drank a Singapore Sling, shoved a handsy East Indian off the seat next to her and decided to leave. Then she saw him across the room, a hunched beanstalk with an Ichabod Crane nose and a billed cap. He didn't look *that* different from his copter cowboy days except for the wisps of gray hair that had once been a shock of red straw. Red Koontz had been Charlie's closest flyboy buddy.

After they hugged and cried, Kate joined him at a corner table and they talked—they talked for hours. A waiter twice cleared the table of beer bottles. A casual observer might have supposed they were a couple in love either making up, reuniting or trying to settle some difficult personal problem. About once every twenty minutes or so, the woman would break into tears or put her head on the man's shoulder. Then he would wipe the tears away and she'd order another beer. When the man finally had to leave (he was working for oil companies in Indonesia), the woman held him tight to her as if reluctant to let him go. Then he kissed her and left quickly.

Kate Noonan spent most of the night writing a long letter. When she finished, it was nearly 4:00 A.M. She had discarded half as many sheets as she'd used in writing the letter, had smoked two packs of cigarettes, drank half a bottle of Jack Daniels, and scripted the last hour of her life. She would seal the letter carefully and walk ten blocks to the Saigon River bridge. In midspan she would stop, burn the letter and watch the ashes float downstream and out to the China Sea. Then she would climb the railing and give herself to the river. She, too, would be an MIA.

> *Dear Charlie,*
>
> *I love you as I always have, unconditionally and totally. You have quite literally been my life, the love that kept me alive when I wanted to die, not once but many times. Now I wish I had died a long time ago. Let me explain.*
>
> *Just a few hours ago I met your old sidekick, Red Koontz, at the Hotel Rex bar. I'd gone there because that's where we used to hang out whenever we were in Saigon. It seemed a very romantic idea, like something out of Somerset Maugham.*
>
> *I'm writing this without tears, Charlie, matter-of-factly, but in truth I'm barely holding together after the shock of suddenly encountering a messenger of death from the past. You see, Charlie, I've lived on the thin edge of hope for twenty years, the hope that you, my beautiful man, were still alive.*
>
> *Red, I think, was even more shocked than I was. I give him credit, though, for giving me the unvarnished truth about you. The lowdown was pretty damn low. To fill you in, parenthetically, your old fly buddy has been freewheeling around the world—Indonesia, Africa, Latin America, wherever he could find an adventure of the illegal or extralegal sort. Red, by the way, has gone totally gray; what's left is frizzy old straw. He looks as tough as jerky, like a much uglier Clint Eastwood. If you had survived, Charlie, I suppose you would have been with your old sidekick. I was just thinking, what if I'd walked into the Rex bar and seen you? Jesus!*
>
> *I remember when you and Red "disappeared" together as if you were twins or something. I moved heaven and hell to track you down and nearly lost my fucking marbles, Charlie. (Pardon your old*

sweetheart nurse for using the "F" word, but when a lot of shit happens one's language changes.) The brass at MACV stonewalled me with vague references about national security, special assignment and a lot of other crap. Later I realized they were feeding me a bunch of lies. I mean, who the fuck was I, little ol' me, when one thinks of the BIG LIE that was the war. Your flyboy buddies at the time were as tightlipped as the brass. That's what the military relies on—male bonding, the buddy system, group loyalty. Shit! It's all a fucking cover-up.

Well, now I know and I wish I didn't, Charlie, because it's a damn shitty story. Red told me that you and he were on special assignment (meaning secret, of course) with the CIA, flying drugs—heroin and opium—for some real sleazy characters, French Corsicans, I think, because the Americans needed the support of anti-communist mountain tribes in Laos and Cambodia whose whole economy was based on growing poppies for making opium and heroin. Red told me the two of you flew the stuff into Vietnam where it was then flown by government planes into Saigon. From there a network of South Vietnamese generals and their wives controlled the distribution that was destroying the American army.

Jesus Christ, Charlie, that's how the American army went down the fucking tubes! That's how we lost the war. The enemy couldn't have planned it any better! I mean here I was working around the clock to save lives in Chu Lai and Danang and all the time I was getting stabbed in the back by you, Charlie. No, goddammit, Charlie, I take that back, I mean the U.S. government, the CIA, the democratic forces of South Vietnam. Shit! I'm crying now, Charlie, crying for you, for me, for the whole fucking lot of us. We were all so naive, so fucking stupid!

Because you were the best of the best, Charlie (if Red says this, it's gotta be true), they used you in the super-secret illegal war in Laos to ferry supplies to the CIA's secret bases there. Red thinks you got caught in the ambush at a mountain fortress called Phou Pha Thi, the high-tech surveillance post directing bombers along the Ho Chi Minh Trail.

You got trapped in the impossible ambush that wiped out everybody, not a single survivor, your names were simply erased. You never existed. There are no death lists or records—nothing. At least now I think I know what happened to you, Charlie. So I'm going to have a ceremony for both of us, as maudlin and melodramatic as possible.

Oh shit, Charlie, I want to remember and cherish the good times. When our tour group stopped over in Japan for a few hours, I took a cab to the rehab hospital at Zama, where I first met you. It still looks the same except that Japan's self-defense force now operates the facility. Anyway, what I want to say is that I walked out to the lovely and lonely promontory overlooking the sea, the place where you first kissed me after I'd slapped you down in my phony virginal innocence.

You thought you were Mr. Tomcat himself when you said, "You cute little thing, look what you're doing to me; I'm burning up with desire. I'm gonna burn to a crisp unless you help me." Then you showed me the horrible burn scar on your belly. When I reached out to touch it and touched instead your rock-hard dick, you laughed so hard you nearly opened your wound.

"Is it okay?" I asked and then my face was burning redder than your burn scar and you were laughing and then suddenly you were kissing me. God! Did I really slap you and tell you to stick your dirty claws into some other dumb kitty? Was I that big of a prude? At least I didn't say pussy!

But then you turned out to be such a helluva nice guy, really decent and sweet and honest. In fact, I fell in love with the whole group of flyboys who took me into your male group as little sister. God how we all drank, and the unbelievable stories you guys told. I thought you were putting me on, but I later learned how wild and crazy and heroic chopper cowboys could be. But you were so damn eager to return to duty that we didn't have time to try out your so-called peter principle. Shit! I was so mad because by then I really was burning for you. I thought I'd lost you forever.

Then a miracle happened. Two months after I arrived in country I got assigned to the Second Surgical Hospital at Chu Lai and you were one of the Medevac Madmen. I mean you were Doctor Medevac, Doctor Hawk, a legend in his time. You performed miracles ferrying in the bloody body parts, and we performed miracles patching them together again, even if it was half a body.

Actually, nothing in my training prepared me for the shock of combat, the body parts strewn everywhere, the bloody and burned bodies, the guts and brains hanging out, bodies full of burning shrapnel and burned like toast by napalm, often by friendly fire.

We operated a human salvage dump. I remember a sergeant who'd lost both legs at the hip plus a hand and an arm. What he had left was filled with shrapnel. On top of all this he was blind. He lived, Charlie; he fucking lived. But, Jesus, was he really living?

Then there was the eighteen-year-old who'd lost both legs. He was cursing and ranting, throwing bedpans and using his IVs to whip the nurses. I read the fucking riot act to him and shut him up. I said, "Look, asshole, you aren't getting a damn thing, no IVs, food, cigarettes, water—I mean NOTHING until you fucking behave yourself!" I was a real bitch. I turned on my heel to let him die. Two hours later he said very quietly and respectfully, "Nurse, may I have a drink, please?" I started bawling right there and went to fucking pieces. I couldn't take it.

Why am I telling you this, darling? Because I wouldn't have survived without you. You were so fucking understanding, so calm and self-possessed. And you were going though more hell than I was. How I thank God that the peter principle below your burn scar was A-OK, standing tall, strack all the way. We had so little time. But the two weekends we flew into Dalat and once to Cape Saint Jacques were worth all of the shit and pain and hell and suffering simply because I loved you so totally. The Jack Daniels and Montagnard Gold helped, but the real high was making it with you.

But then, Jesus God, you were gone, disappeared from the face of the earth without a fucking word. I couldn't find a trace of you or begin to track you down. Nobody knew where you were. I got stonewalled again and again and again. Can you believe I still trusted the fucking military? Jesus!

About a month after you'd disappeared, all hell broke loose along the DMZ. Bodies were coming in so thick and fast we could only operate on the sure recoveries. Even then we couldn't keep up. Under all of this pressure, one of the surgeons failed to trach a kid with his lungs full of shit. The kid went into cardiac arrest and died. When the hospital supe raised hell on procedure, the surgeon laid the blame on me. Later I was at the club getting drunk like I'd done every night since you disappeared. Only this night it was worse because of the kid that died. I was feeling guilty as hell and ready to die when the supe sat his fat ass next to mine and said, "It must take a hard bitch to kill a grunt and then get drunk."

"You goddamn son of a bitch!" I screamed. I threw the drink in his face and stormed out. I was no good after that. I started blaming the Vietnamese for my anger and pain. When the medics brought in a VC, I'd let someone else handle the case or simply let him die. I refused to participate in MEDCAP projects, going into villages to help Vietnamese who'd been napalmed by American planes. So I finished my tour of duty doing administrative staff work at Bien Hoa. I left Vietnam hating the Vietnamese, the military, the war and Vietnam, everything.

My homecoming, Charlie, was all hostility and hate and cold fucking shoulders, even from my own parents. Sad to say, sweetheart, I slept around a lot but it was always your face that I saw, I swear it. What kept me sane and surviving, Charlie, was the hope that I'd somehow see you again, to make love, make babies, make a home and the whole damn dream. Shit! It was all a dream, only a dream!

My biggest regret, Charlie, is that I wasn't cynical enough. We were all too trusting. I believed in my country, in the war, in American ideals. My innocence got shattered in Vietnam. Now, at least, I know part of the truth. Like most truths, it's very, very bitter.

One final thing, Charlie. I visited a children's hospital near Saigon, the one filled with kids who've been deformed and malformed at birth as a result of Agent Orange and other toxic chemicals spewed on the Vietnamese. These hidden atrocities of war may be our most enduring legacy. I suppose this particular visit was most relevant for me because

I, too, am dying from Agent Orange. I've had two operations for breast cancer and my joints are swelling with arthritis. Soldiers aren't the only ones who die in war.

Everything seems turned around, Charlie. I really felt like I was coming home when I landed in Vietnam. I felt it so strongly that I cried for a whole week. So now that I'm home, I've decided to join you, Charlie, while I still have the capacity to think and act clearly. I've decided to join your ashes (the ashes of this letter) in the Saigon River, into the China Sea and maybe all the way to Mandalay where the flying fishes play.

So now it's time to say good-bye, good-time Charlie. Good-bye.

Love always,

Your Kate

Kate left the hotel feeling as physically woozy and wasted as the self-image she now held of her life history. She had a difficult time negotiating the half-mile walkway along the river. Once a French-designed art nouveau promenade with arches and close-fitting cobblestones, the walkway was now a rocky, uneven trail made slippery by the river fog. She stumbled and fell several times before she saw the billowing mists rising off the river holding the forms and faces of Vietnamese, mostly women in flowing white *ao dais*. The spirits of dead Vietnamese kept rising until the river was a train of ghostly MIAs. She nearly collapsed. Then she saw the bridge partially exposed and ran for it. She fell against a large rock and splintered her glasses.

The next thing she knew, she was wobbling and squinting through a kaleidoscope of broken images, squinting at the same out-of-kilter figure tilting around like a bunch of crazy Charlie Chaplins. She closed one eye and the figures merged into one in full uniform and flyboy cap, blocking her path. She should have been surprised but she wasn't—not after encountering Red Koontz out of nowhere.

She hiccuped and giggled. "You look weird, Charlie, all wavy, like a wavy-gravy Charlie Chaplain." She giggled again. "Stand still, you crazy bastard, you're making me dizzy."

Charlie didn't laugh or smile or stand still. "I'm different now," he said. "I live in a different world, unreal for you, real for me, capice?"

It was Charlie, all right, always ending his comments with "capice?" The beautiful, damn wop . . .

"Goddamn you, Charlie—" she started to say.

"Don't do something stupid, sweetheart, something you'll die to regret," Charlie said. "Take it from someone who knows."

Charlie hadn't even said hi or how are you. Kate's bottled anger exploded. "You picked a hell of a time to tell me, Charlie!"

Charlie threw his hands flat out and shrugged his shoulders. "No way I could tell you any sooner, baby. I haven't exactly been in circulation—blood stream or social stream."

Kate giggled again, then she bit her lips back into a hard line. "Yeah, well, I'm pretty damn cynical at this point, Charlie."

"I don't blame you, sweetheart; hell, so am I. But listen to me. You've spent half your life chasing a fading rainbow, living a hopeless fantasy, dancing with ghosts. Time to get your feet on the ground. Get a life, look to the future."

Kate was crying now because she wanted to feel Charlie's body rubbing her the wrong way just like his words were, the son of a bitch! "What the hell are you doing here, Charlie? Red Koontz told me you'd been shot down in Laos."

"Yup, no doubt about it. Old Red never lied unless instructed to. Actually, I was on the ground, killed by mortar fire."

"But how did you—?"

"How did I get here? Haven't you heard, things are different with the dead in Vietnam. Without a proper burial, the ghost never rests. Your spirit is supposed to hassle family and friends until they send you away with a proper ceremony."

"But, how—I don't understand—"

"Shut up and listen, sweetheart. My river recess is damn near over. Everyone and everything at the base in Laos was blown to hell except my copter. My brain and spirit were still functioning, so I flew out and headed for Bien Hoa airbase where I could harass the asses of some flyboy buddies, get them to play some taps and send me off on a wing and a prayer. I didn't make it, crashed in the river. Then the Americans pulled out all of a sudden and left me with a river full of gooks. I've had nobody to cuss or harass 'til you showed up, sweetheart."

"What I was about to do, Charlie," Kate said, "was to give you a proper burial."

"Yeah, but this other thing, Kate, this grandstanding act, going off the Golden Gate Bridge thing, it really sucks. Doesn't make a damn bit of sense. But then you were always a flaky lady."

Kate felt a surge of anger at Charlie's naked gall, trying to tell her what to do with her life after she'd given it all to him. She picked up the cobble that knocked her dizzy and screamed, "You presumptuous son of a bitch!" She threw the rock full force into thin air. Charlie was gone with the first streak of morning light. The dull plop of the rock, or Charlie, maybe, splashing into the river was the only sound she heard.

By the time Kate regained her feet and sense of who she was, early risers cycling across the bridge were looking at her sideways. She removed her glasses and wiped the blood off her face. The bump and splash of sampans and the stink of effluents reached her from the river below. A baby's cry, uttered in hunger or pain, pierced something deep inside her, a wound of remembrance that evoked the first cry of her only child.

She wanted to see her son again and, if she was fortunate, eventually some grandchildren. She thought of the unfinished quilt that she and the circle of Vietnam nurses had begun and how much she missed them. The old Victorian she'd purchased with two friends needed years of restoration. Once the cycle of unfinished business started, when she thought of all she'd planned to do, there was no end to it. She simply couldn't afford to end her life at this time.

Mostly, though, she was angry—angry at Charlie and the way he'd treated her, angry at the government and the military for fucking up their lives and angry at herself for being so trusting, gullible and just plain stupid. "You've stolen twenty-five years of my life already, Charlie," she said, "you're not going to steal what I have left."

With these words Kate Noonan burned the letter and threw the ashes into the Saigon River. A breeze coming off the China Sea had blown away the stink of sewage. The bracing aroma of breakfast noodles laced with garlic and *nuoc mam* sauce was floating up from dozens of sampans. She was hungry. She wanted to eat. She wanted to live.

The Seduction of Elvis

Meeting Elvis face to face in Hanoi's Noi Bai airport shocked the hell out of us. We'd heard about the second coming of Elvis with all of the psychic phenomena bullshit, but encountering his living image in Vietnam was too real. His name was Vinh and he looked pretty damn authentic with sideburns, tinted glasses and turned-up denim collar. He even had the chubby cheeks, full pouty lips and dimples of his hero. The rest of him was different. He was about five-foot-two with a face as round as a plate. His ersatz drawl was so phony it was funny. He was to be our guide and interpreter. He greeted us with one thumb in his belt and the other uplifted in greeting.

"Hi guys! I hear y'all are mostly from Californy—purty cool, purty hip. Waal, ahm yore man, hee, hee, hee." He laughed in a kind of self-deprecating way while we gawked, unbelieving, with silly grins—except for Tina Brown, the young black journalist-seminarian who was fixing Vinh with a hard, no-nonsense stare. Tina really fit the stereotype of big, black and beautiful. Her direct and sometimes abrasive style had already rubbed a few people raw. But she could be as warm and sweet as Nutella on a fresh baked muffin and melt the Mendenhall glacier with her smile. I loved her high Cherokee cheekbones and almond Indian eyes that gave her a fetching predatory squint. But, oh mama, she could be a scary Medusa when she put on her "I dare you" scowl and whipped her dreadlocks in anger. During that historic airport encounter, none of us would have guessed that Tina Turner's namesake had already determined on the seduction of Vietnam's Elvis Presley.

The vets in our group were a bit uneasy when they discovered Vinh's father had been an NVA medical officer and his mother a nurse with the front. Fortunately, Tina's sawtooth persona put them sufficiently on edge to take the pressure off of Vinh, which worked out fine for our tour.

Tina came on strong because she had a lot going for her. A Southern Baptist attending liberal Union Theological Seminary, she had earlier reported for the *Post Dispatch* while attending college in Saint Louis. The *Post Dispatch* and two other newspapers were footing her expenses to uncover the Christian underground in Vietnam. Two suitcases were required to carry her computer, camcorders and 35-millimeter cameras. A half-dozen others were needed to pack her fashion outfits, trendy leisure wear and twenty pairs of shoes. Most of us were lugging backpacks and wearing Levi's and Nikes. No wonder she acted like the Queen of Sheba.

I, too, was upset by Tina's high-handed style, like the way she shanghaied my personal services at the San Francisco airport until I discovered our common roots as shouting Baptists and love of hoot-and-holler gospel music. All the way to Vietnam, we glued both sets of cheeks together singing gospel music with the Five Blind Boys of Alabama, Sweet Honey in the Rock, and a half-dozen other soul singers including Aretha Franklin. We were higher than hallelujah heaven.

"You know," I said with our earphones off for dinner, "there's a girl I love who used to sing gospel, and I wish she'd do it again."

"Who?"

"Tina Turner."

"Oh, my Lord," Tina exploded, "my mama went to school with Tina Turner in Nutbush, Tennessee. She named me after Tina Turner. Sometimes I even think I am Tina Turner!"

"Whooee, girl," I shouted, "I think we are singin' the same gospel!"

This shared love of gospel music is why Tina took me as her friend and confidant and told me her story. That's how I discovered the little girl behind the big bad mama facade.

"My daddy went to Vietnam while I was warming in Mama's oven," she confided. "Four years later he returned, a Purple Heart hero minus an arm, which he had replaced with a Vietnamese wife and two kids. Me and Mama got dropped like a couple of lead weights and nearly sank under."

"How about the divorce?" I asked.

"He'd already taken care of that. Mama signed some papers and just hoped, I guess, that it couldn't be true. She was pretty gullible. It didn't make much difference to Mama anyway because she died of cancer before I was five. My grandparents asked my daddy to take me in but he wouldn't have it. So I was bounced like a rubber ball between several aunts and my grandparents. That's another story."

Then, as if she'd hit some inside trigger, Tina broke down and started bawling away. I mean bawling buckets. She put her head on my chest and drenched me in a baptism of pain. Between sobs I discovered Tina's real purpose in coming to Vietnam was to capture a husband by any means possible. She was convinced this was her last chance and the only way to reunite with her lost father, that by replicating his ethnic union she could somehow win his acceptance.

I wanted to tell Tina that her whole gig was a fantasy, that she had been blinded by her lost childhood, that her dad was an asshole who should, given her accomplishments, crawl to her on his knees. But, of course, I couldn't blunt her dream with reality. She'd already made me her confidant and unwitting accomplice. And who the hell knows what might happen? It was a crazy world. I said sure, I'd help. I was her gospel-singing soul brother.

What made the planned seduction doubly intriguing was that Vinh was just as determined to get to America by any means possible. The fantasy he had concocted was motivated by the kind of religious fervor that drives true believers to remote sacred shrines and makes prophets out of penniless pilgrims. Vinh's dream was to make his pilgrimage to Graceland, emerge with the King's mantle as the resurrected Elvis and then become the rock and roll reconciler of Americans and Vietnamese. Of course, he knew nothing of the thousands of Elvis imitators running loose in America. His cloud-cuckoo fantasy was even more outlandish, illusory and unattainable than Tina's. But for her seductive purposes, he was a prime suspect. I couldn't resist playing Cupid.

On our third night in Hanoi, Vinh popped his big surprise. He was competing, he said, with a dozen rock and pop groups for prizes in Hanoi's largest auditorium, the huge union hall near Ho Chi Minh's Memorial. I couldn't wait, because I'd cut my rock and roll teeth on the teenage Elvis. In Yuppie maturity, I ridiculed the rhinestone caricature of my hero while burning inside for the ducktailed knee-knocker who took inspiration from holy-roller gospel.

The huge hall was packed on a sweltering night like gummy bears in a snack pack. A few elders were sprinkled like mildew in an audience of mostly teenagers. Fillmore Far East it was not. The music was mostly a caterwauling cacophony, worse than rocks rolling inside a tin bucket. The beat was simple '60s stuff—Everly Brothers, early Beatles and the Monkees. No hint of soul or rhythm and blues. It was a hell of a racket, but the kids were grooving. When Vinh pranced on stage everything stopped. In the hush of anticipation, the King arrived in drapes and platform shoes. His shades curved around his greased ducktail with style. His attempt to smile and pout simultaneously was ludicrous but his fans loved it. When he twanged into *Ain't Nothin' but a Hound Dog* with knee-knocking, hip-thrusting gyrations the house went stone crazy. The decibels rose exponentially with *That's All Right Mama*, *Jailhouse Rock* and *Heartbreak Hotel*. His crooning finale, *Blue Suede Shoes*, cooled the emotional heat like a breeze off the South China Sea.

Vinh was simply terrific as the King in caricature. His unintended parody was unrivaled by anything I'd seen in America. But for himself and his audience, Vinh was playing it as straight as gospel. He took top honors. Vinh was understandably ecstatic and waited for our approval as eagerly as a performing puppy dog. But Tina was keeping her distance with a disapproving scowl-stare on full throttle.

"Hey, not bad," I said, "Vinh was a scream and a half, wasn't he?"

Tina left my high-fives hanging and slapped me with a weird look instead. "Man, you must be crazy. That was the worst bunch of noise that ever crossed my eardrums. I prayed to go deaf, but Jesus was probably using earplugs himself."

The minibus ride to our hotel was a high flying Elvis sing-a-long with a monsoon of verbal bouquets for our hero. Tina couldn't take it. "Stop this crap. You think you're helping Vinh by kissing his cute little butt. He doesn't need that, he needs advice, expertise and guidance, not a bunch of patronizing foreigners fawning on the little brown brother."

Silence settled in as several tour members tried to salve Vinh's feelings. But he was in a funk, really hurting. I gave Tina a hard "let's cool it, girl" look. She glared me down in return. "Girl," I said, "your love connection just got fried on a short circuit. Kaput. Over and out."

Some inner Elvis voice said, *Hold on, stupid! Resistance to attraction is part of the mating game. Find a way to unite their voices in song; their hearts and minds—and bodies—will follow.* The upcoming *Orient Express* from Hanoi to Hue promised to be the perfect venue for a romantic duet or duel, inspired by twenty hours of boredom and B.O.

The train trip was a disaster, almost *Murder on the Orient Express.* To cut costs, our hosts had reserved second-class sleepers for us, six to a state room with flop-down bunks as hard as mahogany. Tina was outraged. No way was she going to squeeze her beautiful bulk into the narrow bunk space, let alone find room to sit. "This setup looks like a slave ship on rails!" she exploded. "I didn't come to Vietnam to find my roots." Vinh hauled his ass off to jaw with the conductor. Within minutes Tina was enthroned in three lounge chairs while Vinh was struggling with her suitcases.

Tina's bratty behavior, or display of chutzpah, exploded the Volsteds' by-now thin shell of self-control. Betty sat on a suitcase and swore. Phil was shouting at the top of his voice, demanding at least equal privileges with Ms. Tina Brown, if you fucking please! He grabbed Vinh by the collar with both hands and jerked him off the floor in a puppet dance. Tina twisted out of her seat smoother than Chubby Checkers and decked Phil over several rows of shocked Vietnamese. The undersized conductor flapped his arms like a bantam rooster and shouted, "You goddamn spoil American! No more change. No more change!"

"Stop this stupid shit!" I yelled. The shock of violence calmed everybody down temporarily. I got the Volsteds seated in lounge chairs by slipping the conductor a twenty dollar bill. But I was sleepless with frustration, upset with the Volsteds' explosive flap and unhappy with my role as putative Cupid and compromiser. Tina was becoming a tigress in my emotional tank, a pain in the ass. I walked the night from car to car in a mental DMZ, bumping into other insomniacs like rudderless sampans. Way past midnight I jarred to a halt, unable to believe my eyes. Tina had enveloped Vinh in her muscular arms with the beatified gaze of a Renaissance Madonna. She was softly humming gospel lullabies to the wannabe Elvis buried in her bosom, or perhaps trapped in the headlock that made Strangler Lewis famous.

Beautiful Hue, Vietnam's ancient cultural capital, replete with Buddhist temples, sanctuaries and gardens, seemed ideally suited for romance. We took rooms at an elegant three-tiered hotel overlooking the Perfume River. The sunsets were spectacular, the moon viewing indescribably exotic.

Unfortunately for Tina, the Vinh fan club appeared to be headquartered in Hue. The shy flirtatious girls of Hue were famous for their beauty. We met them everywhere like flurries of butterflies—waitresses, dancers, tour guides, hotel maids. They flocked to Vinh like groupies in America panting for their hot rock heroes. Vinh, whose ego ballooned to bursting, flirted outrageously.

As Tina's self-appointed love life advisor, I wanted to make sure she followed my advice. I cornered her on the third-level deck overlooking the Perfume River.

"Baby," I urged her, "this is your big opportunity. Take these Elvis tapes I've borrowed from Vinh, get the songs down like you are singing a duet with Elvis, and I guarantee you'll turn our boy's pelvis into silly putty."

Tina immediately flared up. "I can't sing that redneck kind of crap. Every time I hear one a them nasal twanging yokels singing, I see Confederate flags flying and black men twisting on a rope. Makes me want to puke!"

I suddenly realized—with a shock, really—that Tina had never heard the real Elvis, the holy-roller rocker who had black kids all over the South stomping to his gospel-blues-country beat, all of the time thinking he was a soul brother.

"You're in a fine romantic mood," I said. I dropped the Elvis cassettes in her shoulder bag.

We stood by the balustrade in silence as darkness descended on a river of lantern-lighted sampans. Putt-putt motors and distant voices mixed with the laughter from the dining hall below. Across the river the Citadel was bathed in floodlights that sent shimmering streams of light dancing on the water. Boats and lights intersected constantly as in a shadow play. I waited until Tina had finished crying.

"Tina," I said, "whatever you do, don't miss the midnight moon cruise. With all of that shadow and light, you'll blanch those Vietnamese girls like corn into grits. You are a bronze goddess, girl."

Tina started laughing so hard her shoulders shook but not for long. She heeled around in a huff. "Bronze goddess, huh? You sound as crazy as Langston Hughes with his cocoa-mocha girl gobbledygook. Get off it!"

At that point Vinh walked out on the deck with two French tourist girls. He lit their cigarettes with a Ronson lighter I'd given him. Tina snorted, "I'm through with *him!*" Then she turned her back on him and me.

"Give the boy some slack, Tina," I said.

"How about giving *me* some slack," Tina said, "like, bug out!"

Tina didn't have to give Vinh any slack. He simply took it.

Tina arrived for the moonlight river concert squeezed into a slinky wrap-around sarong that signaled dangerous curves ahead. Dark obsidian eyes smoldered behind a curtain of beaded bangs. She looked like Cleopatra on a kill.

"Hi," I said, "glad you could join our romantic journey."

"Romantic, huh!" Tina snorted. "Whose romance?"

I laughed. "Don't kid me," I said. "We're talking murder on the Nile, baby. You could knock Cleo on her asp and Liz Taylor on her ass."

"Man, you must be crazy. I don't need your shuck and jive."

The oversize sampan barely floated with ten American heavies at one end facing two gorgeous performers and their father at the other end. Papa and a couple of drums comprised the rhythm section. The twin beauties in tight-fitting *ao dais* sang like squeaky canaries and played a variety of oddly-shaped and weird-sounding instruments. Vinh sat between the two canaries with a hands-on approach and insisted that we keep taking his picture while Tina cowered in the darkest corner, stashed her cameras and guzzled beer like a backslid Baptist in a Texas drought. In the flickering light from the kerosene lantern, her eyes glistened between shimmering dreadlocks with visible pain, and possibly murderous intent.

After a nerve-jangling concert, we launched some candles in paper boats. The flotilla of candles floated downriver without mishap, which by tradition meant we would some day return. Everyone but Tina cheered and clinked cans of beer as we bumped against the muddy shore. Vinh, with two clinging beauties hugging his hips, rose unsteadily. Tina lurched to her feet and just as quickly grabbed her stomach. The captive gases in her gut exploded in a Pinatubo-like swoosh of beer and dinner leftovers that sent her careening into the wobbly trio and, together with them, overboard into the shallow muck. Vinh rose from the slime, a midget Neptune, dripping lotus vines and sputtering curses. Tina and the two beauties, baptized in mud, were wailing and flailing away like mud wrestlers with gobs of goo until all of us were slobbered in slime. We all looked so ridiculous and reduced in dignity that I couldn't help but roll on the deck with laughter.

I woke up early the next morning to roust Vinh for an early trip to Danang. I figured the kid probably had a hard night and was sleeping it off. Vinh's room, located near the boat wharf on the lower floor, was fully screened to take advantage of the river breeze. Vinh was missing. I saw instead an Ethiopian princess, partially covered by a tiger-design sarong, arched across the bed with golden thighs akimbo and cantaloupe breasts about to escape. It was Tina in divine dishabille snoring up a storm.

I said to myself, what is going on with this Southern Baptist seminarian and where the hell is Vinh? Then I saw a hand waving from one of the tourist sampans on the wharf below. Vinh was shivering inside a thin blanket.

"What's happening?" I hissed.

"I had to sleep in the sampan last night," Vinh chattered. "Tina came into my room to apologize and then just collapsed. I couldn't wake her, so I slept in the sampan."

I looked at the magnificent tigress called Tina and then to the mouse of a man named Vinh and rolled my eyes in disbelief and certain relief. "You did the right thing, my man," I assured him. She would have eaten him alive.

Danang became our Club Med, a place for fun and relaxation. We loved the colorful shops, the lively streets, great restaurants and superb beaches. Each evening after the full day's activities and seminars, we charged for the uncluttered sands of China or Cui Dai beach.

Tina declined all beach party invitations with the comment, "That Beach Boys California surfer girl crap doesn't appeal to me. Besides, I forgot my swimsuit." Instead she stayed in her room and listened to the Elvis Presley tapes I'd borrowed from Vinh. I could hear her singing late into the night and wondered what had possessed her. She was actually following my advice! When I kidded her about singing the songs she once condemned, she smiled and said, "Hey, I'm doin' the singin', not Elvis."

Danang was suffering through a heat spell which kept most of our group inside air-conditioned rooms after dinner. Some of us cruised the river front because that's where most of Danang's people seemed to be. Several large hotels were on fire with neon lights and breaking eardrums with sound systems at full blast with 1960s rock. One of the largest hotels, the Pacific, featured live music with a mediocre band and a great pianist. Several hundred teenagers had paid a cover charge to suffocate with apparent ecstasy inside a cyclone fence. The noise was deafening. Vinh and I yelled into each other's ears through cupped hands.

"Tomorrow night is karaoke with an open mike. I'm going to kill them, knock them dead with my gig."

"Do you really want to knock them dead?" I yelled. "I mean really kill them?"

Vinh looked puzzled.

"Ask Tina to join you," I yelled. "She's learned all of the Elvis songs, and she can really belt them out. She's dynamite, man!"

"Yeah, man, but she's been tense with me. I think she will refuse, maybe even bite my head off."

"No, man," I insisted. "I've been talking with her. I know she'll do it."

"Okay," Vinh said reluctantly, "I'll do it."

Back at the hotel I passed Tina's door. She was singing Elvis Presley stuff with a voice to die for. I loved it. "Elvis Presley and Tina Turner could be a great act," I told her. She kept right on singing.

On Friday night our entire group sliced through the heavy humidity at the Pacific Hotel and paid our cover charge. Tina stood with us in a short red sheath dress that barely contained her full-bodied energy. She was like a Ferrari revving up at the start of a Grand Prix. I smiled at her and held thumbs up. I'd brokered a musical coupling that smacked of sweet success.

The piano player was terrific, a combination of Elton John and Jerry Lee Lewis, energy with finesse. But the singing was like junkyard dogs howling at the moon or feral cats screeching for sex. We suffered through it all waiting for our hero. When he finally jumped on stage with ducktail and drapes, the crowd went crazy. Kids were screaming "Elvis! Elvis! Elvis the pelvis!" in English, no less. The scene was crazy and wild.

By the time he rolled into *Jailhouse Rock*, the whole river front was rocking. People outside were crowding against the cyclone fence; it sounded like the whole of Danang was on full rock and roll. Then I saw Tina powering her way through the crowd as strong as a Mack truck running through a car lot of Volkswagens. She landed on stage—a human jackhammer of pulsating pulchritude—in a single leap. She roared into *Jailhouse Rock* without missing a beat. She had learned all of the Elvis numbers, adapting the moves and intonations to her own volcanic fire with a Tina Turner shake and thrust that drove the sheath dress up her pile-driving thighs and turned her twisting torso loose and wild. She would have knocked the King himself offstage, let alone poor, pitiful Vinh. He seemed to shrink with each rendition, while Tina expanded and energized.

By the time they rocked into *That's All Right Mama*, Tina was *the* mama, all of the red-hot mamas from Bessie Smith to Janis Joplin, whoever sang gospel, blues, jazz, rock and country. Tina was more than all right; she had us all totally mesmerized. She had taken us with her into a new dimension where we'd never been and where we wanted to stay. I'd seen holy rollers taken by the Spirit, but nothing like this. I didn't even notice that anything was wrong until I heard the waves of applause and people screaming for "More! More! More!" Tina had stopped singing. She was smiling and looking around frantically. Vinh had disappeared. Tina, I think, was completely unaware that she'd humiliated him and sent him packing. I looked for Vinh but the crush of the crowd pushed me around like flotsam. Vinh was nowhere to be seen. Tina suddenly broke into tears and ran through the crowd pushing and shoving. I couldn't hear her but her lips kept repeating "Vinh! Vinh! Vinh!"

Vinh really had disappeared, apparently home to Hanoi, although repeated calls to the Friendship Association there turned up zilch. I believed, or hoped, Vinh was pulling a stunt, that he'd surprise us with the same goofy Elvis welcome in Ho Chi Minh City that he'd given us in Hanoi. It didn't happen. Vinh was gone and I was the asshole who'd made it happen.

Ho Chi Minh City (Saigon) was lively and exciting, chock full of small markets and bursting with enterprise. Saigon was also choking on monoxide. We visited schools and clinics, took a boat trip to the Delta and drove out to the famous Cu Chi tunnels where one of our vets, an ex-tunnel rat, confronted his ex-VC counterpart in a strange underground war game which I missed. Rumor had it they ended up in a surprising reconciliation.

While the tour group gallivanted around Saigon and its environs daily visiting a half-dozen community and service groups, Tina spent her days at Cai's *Gam Lam* ("Nearby") Crafts Center. Actually, its real purpose was to serve as a halfway house for Saigon's street kids, many of them drifting back into Saigon from former re-education camps. Cai was a chubby, gray-haired grandmother who was educated in the U.S., taught at Saigon University during the war and somehow survived ten years in a re-education camp without losing her love for others and her lust for life. She survived by marketing the handicrafts made by the kids, but her real vocation was salvaging youngsters who lived by prostitution and street hustling. Tina fell immediately in love with Cai and the kids and made herself at home.

In the evenings Tina lapsed into a funk—when she wasn't playing Oprah to someone else's hurts. I knew she was drinking a lot, because I could hear her singing in a sloppy, self-commiserating style. Eventually, even the singing stopped. Late one evening she returned some blues tapes she'd borrowed.

"Vinh took your cassette player and some of your cassettes. I'm sorry."

"That's okay," I said. "He also swiped my Stetson. You want to talk?"

"Thanks, but I really can't, at least not yet." Halfway out the door she turned around.

"I'm okay; don't worry. I know this whole trip has been a fantasy and I've done everything wrong side out, but we all have to dream, don't we?"

I wanted to get Tina's mind off of Vinh if possible. "I think your volunteer work with Cai is about as close to your dream as possible—I mean your chosen profession."

"I guess you're right," Tina said, "but I was thinking about the other dream. Working with Cai and the kids comes easy. Several of the Amerasian kids had African-American fathers. Maybe that's what drew me to the center."

"You and Cai seem to relate really well with each other," I said, "like she's a close relative or someone you've known for a long time."

"We clicked from the very first," Tina replied, "then I discovered she's a closet Christian with a circle of Christian friends who meet regularly in private homes. I attended one of their circle meetings and taught them a bunch of Baptist hymns. They loved it. Cai's circle is linked to other circles all over Saigon forming a chain link which they call the Armor of Righteousness."

"Great," I said. "I thought you'd dropped your journalist gig, but it looks like you'll be able to complete your project after all."

"No. No," Tina insisted, "I'm not going to write about Cai's circle group. I'm not about to compromise their program and bring government goons on their heads. I don't want that. Maybe I can write about it later if things loosen up, but not now. That's definite."

One evening, Andy Fetzer told me about a friend of his, a black ex-marine who was in a hospital in Bien Hoa with a brain aneurysm. He'd returned for a visit with his Vietnamese wife and suffered a stroke or something. Without thinking, I immediately hustled Tina to the hospital on the outside chance it might be her father. It wasn't, and the guy was dead.

Tina stiffened and then stumbled backwards. When I reached out to steady her, she brushed me away.

"My dad had only one arm," she said.

That was the first jolt. I'd forgotten about the arm. The second jolt followed as we walked to the taxi.

"He was white."

"What?"

"White. My dad was—is—white."

"But how—?"

"How did it happen? Like any other boy meets girl romance."

"But different," I said.

"Different? Yeah, real different. He—my dad—came south to work in voter registration. Mom came over from Tennessee State with other black students. They all shared the same house, black and white together. Mississippi summer of love. That's how I was conceived, a child of civil rights."

"Some pedigree," I said, "but why—how could a civil rights worker end up a soldier in Vietnam?"

"I'm not sure; I'm trying to remember what my aunt told me. As I recall, my dad received his draft notice that summer and returned to Milwaukee to work on a deferment, but not before he and my pregnant mom got married by a minister friend."

"That was jail time in Mississippi."

"I guess that's how the annulment came about when my dad was back in Milwaukee. My mom got a settlement from his family—*noblesse oblige*—just like on the old plantation. I have to believe, maybe want to believe, my father fought his family over this situation and out of his anger and frustration let himself be drafted."

"Why do you say that?"

Tina was changing her story but, what the hell, it was her story.

"Because when he finished basic training and got his orders for Vietnam, he refused to go. The authorities put him in the stockade. My dad responded with a hunger strike like Gandhi or Martin Luther King. He said he'd never fire a gun or shoot a fellow human being. This is one reason I want to meet my dad, to tell him I'm proud of what he did."

"But he still ended up in Vietnam. How come?"

"There was a plea bargain. My dad agreed to serve in Vietnam as long as he didn't have to carry a rifle. So they assigned him to a combat infantry unit as a radio man."

"RTO, the first to go," I said.

"He was in country for nine months before he got wounded, long enough to marry a Vietnamese."

"He got her pregnant too?"

"Maybe. I don't know. I think he married her to spite his folks, like he did my mom. I don't know. But I want to know."

Our few days in Ho Chi Minh City ended quickly. We gave a banquet to honor our Vietnamese hosts. Our many toasts to friendship and solidarity and to the new Vietnam sounded forced and slightly hollow. Maybe we were drinking to hide our feelings about losing our guide, companion and friend, the one and only Vinh.

When we were all improperly soused, we prevailed upon Tina, who seemed more composed than all of us, to sing a finale. She rendered Tina Turner's *I Can't*

Stand the Rain with such depth of feeling that we all ended up crying and hugging each other.

But I dreamed of a different finale, one in which Tina didn't finish the song because she was interrupted by a tall, handsome man with one good arm which he used to lift Tina. He swung her around and around as if they were dancing for joy. But when I blinked my eyes, I saw that it was Tina who was swinging Vinh in circles before a crowd of Vietnamese who were screaming madly for more, more!

The dream was so real that it followed me across the hot tarmac to the Malaysian Airlines 737. I kept looking behind, expecting to see a one-armed veteran or a truncated Elvis. We were halfway up the steps before I said to Tina, "I'm sorry your dream didn't pan out, Tina."

"Well, like they say, it isn't over 'til the fat lady sings."

"What do you mean?" I asked.

Tina looked back at me and grinned, "I didn't learn all of those stupid Elvis songs for nothing."

"Girl, what are you talking about?" I insisted.

"I mean Vinh called me late last night. We talked for two hours. He's already got us booked for a two-month concert tour in Vietnam next year in all the big hotels and auditoriums in the major cities. He is some hustler. He also proposed to me over the phone, but I held him off—barely. God help me, but I love that boy!" Tina turned quickly to hide her tears and entered the plane.

As the plane rose above the tarmac, I looked below at the green rice fields pock-marked with hundreds of bomb craters. I thought of the millions of lives and billions of dollars expended trying to persuade the Vietnamese to see and do it our way.

Then, as in a vision, each crater became a concert shell, until I imagined all of the bomb craters, extending from one end of Vietnam to the other, filled with people shouting in concert, "More! More! More!"

I immediately made my way to Tina's seat. "Girl," I said, "I do believe the good Lord showed me a vision of what you and Vinh can accomplish. You've got to return to Vietnam and do that concert tour. You will have a ministry of healing and reconciliation you will never have again."

Then Tina surprised and actually deflated me. "I don't think so," she said. "I think Vinh is basically just a hustler, a sweet and wonderful guy, but at heart, a hustler. If I do return, I want to work with Cai and her kids. But for the present I have a more important mission."

"What's that?" I asked.

"I want to meet my father, talk with him, get to know him. Coming to Vietnam has given me the courage and will to face my father. Seeing that vet in the hospital—life is so uncertain. I want to meet my father before it's too late." Tina looked out of the window for a few minutes and then grinned back at me. "Actually, I'm putting Elvis on hold."

"Amen, sister, amen," I said and when I looked below again the bomb craters were gone and we were flying over an emerald sea which was an ocean highway that would take us all the way home.

Cinderella Gook

I thought she was Vietnamese at first, because she was slender in the waist, with the curvaceous hourglass figure that even the thinnest Vietnamese women seem to have. But the face and lips were thin and her narrow eyes, rimmed by shadows, glistened like cats' eyes in the dark, as if she were stealthily peering out from behind a dark curtain. Still, she looked much younger than her forty-plus years, perhaps because her unblemished skin was so light and luminous and her lustrous sheen of dark hair fell to her shoulders in the fashion of younger women. She dressed in dark, stylish clothes, was quietly observant, and after a row with Kate Noonan preferred to room alone until Tina Brown took her in as a roommate. Somehow their contrasting personalities seemed to fit together in a yin-yang symbiosis. I got to know Lily through Tina, who'd become a kind of gospel singing soul sister to me. Lily told us her story on a muggy hot night in Saigon. We were trying to cool off on the second floor landing of our hotel by dousing ourselves inside and out with Vietnamese beer.

I think it was a combination of elements: getting mellowed by drinking several beers, Tina's brassy forthrightness and Lily's trust in Tina that finally broke her silence. Once Tina broached her question, Lily talked non-stop for two hours.

"Everybody knows I'm black and Cole's white," Tina said, "but I can't place your pedigree, if you'll pardon the implication that all Asians look alike. Now look, girl," Tina said, "you've been elusive this whole trip. I'm really serious about this; who are you?"

Lily laughed. "Don't worry," she said, "it took me half a lifetime to figure out who I was. Now solve this riddle, if you can: I was born an enemy alien and American citizen simultaneously inside an American concentration camp located on an Apache Indian reservation in Arizona. Give up? Answer: My mother was Japanese-American, my father a Caucasian. He visited my mom twice in camp, like conjugal visits in prison. Bang-bang good-bye. That's how I came to be born. My father started divorce proceedings before I was even born, on VJ Day 1945. I've never seen him and I don't want to. After the war Mom played it safe by marrying a Nisei war hero who'd lost a kneecap fighting with the 442nd in Germany and walked like a storm trooper ever after. He eventually became a highly placed engineer with the Bechtel Corporation."

At this point Tina started crying, maybe because of the beer but mostly, I think, because her father had abandoned Tina and her mother during the Vietnam War. Lily put her arms around Tina. "Go on, please continue," Tina said. "I want to hear your story. Don't mind me; I'm just a big old crybaby."

"I guess you could say I was brought up to be a Japanese-American princess," Lily said, "an all-American girl, not the Madame Butterfly image my mom had to deal with. I took ballet lessons, tennis, gymnastics and even lessons in deportment at a girls' finishing school in Palo Alto. Of course, I always had to be on the honor roll. That was obligatory for a Japanese-American princess."

Tina laughed. "Girl, seems to me you had it made. I feel like I'm listening to an all-American success story. What went wrong?"

"Nothing went wrong on the surface. It was the hidden stuff. The thing I remember most vividly was the silence, the awful silence about the concentration camps and the war. It was as if Mom blamed herself or was ashamed of some crime she'd committed instead of the other way around—like she was the perpetrator instead of the victim. That seemed all wrong to me. My stepdad never talked about his experiences either. I think it was the horror of things he'd witnessed and wanted to forget. Then there was the humiliation of having to prove his loyalty. Maybe he felt guilty, as well—guilty for having to live with the humiliation that so many of his closest friends had been killed and yet he had lived."

"That's something at least you never had to face," I said, "the humiliations your parents' generation had to endure."

"I had to live with the aftermath of their experience," Lily said, "with the silence, the covering up, the inner pain and unexpressed anger. But you're right; I was privileged. As a high school graduation gift, my parents sent me to Japan to visit relatives and check out my roots. That trip really changed my life."

"How did it change your life?" I asked. "It sounds pretty conventional to me."

"I spent three months backpacking in northern Japan with two cousins, mostly in Hokkaido. From Japan I flew to Malaysia, Singapore and Indonesia. I spent three months in Bali and loved it. I returned to Japan, taught English for three months, took in the Tokyo Olympics and then flew home.

"Some trip," I said, "but how did it change your life?"

"I became an Asian, or at least I developed an Asian view of the world. I saw Asians throwing off the mind-set of colonialism and realized Asian-Americans need to do the same."

"So then you came home to change America," Tina said.

"America was already changing," Lily said. "There was a civil rights revolution, a youth revolution, beginnings of feminism and several other revolutions all going on at once. I just wanted to join in and become a part of the scene. It was all very exciting. My friends said, 'Go to Berkeley; that's where it's all happening.'"

I snorted. "Yeah, good ol' Berserkeley, sucked in all of the nuts and screwballs in America like a magnet."

Lily ignored me. "I entered Berkeley in 1964 when the movement was gathering steam. Students who had recently returned from Mississippi, from working in voter registration, were ready to take on the world, which included protesting the war in Vietnam. For a suburban Cinderella like me, Berkeley was enormously exciting and different. I was repulsed at first by the longhairs and grungy street people, but you couldn't be at Berkeley and not be involved in politics."

I remembered entering San Francisco State in 1968 as a Vietnam vet and having to keep my identity undercover. I'd have gotten trashed or mobbed. Even after I turned against the war, I identified with fellow vets whether they were pro- or antiwar. Most of the protesters had no understanding of the vets' situation.

"If you aren't part of the solution, you're part of the problem," Tina said.

"That's what everyone was saying," Lily continued. "I couldn't stay at Berkeley and be a banana."

"Or an Oreo," Tina added.

"Yeah, I stopped being an Oreo banana and turned mellow yellow. I started attending the Asian-American Forum consisting of Asian students concerned about the silence of Asian-Americans while the rest of the country was in turmoil over civil rights, ethnic identity, poverty and the wars in Asia. We wanted our parents and grandparents to speak out against the law that still existed that could put blacks and protesters inside barbed wire. Those of us raised in suffocating silence were ready to scream at last. I hadn't realized before what a banana I'd become. I put most of the blame on my parents."

"Mama Madonna," Tina said, "and didn't the honey bucket hit the fan!"

"The arguments with my parents got pretty horrendous. I saw myself as a colonized victim. I remember an essay that everyone was reading, 'The Student as Nigger.' Well, my parents had become the plantation masters. If they'd known I was living with a black guy, they'd have self-destructed."

"Messed in their pants at least," Tina said. "How about you, Cinderella? You're the one I see heading for self-destruct."

"My parents separated my sophomore year, mostly because of me, I think, at least that's the way I took it. Later they got together again. But that's when I decided to drop out of college and go to Vietnam. It seemed crazy even at the time, since I knew almost nothing about Vietnam's history, culture or the war. But with the war dominating our lives more and more and my classes less and less relevant to my personal life, I got this overwhelming urge—almost like a spiritual calling—to just go. The final straw was when my old man dropped me for being too white. I nearly flipped over the edge because I'd just had an abortion."

"Black men," Tina said, "can really be messed up. But shoot, girl, you just can't up and decide to go to Vietnam. I mean how did you get there, on some magic carpet?"

"I heard from a friend about the Red Cross being hard up for service girls or Donut Dollies—Miss Americas who could project fantasies of Dallas Cowboy cheerleaders with the image of the girl next door to remind the boys of who they were fighting for. We personified the wives and sweethearts they left behind. Sometimes we were called fun and games girls but that was mostly said in jest. We were there to be ogled and worshipped. Don't touch the merchandise was the unwritten rule. There were plenty of Vietnamese girls to satisfy the grunts' animal desires.

"The contradictions were unbelievable," Lily continued. "You could be there and still not believe it. We flew into Cam Ranh Bay which in one sense was like landing in America. I mean, they had everything—restaurants, rec clubs, swimming pools, water skiing and surfing. I felt like Dorothy in the land of beach blanket Oz.

"The down side of fun and games was being helicoptered into the fighting zones and firebases where we delivered Kool-Aid and, yes, played checkers and Scrabble and games that required talking. The idea was to break the thousand-yard stares and the shell shock. We were like angels being dropped into hell. The grunts stood around us and simply devoured us like it was their last supper. It was for many of them. One firebase we visited was totally wiped out the next day, no survivors."

Angels from hell, baby, that's what you were. The thought of squeaky clean Dollies confronting a pack of oversexed teenage grunts facing death was too much. Donut Dollies were the final masturbation, the ultimate cock tease, like holding out a cookie jar and then shooting the kid between the eyes.

"Even worse were our regular visits to hospital wards trying to comfort guys whose limbs had been shot off, who were horribly mutilated in mind and body, blind and screaming and burned into crispy critters (the medics' term). Under the MEDCAP program we also visited Vietnamese orphanages and schools in which many of the kids had been napalmed. Their sad, beautiful eyes looking out through keloid masks of scarred flesh still haunt my dreams.

"There was an even darker side. My first week in country a nurse at Cu Chi was raped and had her throat cut. Later a Donut Dolly was raped in Danang. So the fear was always present. After the rape at Danang, I went on temporary duty to fill in for Dollies who quit. The place was awful. Young marines—kids really—would come off patrol with ears, penises and even scalps hanging from their belts, bragging how they'd shot some scared old *mama san* in a rice field. Those zombie kids with their brains fried on drugs scared the hell out of me."

"Take me back to beach blanket Oz," Tina said. "I can't take this trip through hell."

Lily's view of the American military was so one-sided that I was forced to break in. "You make it sound like Americans in Vietnam were mostly fuckups and failures. Not true. I worked with civic action teams that tried to help ordinary people improve their daily lives. In some cases we were damn successful."

"And the motives?" Lily asked sharply.

"Motives? The motives were many and not all of them were self-serving."

"I thought we were in Vietnam to win hearts and minds as we piled up body counts. Some logic, huh?"

"Yeah, right," I said, "but some people-to-people programs were successful, supported by the peasants."

"I'm not going to dispute your experience," Lily said, "even though I've heard more than a few civic action horror stories. I can only give you my story. Okay?"

"Okay," I said, "just don't make it boring."

"Well, life at Cam Ranh Bay was pretty boring. We dealt mainly with REMFs and Remington Cowboys (clerk typists) who were largely exempt from the horrors of war. We played Scrabble and served them snacks and sodas. They were as bored as we were, so drinking and smoking grass on the QT was about the only way we survived.

"I made the mistake of falling in love with a young pilot from Oklahoma. He was sweet and wonderful and married, which didn't seem to matter in Vietnam. Everything was so uncertain. One evening I returned from a clinic where I'd seen some Vietnamese kids horribly napalmed, eyeballs hanging out, the works. Eddie (my man) and I met at the officers' club for a steak dinner. Of course, I drank like a fish to drown the images ricocheting inside my skull. We returned to my quarters and made love. Eddie fell asleep, but I stared into space filled with images of death. I looked at Eddie and realized that this beautiful man could have been the son of a bitch who napalmed some of the horribly burned kids I'd seen just a few hours before. Something started to tear inside me. I began screaming and beating Eddie with both fists. I was coming apart. I had to get out of Vietnam."

At this point Lily started shaking. Tina hugged her close. When Lily pounded Tina with her fists, Tina hugged her tighter until she finally calmed down.

"I'm sorry," Lily said, "let me finish. My return to San Francisco didn't help my mental state at all. I was taking courses in journalism at San Francisco State, but my heart and mind were still in Vietnam. My old boyfriend tracked me down, but he was so deep into Black Panther politics as theater, wearing shades, black beret and spouting Armageddon dialectics, that I turned for relief to a very hip doctor working in a Haight Ashbury clinic. I'd met him at a Panther fund-raiser. He was a terrific guy, really, very understanding and decent. With a haircut and a practice in suburbia, he could have been the Prince Charming of my parents' dreams. But I couldn't dream about babies in suburbia while I was having nightmares of babies burning in Vietnam.

"My stepfather, thankfully, understood that I needed to return to Vietnam, or maybe he just wanted to get rid of me. So he helped me get a public relations job with Bechtel in Vietnam, which really meant working as liaison with the military: living like a princess, eating at expensive restaurants, dating officers, hanging out at the *Cercle Sportique* and flying to Dalat and Cape Saint Jacques for lost weekends. Sometimes I felt as removed from the war as a pilot in an F-105, above the clouds at thirty thousand feet, which I actually experienced on one occasion. Fortunately, my liaison job put me in touch with some gritty reporters who took me into the mud and shit side of the war as well as its dirty politics.

"I traded my two semesters of journalism for a reporter's job with the *Saigon Post*, an English-language newspaper that supported the war. The job got me a press pass from MACV, which allowed me to travel on military vehicles and aircraft, mainly helicopters."

Slumming. That was Lily's whole fucking gig. Slumming, playing Donut Dolly, military liaison, party girl and now adventurous war correspondent—Nancy Drew in campaign jacket and jaunty cap tilted at a rakish angle. A pinup journalist.

Tina, who'd been quiet for a long time, interrupted. "Honey, you do have a gift for wading into a deep dish of sweet potato pie, and I do mean a substance of the same color."

"Actually, that came later," Lily said. "At first I took a room at the Caravelle Hotel, hung out at the bar with the other reporters and took my stories from the Five O'clock Follies, the daily briefing by the MACV mouthpiece. Once the romantic illusion of becoming another Marguerite Higgins wore as thin as my wallet I had to move into a slum apartment near Bui Phat, a refugee garbage dump. That's where I encountered real Vietnamese, a million street people, mostly kids, who survived by begging, hustling black market goods and pimping. Half of them lived in cardboard boxes, chewed on cigarette butts and snarled like Jimmy Cagney: 'Hey GI, five dollah, you boom my sistah. Yeah, she virgin, man. Bes' boom-boom in Saigon.' And when the GI turned away, 'Fuck you GI. Yankee go home!'"

"Could be East Saint Louis," said Tina, "my old news beat."

"In the midst of this terrible turmoil, families survived, held together, went about their daily tasks. School kids in neatly starched uniforms walked through the war zone of mean streets like it didn't exist. It was really unbelievable. This was a part of the war—the human factor—that Americans weren't hearing about. So I began pounding out a series of articles entitled 'Saigon's Mean Streets.' But there were no takers. This is not what Americans wanted to hear about. Neither did the *Saigon Post*."

"So how did you survive if you couldn't get your stuff published?" I asked. I suspected Lily was still hitting up her parents for support.

"I don't know what I would have done if I hadn't met this giant of a guy, a photojournalist from Australia with a lantern jaw and a haystack of hair hanging over his eyes. Kenny helped me market the articles to magazines in Australia and New Zealand, enhanced by his marvelous photographs.

"Kenny loved the Vietnamese, which is why, I suppose, they loved him. Most American reporters followed American troops and reflected their prejudices, always badmouthing the ARVN. Kenny was constantly in the field with Vietnamese and knew them intimately as people. He reported their bravery and had the film to prove it. ARVN soldiers often took their wives and families with them, as if they knew the war was long term and they all were part of it. U.S. soldiers, whose families were exempt from the war's devastation, didn't understand the ARVN."

Lily! You are so fucking naive and misinformed! I wanted to scream. The ARVN as fighters were a bust. I'd seen them fold under pressure, cut and run, refuse to fight again and again. But I kept my opinions to myself because I wanted to hear Lily out. Besides, I didn't know the ARVN from inside their culture. I couldn't sympathize with their point of view or approach to the war.

"Kenny started taking me with him to several orphanages around Saigon, ones he'd been helping for years. We'd hustle stuff from American PXs and the black market, toys, clothes and food for the kids. We'd take them to the Saigon Zoo and parks to play soccer and kickball. I wrote a series of articles on the orphans, one of which got published in the U.S., a small victory for me.

"When Kenny insisted on going with the ARVN into Cambodia in 1970, a terrifying, paralyzing fear turned me into a crying, begging, threatening shrew, a real basket case. 'I'll never marry you,' I screamed. We'd agreed to get married just so we could adopt Bobby Brat, a lovable street orphan who had become a mascot and prince of pimps for a marine unit stationed at Bien Hoa airbase.

"Kenny's disappearance and death would have sent me spiraling into suicide, I'm sure, if I hadn't survived by working with the street orphans of Saigon. I needed them even more than they needed me.

"The final years of war turned Saigon into a battle zone. GIs in jeeps were knocking over bike-riding Vietnamese for sport, shooting street kids suspected of carrying grenades and beating up streetwalkers. VC guerrillas were blowing up bars and hangouts frequented by Americans.

"When a gang of Vietnamese teenagers, Saigon cowboys, railed at me as a 'Yankee bitch whore' and pelted me with rocks, I realized my personal tour in Vietnam was over. Cinderella Gook couldn't play in the hell of Saigon. Hell, as one writer said about Vietnam, it was a very small place, too small for me to survive. I stuck it out and finally, with my parents' help, adopted Bobby Brat after months of bureaucratic hassling. He became my reason for living. I took him home with me, and he became an American brat. He's now an intern at Stanford Medical School training to become a heart specialist."

At that point, Lily suddenly broke down and started crying. Tina wrapped a big arm around her. "What really happened?" Tina asked.

"I just told you," Lily sobbed, "my all-American boy is completing his medical training at one of the best university hospitals. That was my dream for him. He's everything my parents wanted me to be, the success story they'd always dreamed of and hoped for. So now we can all live happily ever after in our land of dreams."

"What really happened?" Tina repeated gently.

"Unfortunately, my parents couldn't handle Bobby the brat. They just couldn't accept the little gook. They drove him away just as they drove me away." Lily wiped her eyes and took a long draught of Vietnamese beer. "What happened is as American as apple pie; Bobby got involved with a Mission District gang, went to war in the streets and got killed. He came all the way from bloody Vietnam just to die in America—that's what happened. It's crazy how the streets of his adopted country became more and more like the streets of wartime Saigon."

"And now you've returned," Tina said. "Why, for another brat?"

Lily nodded, "Yes, for another brat, if that's possible."

Tina was crying and so was I. Tina looked at Lily and smiled. "I think you're the heart specialist, girl. In fact, I know you're the heart specialist."

That's where I wish Lily's story could have ended. But it didn't. The formidable Nurse Noonan, who was standing in the doorway, apparently had a different version.

"Tell them what really happened, Lily," she said.

Lily's head snapped around as if she'd been slapped in the face. "You bitch," she hissed, "You've never believed me; I never should have taken you as a friend." Then she burst into tears and ran from the room.

I think Tina and I were both too shocked to react at first. Then Tina snapped, "What's your problem, Kate? What are you trying to do, mess with her mind or something? She just told us one of the most moving and realistic stories I've ever listened to."

"Maybe so, maybe no," Kate said. She turned abruptly and walked away.

If I hadn't stumbled into Betty looking for early breakfast tea after a night of insomnia, Lily's story might have ended with Kate Noonan's snide, cryptic comment. Betty, a proverbial early riser, already had a pot steeping. She was writing in her journal. She motioned me to a chair and poured two cups of steaming tea.

"Getting your frustrations out?" I kidded.

"In a word, yes," Betty said, "mainly my frustrations with one member of our happy crew."

I turned both eyebrows into question marks and waited. Betty and I were long time confidantes as well as close friends.

"I had another long conversation with Lily Okada last night at midnight, for the third time this week. She knocks on the door, always crying, says she's having nightmares."

"About Vietnam," I said, "and the story always changes."

"About Vietnam, yes, but the story never changes."

"What's her story line this time?" I grunted.

Betty frowned at me over her Franklin half-specs and poured another round of tea. "Pretty cynical, aren't you? Drown your grouch and listen up. The woman is carrying a load of guilt that would sink the *Saratoga*."

"What's that?"

"Aircraft carrier. World War II. Lily's nightmares result from having sent three people she loved to their deaths in Vietnam. She sees only their heads, free-floating in the dark of night accusing her and asking her why she's still alive."

"I know about one of them," I said, "a photojournalist who was killed during the Cambodian invasion. How about the others?"

"She won't say. But she says the nightmares started after the son she gave up for adoption arrived on her doorstep after twenty years."

"What?"

"Yep. Just like that, quite a shocker. He's twenty-two, a pre-med student at Stanford University. Somehow he tracked Lily down and started calling her Mom. Eventually he wanted to know who his father is—or was—insisted on it. That's why Lily's here, to trace the father's whereabouts."

"Father? A Vietnamese father?"

"Yes, a Vietnamese journalist, an older man who became her mentor, took her under his wing so to speak, like an elder brother. She became pregnant with his child and returned to the U.S. to bear the child and then, for whatever reasons, gave him up for adoption."

"And you believe her story?" I asked.

Betty spilled her tea. "Why would she travel all the way to Vietnam, relive all the wartime trauma and lie about something so important as life and death? It doesn't make a damn bit of sense!"

"You're right," I said, "it doesn't make a damn bit of sense. None of Lily's stories make sense because she's making up half of her stories." I then told Betty the story Tina and I had heard from Lily.

As I expected, Lily never found her Vietnamese lover, the father of her putative son. Nor did I talk with Lily again or anyone else about Lily until her name came up in a conversation with John Tortino, the travel agent who'd arranged our tour and had once been employed by AID in Vietnam.

We met in Los Guitares, a Mexican restaurant near John's agency in San Francisco's Mission District, to discuss and debrief the tour. We were finishing our dessert of coffee and flan before I mentioned Lily.

"Lily Okada. I knew her," he said, "not really well, but I knew enough about her."

"Knew enough?" I questioned.

"Yeah. She had one hell of a reputation."

"What do you mean, reputation?" I asked.

"I mean she had a reputation for sleeping around."

"With whom, everybody?"

"Everybody in the circle she hung out with—outlaw journalists, freelancers, photographers, wild guys living on the edge with a reputation for drinking, drugs, and sex, lots of sex, all kinds," John replied. "I should know because I sometimes hung out with them to break the bureaucratic boredom. They were as exciting as hell, running the border between life and death, taking risks. For me it was a kind of slumming, jazzing up my dull existence with vicarious danger. Lily was in the center of it all, living it up in a wild kind of polyandry."

"If you mean fucking her brains out, it doesn't sound like the Lily I know." I didn't believe him.

"She had reasons. She'd lost a boyfriend in Cambodia, an Aussie photojournalist. I think she was reacting to that loss. Being with the Aussie's buddies kept her in touch with him, so she traded sex for their companionship and they damn sure took advantage of it."

"Jesus, I don't know," I said. "Did you ever hear of Lily working with orphans, that kind of thing?"

"Nothing like that. She was strictly a party girl, living as high as she could, hitting heavily on booze and drugs like the rest of the Dirty Dingos. That's what they called themselves."

"I wonder how she ever came clean?"

"I don't know," John answered. "She just suddenly disappeared, dropped out of sight."

"Just like that, no clue?"

"Only a rumor that she was living with a Vietnamese journalist, an older guy. At the time, she was maligned and laughed at by the Dirty Dingoes as a gook girl, the female equivalent of squaw man. If Lily survived, he probably saved her life."

I tried several times to track Lily down. I was determined to unravel her story. She was too elusive. She kept moving, had unlisted phone numbers and frequently changed jobs. Then in August of 1994, I finally caught up with Lily—after she'd jumped off the Golden Gate Bridge. Death by drowning. She would have survived the jump.

I immediately called on Kate Noonan. She'd worked with Lily on the Telephone Tree and had questioned Lily's story. Besides, Kate was an expert on suicides. She'd contemplated suicide herself and had done suicide counseling for the Vietnam Nurses Association, where she now held a paid position.

"Lily Okada," Kate said.

"Yeah, it was a hell of a shock and yet, not surprising. She'd wrapped herself inside a dynamite stick of contradictions."

"I've thought about her a lot this last year, trying to figure her out. I even tracked her down once, but she either wasn't home or wouldn't answer the door. I did, however, talk with two other Donut Dollies who were housed with Lily at Cam Ranh Bay."

"You were the one who doubted her story, remember? That's why I'm here, to get your take on Lily, find out why you questioned her story."

Kate was aging fast. Her visible wisps of hair were mostly gray with a few streaks of rust; her skin was sagging beneath the once firm chin and she was wearing a knit skull cap. Cancer—chemotherapy or radiation, probably both.

Kate looked out of the dirty window of the second-story warehouse office like she didn't want to answer, or was gathering her thoughts. I wondered why she didn't clean the window because I could see Treasure Island and half of the Bay Bridge.

"Well," Kate offered, "I know a few things about Lily you may not know because I worked with Lily for several months on the Telephone Tree in the quest for MIAs. Lily got involved because she lost a brother in Vietnam, a proud and brilliant kid who'd come through West Point near the top of his class. He chose Special Forces, probably because his dad had been a hero in World War II. He felt compelled to live up to some heroic ideal."

"Lily never mentioned her brother," I said.

"He disappeared in Laos or Cambodia like a lot of other guys on special assignments, in illegal, secret wars. That's what brought us close together at first—we both had men that disappeared. Then, early in the tour we quarreled and split over my hassling Vietnamese officials."

"How would Lily have known about her brother's secret missions?" I inquired.

"She must have talked with him about the dangers and illegalities. They'd become very close, maybe because they'd lived apart as teenagers. She knew about his misgivings, the kinds of pressures he was under. He had encountered a lot of racism as well, and felt he had to prove himself by killing gooks. I think she was the only person he could confide in."

"Sounds like he laid a heavy trip on Lily."

"Actually, Lily laid a heavy guilt trip on herself. She blamed herself for her brother's death, felt she'd driven him to self-destruct. Her brother's disappearance dismantled Lily's life as a Donut Dolly. She went to pieces emotionally, started criticizing the war, got reprimanded for using drugs and getting drunk and finally got sent home pregnant."

"That does put a different twist on it," I said.

"A bigger twist than you may think," Kate replied. "Lily gave the baby up for adoption to her sister-in-law and her new husband."

"Jesus Christ," I groaned, "this is getting too fucking complicated. How about the Vietnamese kid, the adopted son she claimed was killed in a gang war?"

"It's true, according to the former Dolly I talked with. Lily adopted a Vietnamese kid, a tough-as-nails street hustler who, as a teenager in America, got snuffed in a gang fight."

"But the kid that suddenly showed up after twenty years demanding to know who his father was, where does he fit in? Was he a figment of Lily's imagination?"

"I think he was the most real of all her stories."

"What do you mean?" I asked.

"I think the young man who showed up after twenty years was her first child, the one she gave up for adoption."

"I thought Lily's lover was an American pilot. So why would Lily return to Vietnam to find the father? It doesn't make sense."

Kate coughed and took several deep breaths. "It makes sense if she planned to hide some dark truth, a family secret that might destroy the lives of Lily and her son, and maybe others if it came to light."

"I don't get it."

"I think Lily needed the Vietnamese journalist as a substitute for the real father. He'd been her savior in Vietnam; now she needed him again. If she could find and convince him to play the surrogate father, she might be able to keep the family tragedy buried. Crazy, yes, but she was desperate. If her mission failed, she'd have to hide or run, both of which she'd been doing until the end."

"Jesus Christ! You mean the brother . . ."

"He was her half-brother; maybe that made a difference. But he was still her brother."

"And the father of her child."

"Yes, the father of her child, the child whose return would destroy her."

Kickboxing
Spider Woman

The purse snatcher was big and fast and sliced through cracks in the long ticket lines with the skill of a pro football running back until a mule kick out of nowhere stopped him cold. It was a millisecond blur that broke his jaw and sent him sprawling into cloud cuckoo land. Then all the cowardly bravehearts who'd turned their backs in fear jumped all over the inert homeboy in baggy pants and Raiders jacket, stomping out their fears and frustrations until airport security guards intervened. Meanwhile, I tried to catch the eye of the slender Asian lady in line behind me whose leg was such a lethal weapon. She seemed so quietly oblivious to all the commotion that I questioned what I'd witnessed. I'd seen a bluish blur, the color of her pantsuit—that was all. Then she looked me in the eye, gave just the slightest enigmatic Mona Lisa smile and looked away.

The thin, delicate pixie with hidden springs of steel, who reminded me of a young Leslie Caron with luscious lips and cheeks, long eyelashes and high forehead, joined our tour group a few minutes later, carrying a single bag as if she were on a one-way trip. Her Vietnamese name, she said, was Cao Nu Lien, but she now preferred her American name, Sybil Patterson. She had been married to an American IBM executive (recently deceased) and taught modern ballet and dance in her own San Jose studio. When I asked if she also taught martial arts, she looked at me like I was crazy. Her purpose in returning to Vietnam was to trace some relatives in Hue if, in fact, they were still living. Her family had been trapped in the Tet holocaust of 1968. She hadn't heard from anyone in twenty-five years, she said.

It was obvious from the first day that she wanted privacy and anonymity. Fortunately, she roomed with Kate Noonan, who wanted the same. Like a couple of nuns in seclusion, they rarely left their room except for obligatory tours. Maybe Sybil could have kept her anonymity if a sharp-eyed airport official hadn't looked at her twice. Two days later three look-alike security officials, hatless and wearing dark suits and ties, drove to the Friendship Hotel in a sleek '60s Mercedes (waxed and purring) asking for Ms. Cao Nu Lien. Ms. Lien (Sybil Patterson) changed into a dress, took her tote bag and drove away with the security clones. She returned the next day with the same crew, same Mercedes.

"I had to meet with some officials," she said. "It was nothing—just some talk with some people I once knew."

Some small talk. That next day Hanoi's official newspaper carried a spread of front page photos, pictures of Sybil surrounded by a bevy of old revolutionaries, including the famous, or infamous, General Giap. The headline proclaimed in Vietnamese "GUERRILLA GIRL RETURNS FOR REUNION." The article praised Madame Cao Nu Lien's wartime work as director of the National People's Dance Theater and as a revolutionary fighter whose picture, *Guerrilla Girl*, reproduced by the thousands, had become the symbol of resistance for Vietnamese women and the heart photo for unmarried fighting men going south on the Ho Chi Minh Trail. I recognized the photo immediately. The smiling girl with the deadly AK-47 had been the prized collector's item for American grunts in Vietnam, worth two cartons of Kools on the black market.

The communist big-shots apparently wanted to give Sybil a returning hero's tour, but she insisted on staying with our group. The brief flurry of public attention seemed only to introvert her, driving her more deeply into her private self. Nurse Noonan, square-jawed with flaming hair, became her guardian angel and protector. Even General Giap would have backed off.

Sybil's withdrawal only served to increase her aura of mystery and my own captivation with her. I remembered seeing photos of her with Jane Fonda and Doctor Spock during the war and somewhere else. I knew I'd seen her somewhere else in a different context. But where? I didn't want to intrude into her private life and I couldn't anyway, not with the formidable Nurse Noonan on guard duty.

Fortunately, I later encountered Sybil one-on-one in Hue. Having failed to trace her relatives, Sybil had been daily offering incense and meditating in the Thien Mun Temple overlooking Hue's Perfume River. I went there with a letter for one of the monks that I also wished to interview. After the session I came to sit by a quiet pool under a high arched arbor near the temple graveyard. The scene was so serene and peaceful following our painful exchange on the war that I started to softly chant a mantra I'd learned from a Vietnamese friend in the States.

Muffled laughter broke the meditative mood. I twisted around and saw Sybil still laughing. "Do you know what you're chanting?" she asked.

"I understood it was a Buddhist mantra," I said, "that a Vietnamese friend taught me."

She laughed again. "It's very erotic, wild and crazy, something soldiers might have chanted on the Ho Chi Minh Trail to keep their spirits high—a marching song."

"Like your photo," I said, but she acted as if she hadn't heard me.

"Don't worry," she said, "if the monks heard you, they're probably laughing, too. For a practitioner of Zen, anything goes. The important thing is mind and attitude; the words are only a vehicle."

"I'm not sure where my mind is right now," I said, drawing on my thin veneer of hipster Zen. "I feel like I've entered a great zone of emptiness."

Sybil was grinning. "So you've achieved *satori?*"

"No. I came here to fill up my zone of emptiness," I said, "to find the truth about something outside of myself—maybe inside too, I don't know."

"What truth is that?" she asked.

So I told Sybil the reason for my visit, of how I wanted to find out who was responsible for the death of my commanding officer and his Vietnamese mistress.

"But why?" she quizzed. "You will only enter a labyrinth that will trap you in frustration. That's the way it is in Vietnam. Sometimes you have to reconcile with pain, anger, frustration."

"Maybe you're right," I said, "but it's something I've got to do no matter where it takes me." Then I added very tentatively, "How about you?"

Sybil didn't answer at first, so I said, "I still have a photo of you as the guerrilla pinup girl. You were as popular with American grunts as with Vietnamese."

Sybil frowned and then laughed, "That was a long time ago," she said, "a very long time ago."

"I have a feeling," I said, "that it's somehow connected with your honorary banquet in Hanoi."

"I wanted to forget all that and wipe out the past, but I'm beginning to realize that the past is always present, all of it."

"One of our writers once said, the past is not dead; it's not even past," I added.

Then Sybil surprised me. She simply started talking about her past like it was yesterday, something she needed and wanted to talk about. "When I was a schoolgirl in Hue and then in Dalat, I was a dancer, a kind of child prodigy. Dancing was my life—everything. Even as a little girl, I dream-danced at night. At age thirteen my parents sent me to Paris to study at the famous *Ecole Danze Francaise*. It was incredibly rigorous and demanding, but I loved it, even though the French girls hated me because I danced circles around them. I had just been accepted as a trainee in France's National Ballet Company when the urgent call came to return home. The war had escalated, forcing some of my family to move from Hue to Saigon.

"It was a shock to see how the war was devouring the country and how my family's fortunes had declined. Even their characters and personalities seemed radically changed. Father had simply given up, drawn into himself and become an opium addict. My older brother, who had assumed control of the family textile business, was now manufacturing uniforms for the military and expanding into a wide range of black market supplies, including drugs. That's how he kept my father supplied with opium. Another brother was an officer in ARVN; a sister had married an air force commander and a second sister was working for the American AID. They had all returned to Hue for a big family celebration during Tet of 1968 and got trapped in a hellfire holocaust."

"How about you? You must have been sucked into the war, too?" I inquired.

"Because I could sing and dance, was so politically naive and didn't know what else to do, I joined Madame Nhu's corps of clean-cut patriotic youth who traveled around performing songs and dances at ARVN bases and strategic hamlets. We were constantly praised for helping in the patriotic task of national reconstruction. But it didn't take long to discover the hypocrisy and corruption behind the smoke screen of democracy. The prettiest girls were asked—required—to act as hostess girls for high-ranking officers. To our devastation, we discovered this included sexual favors. When I refused, I was brutally raped by an ARVN officer. When I protested, I was blamed, verbally abused by the officer's wife as a whore and slapped around by the team leader, who was mortified by my behavior. My older brother, who had encouraged me to join the Youth Corps, cursed me for causing him embarrassment with his business contacts. I thought of committing suicide. Instead, I crossed over and joined the NLF. It wasn't that difficult. The VC had infiltrated everywhere.

"The NLF instructed me to go north for military and political training which proved to be intensely rigorous, but I embraced the sheer physical challenge as a kind of purification. On one level it was pretty simple: just do as you're told. I became expert in martial arts. Eventually I was appointed head cadre for women's guerrilla training. During this training time, I posed for the picture that became the popular pinup, *Guerrilla Girl*.

"Then, because Bac Ho (Uncle Ho) had spent so many years in China he arranged for three of us to study revolutionary opera, theater and dance in Shanghai. Madame Mao-Jiang Jing—was insufferable but the performers were friendly and helpful, as scared of her as we were. Upon our return after six months, I was appointed director of our National People's Dance Theater. I more or less adapted Chinese revolutionary opera like *White Haired Girl* to our own situation. The Americans, after all, were still the *Yellow Running Dogs*. And of course we had our own songs and heroes like the Trung Sisters, as well. Eventually we trained groups of performers to entertain along the Ho Chi Minh Trail."

"I think I understand now why you were honored in Hanoi," I said, "but I have a feeling this is only part of the story, maybe only the beginning."

Sybil did not reply. Dusk was settling over the Perfume River. Lanterns and stoves were being lit in the river sampans below us. The aroma of rice and vegetables being prepared by the monks wafted our way. Sybil rose to her feet, stretched, and then simply walked away humming the mantra marching song I'd been chanting as if to mock me. I rose and followed several paces behind, waiting for her to say something or walk with me. But her mind was elsewhere, perhaps in the past that was not only the past but the present.

Each day, while our tour group pursued a frenzied schedule, Sybil spent most of her time in retreat in the many monasteries and temples that rimmed the city and looked like a necklace of pearls from our hotel balcony at sunset.

Some members of the tour resented Sybil's loner stance and thought she was alienated from the group, but I knew different. She was alienated from her own past and she was seeking reconciliation with herself.

Each day I made a point of waiting for Sybil on the river path below the hotel, knowing she would eventually return in the evening. Each time she would smile and thank me in a whispered *gam-on* (thank you) until our last evening in Hue when she asked, "Would you like to stroll a bit?"

"I know the group resents my failure to join all of the activities," she said, "and I really have wanted to but . . ."

"It's okay," I said, "don't worry. I know you have strong reasons for what you are doing."

"I do, I do," she said. "It seems the more I meditate and sit in *zazen*, the lighter I feel. The despair I felt on finding my family among the disappeared was almost more than I could bear. But I'm working through it by means of the silence."

Then, as if time had not intervened, Sybil continued where she'd left off the week before. "In the middle of preparing a dance opera based on the Trung Sisters for a visiting Soviet delegation, I was suddenly removed from my privileged position and assigned to an NVA unit on its way south via the Ho Chi Minh Trail. Somehow I survived the four months of horror, of fighting malaria, dysentery, the B-52 bombings and hunger—oh, the hunger, with leeches sucking at one's blood constantly! Worst of all was being treated like a pariah, a piece of shit—worse than a piece of shit." Sybil's anger stiffened her hands into fists and made the veins in her neck stand out like ropes.

"But why?" I asked. "How could everything change so quickly? There must have been a reason."

"Well, yes, I did have a clue. The political cadre assigned to our performance brigade had made overtures toward me which I had parried. I warned my friends about him. Someone, an officer in the battalion, had spread stories that I was a loose woman, a home breaker. So then I knew what the political cadre, or perhaps his wife, had done to me."

"Didn't you want to escape?" I asked.

"How could one escape on the Ho Chi Minh Trail? It was like a thousand-mile prison two or three meters wide. For a woman to *cho hoi* (defect) would have meant rape and torture and death from ARVN or the Americans. And I was still a captive of ideology. I believed in Bac Ho's dream of a united Vietnam. I blamed individuals, not the system, even though I felt used and abused."

"When we arrived in the Iron Triangle area near Saigon, the captain took me aside. 'Comrade Lien,' he said, 'my orders are to have you infiltrate the American military system. You have special talents that can be more effectively employed in Saigon than here in the field. We will arrange for your contacts and relieve you if your life is in danger.'

"I soon discovered that my special talents made me uniquely fitted to become an exotic dancer at a classy nightclub frequented by high-ranking American officers from MACV. My orders: establish a liaison in order to penetrate U.S. security, their intelligence system."

"Must have been pretty difficult and dangerous," I said. "Someone might have remembered you."

"Arranging the job was not difficult. The Saigon infrastructure was riddled with VC. My cover story of being kidnapped by the VC was reinforced by my physical condition. Being reduced by malaria and dysentery and covered with leech scars even made me a celebrity."

Sybil raised her pant leg to show me the still-visible scars.

"But the dancing; how did you—?"

"The dancing was simple B&B (wiggling butts and boobs) with a few variations. I had the talent to make it interesting, enough to singe the clients' eyelashes or suck out their eyeballs, as one of my dancing partners said. I had the younger officers panting all over me. But I was looking for officers with shiny heads and birds on their sleeves, not the panting butter bars. I settled on a colonel from army intelligence who set me up in a luxury apartment. We were together mostly on weekends. He had a wife and kids in the U.S., which helped. He drank himself mushy and then started slobbering about his wife and kids. So the sex was easy, mostly blowing him off a few times. Pardon the expression."

Sybil's tough, bar girl persona chilled me for a moment until I realized she could not have survived without being as hard and resilient as she was.

"To sum it up, I was a big success. I helped supply the information that compromised the American Embassy during TET of 1968—the event that turned Americans against the war. But I didn't find that out until later."

How had Sybil survived the personal horror of having helped to destroy her own family in Hue? I wondered.

"Jesus!" I said, "how did you escape detection or at least suspicion?"

"My officer was too highly placed, above suspicion so to speak. Besides, he never suspected. I wanted to escape my own dirty prison. It was all so sleazy and morally demeaning to me as a woman, even if I was performing essential and necessary tasks. I begged to be relieved as the cadre had promised, but they refused with an unequivocal order from the high command: 'You are absolutely indispensable to our cause at this crucial time when the Americans and their Vietnamese lackeys are weakening.' The officer who contacted me was as cold as an ice pick. 'Let me caution you,' he said, 'your reputation as damaged goods, as having been irreparably compromised as a woman, would make a return to Hanoi impossible, equally so a return to our fighting units, where moral discipline is so essential.'

"Then he insulted my sense of patriotism. 'Think of yourself as heroic as Kieu, who sacrificed her soul and body for her family's survival. You are called to an even greater cause, national survival.'

"Something snapped inside me. I had reached a breaking point. Being declared a moral pariah when I'd sacrificed everything for the revolution was too much. Male arrogance and the derogation and humiliation of my womanhood had become a bigger problem for me than the war itself."

"But how did you eventually escape the cycle?" I asked. I could see that Sybil was overcome with emotion, and she seemed totally exhausted.

"I escaped to Hong Kong and survived by using my body, sometimes the only weapon a woman has. But it's a sordid and painful story." She was squeezing my wrist in a vise grip.

"I need to go to Dalat," she said, "but it's not on the official tour. Would you help me out? Convince the Volsteds that it's very important for me, a matter of life and survival. I want to see if my old dance teacher is still alive and teaching."

I realized then that Sybil had not peeled away her past for free. A bargain had been implicitly struck during our conversations: She would cut into the scars of her personal history if I would help her find a fragment of her past that might reconnect her with a culture she'd loved and lost.

"I'll see to it," I said. "The Volsteds are close friends of mine. They'll understand, I think, even if you've been a terrible truant."

Sybil smiled and squeezed my wrist until it hurt. Her fingers were as hard as handcuffs.

I wasn't certain Sybil would return to Saigon. I thought she might simply disappear or stay in Dalat with her old dance instructor, especially after I discovered her other persona. I'd been cruising Saigon's main streets, checking out the impact of Vietnam's capitalist Renovation program. The effects were present everywhere: Honda motorbikes and scooters by the thousands clogging every street and intersection, entire streets of Japanese video and computer components stacked like high-rises in cardboard boxes, billboards advertising joint ventures in beer and soft drinks. Flashing neon tubes advertised the new video palaces crammed with kung fu and karaoke cassettes. I stared at life-sized posters of Kickboxing Spider Woman wearing black leather hotpants with a bra of crisscrossing straps and a sparkling ruby belly button (*a la* black widow). That was her wardrobe, except for the Zorro-type whip. Her gaze was as fierce as those I'd seen in posters of Chinese revolutionary opera. Then I recognized her. Even with the wild Medusa hairdo and heavy makeup, I knew it was Sybil.

Inside the video shop were a dozen or more videos of Kickboxing Spider Woman made famous or infamous by the Tin Tin Shan brothers in Hong Kong of the 1970s. I remembered the soft porn films I'd seen in 1978 on my two-week stopover, waiting for the visa to visit mainland China. Kickboxing Spider Woman had taken Asia by storm, replacing Bruce Lee as idol and icon after his death. Every film, I discovered, had two versions. In the porno version, Kickboxing Spider Woman engaged in sadomasochistic sex with the pirate leader, Triad King or Yakuza boss before kickboxing him to death. In the clean family-rated version, sex scenes were censored. The latter, I assumed, were being marketed in Vietnam.

Sybil arrived in Saigon three days behind the tour group. She was smiling and relaxed, even mildly ecstatic. "I found my old dance teacher," she said, "but of course her dance school had been closed after the war. She's really too old now to dance herself."

"Well, so?" I inquired.

"She wants me to move in with her and take care of her. But mostly she wants me to help re-open the school and studio. Only this time, we'll integrate the dances of East and West, creating something new and innovative. I find it very exciting, like a new lease on life."

I could see that Sybil's eyes were dancing, but even more strongly, I felt her heart dancing. I didn't want to spoil her dream with the revelation of a different rebirth—her second coming as Kickboxing Spider Woman.

I didn't have to. While I took advantage of a free day to oversleep, Kate and Sybil had ventured into the maelstrom of Saigon's minimarts, small shops and video stores. By the time I'd awakened Sybil had already encountered her Spider Woman videos and locked herself in her hotel room.

I woke up with Kate banging on my door. "Sybil needs you. She wants to talk with you. Please just come now."

By the time I got dressed, Kate had opened the door. Sybil was hunched snail-like into a corner, where she was alternately sobbing and pounding the wall.

"Please, Sybil," I said, "I know about your movies; I've seen them. However sleazy the film, you were always heroic and beautiful."

She kept sobbing and motioned me away.

"Your films are popular with young people because you always fight corruption and crime. They love your style, but even more, your fans idolize you for kickboxing evildoers." Sybil shoved a letter at me in an embossed envelope, an official letter.

"Who—what—what does it say? What's it about?"

Kate intervened, "It's an invitation to lunch at the Ben Thanh Hotel for tomorrow, with the vice minister of culture."

Sybil started sobbing again. "What's going to happen to me? Can they arrest me for those awful films I made? Will my American passport protect me? It's like the past has returned to devour me—some monster I can't escape. I wanted it all to be so different."

"Look, Sybil," I said, "you've got nothing to fear. You're an American citizen. I'm sure every one of your videos is a pirate tape. The bureaucrats are probably afraid you're going to expose them!"

I finally calmed her down. "Well, okay," she said, "but I want you to come with me. I need a hand to hold."

Mr. Nguyen Phan Quat, the overweight vice minister of culture, met us at the door of the Mercedes taxi he'd sent to pick up Sybil. His face, a mass of wattles and chins, drooped even further when he saw me.

"My manager, Mr. Cole Parker." Sybil snapped it out so sharply and business-like that I didn't even flinch.

"Yes, yes. Fine, fine. How nice to see you." Quat was all smiles and gracious genuflection like a returned Mandarin of the old regime.

The luncheon was a combination Vietnamese-French cuisine, spring rolls, lemon grass soup, fish Normandie and—surprise—baked Alaska for dessert.

Quat introduced his secretary-assistant, Ms. Shau, who smiled slightly and kept silent. She reminded me of the large beaded Mona Lisa mosaic that covered most of one wall.

"I hope the luncheon is satisfactory." Quat smiled and stuffed an entire spring roll into his mouth.

"I feel a bit chilly and uneasy," Sybil replied. "I danced here for the Americans years ago. Maybe I can live with the ghosts."

Quat's laughter sounded forced. After a few obligatory toasts to Renovation, the return of old friends and the new Vietnam, Quat attacked his mission without a hem or haw.

"Sybil Patterson," he said, "we know you are now an American citizen, but we hope your heart is still in Vietnam. You are very famous here whether you like it or not. Ever since the banquet in Hanoi, the first minister of culture, Comrade Minh Tue Duong, has not left me off the phone or hook. In brief, we want you to return, at least for a time, perhaps a year, to direct a national dance program, principally Western ballet."

Sybil didn't say anything. Mr. Quat continued. "We are disturbed by all of the Western punk and junk music the youngsters are gobbling up, and we'd like to offer them an alternative. As a hero of the revolution who has lived in the West, you would serve as an appropriate and popular model."

At that moment I saw through the fat Mr. Quat's screen. He was trying to capitalize on the popular Spider Woman videos.

I immediately interrupted. "Before there is any further discussion, Mr. Quat, we will need to discuss compensation for the pirate videos, the Spider Woman series."

Quat became flushed and flustered. Ms. Shau dropped her head and smiled behind her hand.

"I—I don't know," Quat blustered. "Some of those videos are pornographic and violate our sense of morality, but the Japanese businessmen are crazy for them. They demand the uncensored version, hee, hee, hee. I'm sure we can arrange something, hee, hee, hee."

Quat reached across the table and placed his hand on my arm, man to man, as if we had an understanding. I pushed him off. His motives were as transparent as his sleazy style. I figured he was skimming his take from the pirate videos and probably from a dozen other extralegal ventures. The dance program was a way to cover his ass. He was afraid of being exposed.

I took Sybil's arm and gave Quat my card (which had nothing to do with being a manager of anything). "Please let us know when you've made a decision on the illegal videos," I said, "then perhaps we can discuss the other matter."

We stepped outside into a misty rain. Sybil was frowning. She'd turned into a glaring Spider Woman. "Are you really my manager?" she demanded.

"Well, yeah, I mean, you said it."

"In that case, you're fired. You really blew it with that tough-guy talk. You made him lose face, the worst thing you could have done."

"Not if we play our cards right," I said. "With guys like Quat, you negotiate from a position of strength, not weakness."

Sybil exploded, "God, how familiar this sounds; just like Americans during the war. You didn't understand your opponent then; you don't understand him now."

"Look," I insisted, "you've got all of the high cards, the videos. You're an American citizen. Once the embargo is lifted, believe me, Quat will come crawling to you."

Sybil sniffed and moved away from me.

"Give me twenty-four hours," I pleaded. "If nothing happens during that time, I'll crawl out of your life forever."

Sybil was grinning. "I wasn't really going to fire you," she said. "I was only testing you to see if you were tough enough to meet my standards." She exhaled. "I'm so emotionally exhausted by what has happened, so confused and uncertain, I don't think I can make an intelligent decision. I've got to trust you. I'm relying on you to make the right decisions for both of us."

For both of us?

I looked at Sybil and smiled. I'd heard that line before in a movie set in a different French colonial outpost—*Casablanca*. That time the woman got away. I wasn't about to let that happen.

I turned to look again at the very European, 1940s-style hotel. The proprietors of the Ben Thanh had kept the former name, REX, in large letters below the new Ben Thanh. RICKS would have been perfect, but REX would have to do.

I turned up my collar, took Sybil's arm and said in my best gravelly Bogart lisp, "Sybil, I think this is the start of a beautiful friendship."

Queen of Hearts

I had returned to Vietnam on a friendship tour but in reality I was on a search and destroy mission. I was determined to uncover the facts concerning the deaths of Annie Binh and Colonel Rowe and punish the perpetrator. Every circumstance I could recall implicated a former ally I'd recently encountered in San Jose, ex-Major Trang of ARVN intelligence. Unfortunately, conclusive evidence of his complicity had been hard to come by in Vietnam.

The testimonies of Trang's brother and Annie Binh's sister were contradictory and inconclusive. Their Vietnam of shifting and overlapping loyalties didn't fit my Manichean world of good and evil and sharply defined allegiances. Nor could I easily accept their belief in karma, which, though it may have enabled the Vietnamese to bridge the hatreds of war, allowed them (in my view) to escape the war's unresolved issues. Better that, one could argue, than America's moralistic, adversarial culture where opponents were still engaged in a crossfire of accusations and raising hell over a few MIAs twenty years after the war.

I needed to back off from my mission of vengeance, partly out of doubts and confusion, but mostly because my self-appointed task as a kind of *Canterbury* chronicler inevitably drew me away from my own concerns into the lives of my fellow tour members.

Besides, I was romancing Kickboxing Spider Woman, which consumed my time and attention. So I built another layer of scar tissue around the wound that had festered for nearly thirty years and got on with my life.

After eighteen months of disciplined work, I had nearly finished my novel. I wanted to celebrate by taking Sybil to dinner as a prelim to proposing marriage. Our relationship had been an on-again-off-again affair because we were both so damn independent and reluctant to change a companionate setup that seemed to suit our needs. I still lived in Santa Cruz, and Sybil lived in San Jose. That gave us plenty of space, maybe too much for me.

I phoned Sybil for an hour without success. In frustration I drove over the hill into East San Jose, where Sybil had a small studio off of Capital Expressway. She should have been teaching a class, but the only car by her studio was Sybil's faded blue Toyota.

Sybil was inside, slumped on the floor, crying.

"What's wrong? What the hell happened?" I demanded.

Sybil looked up. Her face was a mess of smeared makeup, puffy eyes and red streaks. Her hair was flying off in all directions like she'd tried to tear it out or turn herself punk. She responded by silently shaking her head. When I reached out to her, she slapped my arm away.

"Goddammit!" I shouted, "tell me what the hell happened."

Sybil snapped out of her trance. "A man came in and shouted at us. He ordered the mothers to leave, and they did—immediately. Even when I tried to stop them, they ran out like refugees fleeing war. They were scared. Then he gave me a tongue-lashing, called me a communist whore. He said he knew all about my negotiations with the enemy. Can you believe that? When he threatened to torch my studio unless I stopped consorting with the communists, I threw him out. But I'm scared now, really scared—the way he frightened the Vietnamese women. They must have known him."

I knew that Sybil had nearly finalized an agreement with the Vietnamese Ministry of Culture that would allow her to open a dance school in Dalat with her former teacher. Sybil had kept her negotiations undercover, or thought she had. I didn't know what to say, so I simply blurted my invitation. "I've nearly finished the book. I want to celebrate by taking you to dinner at the Mekong in Milpitas."

"Milpitas?" Sybil started laughing. Milpitas' reputation for class cuisine was a cut above an army chow line.

"Yes, in Milpitas. The Mekong used to be my favorite restaurant."

The modest Mekong restaurant I remembered from seven years past had been transformed into a kitschy Saigon nightclub with a rainbow waterfall, flaming tropical flowers, white tablecloths and candlelight. A balladeer with a ducktail was crooning '60s love songs from a raised dais. Waitresses in *ao dais* glided in and around the tables as gracefully as swans. Mr. Hu remembered me. "Your table is by the rainbow fountain. We're trying something different. It's crazy. I'm going crazy, but the food hasn't changed. Try the pearl tapioca soup with crab meat balls and the lemon grass chicken, or maybe the Saigon crepe, very special. Please . . ." He smiled, seated us and disappeared into the kitchen.

We were drinking beer, nibbling spring rolls and holding hands. A giant jukebox was playing an old '50s tune, Vaughn Monroe's *You're So Beautiful, Lady*, and I was gearing up for the big question. Sybil stiffened and gripped my fingers. Her face became as taut as a mask.

"It's him!" she hissed.

"Who?" I asked and did a half-turn.

"Him, the man who tried to muscle me. I'm sure it's him."

I made a full turn and saw my nemesis, ex-Major Trang, glad-handing, laughing and backslapping his way from table to table, acting like he owned the place. Maybe he did. I started shaking uncontrollably, so badly that I had to hold onto the table.

"Let's get out of here," I said.

I turned and flopped on Sybil's couch for two hours, boiling in the anger that my encounter with Trang had unleashed. Then I got up and started drinking my way through a six-pack of beer.

"I think we ought to talk about this." Sybil was standing in the kitchen doorway. She'd wrapped herself in a blanket against the chill.

"Why?" I asked. "What good will it do? The man should be shot, not talked about. He's already caused the death of one woman I loved and now the son of a bitch is on your case."

"I told you my story," Sybil said, "I need to know yours—all of it—if we're going to stay together."

I sat silently for several minutes. Sybil turned to leave.

"Wait," I said, "okay, okay, I'll tell you the whole damn story." And I did, for three hours, up to the point of my interview with Annie's brother. I stopped there because mentally I'd always stopped there, because I didn't believe him or didn't want to believe him or because his story didn't fit my version.

"Too bad you didn't talk with the brother," Sybil said. Her remark hit me like a brick between the eyes. Had I mentioned Annie's brother? I couldn't remember. I drank a full can of beer to get the answer out.

"I did talk with him, but I didn't believe his story. I didn't want to believe his story." Once I made that admission it all came out in a rush—the final days in Saigon, the unanswered phone calls, the pedicab accident, and then the call from Annie's brother.

I had been recuperating at the hotel when I received the phone call. With no introduction, the caller began screaming questions in my face: "Who are you? Why do you come to Vietnam? What do you want? Do you come to spy? I think you come to make trouble. Why don't you go home?"

When the caller gulped for air, I yelled, "Fuck off!" and almost slammed down the phone. This is fucking crazy, I thought, and decided to reverse tactics.

"Who are you?" I yelled. "Why are you calling me? Are you trying to spy on me? Why don't you hang up and go home?"

The caller started laughing. Then came abrupt silence. I hung onto the phone. The caller spoke gently, almost courteously. "My name is Bao Duc Binh. I'm Annie Binh's brother. You've been trying to reach me, I think."

"Yes, yes," I answered, trying to restrain my eagerness, "when may I see you?"

Another long silence. I hung onto the phone.

"Tomorrow noon. Lunch at the Lam Son restaurant by the Caravelle hotel. They serve my favorite, pork liver pate on a French baguette." He hung up immediately.

The Lam Son was a pleasantly ersatz French country-style cafe. Everything was blue and white, including the petite waitresses' checkered aprons and blue caps. A row of hanging copper pans separated the small kitchen from arboreal booths with fresh-cut flowers and wall photos of rural Provence. Edith Piaf crooned from hidden speakers. After waiting for twenty minutes, I ordered cold beer and a sweet-sour French onion soup so scrumptious I forgot about Bao Duc Binh until someone dipped a crust of baguette into my soup without asking.

"Absolutely delicious!" he grinned.

Bao Duc Binh, in contrast to his sisters, was as ugly as a macaque if one combined the monkey's face and Da-Glo backside. His basset-like nose and droopy cheeks were set in a red mask of peeling fungus or some skin disease he'd picked up during the war. Long hair, unusual for an official, flopped over his ears. He had a quirky Alfred E. Neuman smile with several teeth missing, which immediately dissipated his threatening phone call persona.

We silently sparred with baguettes and beer, knocking down three each before Bao opened the conversation. "I came here," he said, "to ask about Annie."

"Me, too," I said. "I've come for the same purpose."

Bao thrust his body across the narrow table and spilled both beers. His face was about a half-inch from mine. "I'm serious," he said, "don't play games with me; I want to know about Annie. Have you seen Annie? Have you heard anything? Anything at all? You must tell me. Please!"

"What in hell are you talking about?" I asked. "Ghosts? Communicating with the dead? Forget it!"

I pushed him back into his seat to get away from his toilet breath and tried to wipe the beer off my pants. Bao slumped into his chair and traced a finger in the spilled beer.

"I know about her arrest, the security police, the autopsy and all that, but I keep hoping . . ."

I felt sorry for the guy. He was getting weepy, but I was disgusted and angry and suspicious of someone so obviously a lackey, an *apparatchik*.

"Let's cut the crap," I said. "I'm here to deal with the reality of Annie's death. I want to know who's responsible for killing her."

"So you talked with Trang's brother and my sister and others, I presume." He lurched across the table again and I pushed him back. "Why?" he cried. "I only ask you why?"

He knows everyone I've talked to, every place I've been, I said to myself.

"Why? Because I loved your sister," I said, "and I hated Major Trang."

"And I," Bao retorted, "loved my sister and hated Trang a thousand times more strongly than you."

"In that case," I said, "let me ask you, was Trang a double agent and, secondly, was Annie involved with the enemy, the National Liberation Front?"

Bao looked at me like he didn't want to answer. He slurped the beer that hadn't spilled and then spoke very deliberately. "First point, *we* were not the enemy." He pointed a finger in my face. "You were the enemy. And yes, the answer is yes, Trang was a double agent and Annie was involved with the NLF, deeply involved. She was the responsible courier making the twice-weekly trips from My Tho to Saigon. Trang was important, obviously, because he provided transportation. In case of interception or search, however, Annie was to take responsibility or blame. Trang insisted on this."

"But Annie's sister—" I interrupted, "I understood she was the main contact."

Bao looked puzzled. "I think you are confused," he said. "Truy only got directly involved after Annie's death. Before that she was used as a decoy to deceive Trang. But what has all of this got to do with Annie's death?"

"Everything," I said. "According to Major Trang, Annie was arrested by Nhu's Security Police with enemy documents on her person. If you or Trang were using her and putting her life at risk, I would hold you responsible for her death. If Annie chose to be a courier for the NLF, knowing the risks and was willing to accept the consequences, well, that's something else."

Bao became very quiet. "I don't know," he said. "At the time, I thought no sacrifice was too great; the cause was everything."

"Even if you had to risk the lives of others," I inquired, "your family or friends?"

"Yes, even then. The cause was always greater than the individual. That was the base upon which everything else was built. But now, I don't know. I don't know."

"Don't know what?" I said rather sharply.

"I don't know if everything I did was right. Some things I can't talk about. Some things are too painful. I just don't know."

"Like Major Trang," I said.

"Yes, like Major Trang," Bao answered.

"What about Major Trang? How did you feel about him as a person, an ally, a double agent?"

Two skinny guys in brown slacks and white shirts walked in, removed their dark glasses and scanned the room. Their facial skin was pulled taut over sharp features, as if they were wearing masks. I wondered why so many Vietnamese security people had that ghoulish look. Was it because they were engaged in ghoulish work? Bao stiffened and bent over his plate of leftovers. A waiter pointed to a table across the room. The men brushed him aside and seated themselves within earshot. One of the men cursed and swept a flotilla of crumbs from the table. His twin opened a briefcase and spread several papers on the table. A waiter arrived with a pot of tea and a plate of baguettes. Bao exhaled as if he'd been holding his breath and raised his head.

"My opinion of Trang? You mean what did I think of him?" Bao glanced at the two skinny guys with briefcases and lowered his voice. "Trang was a double agent whose first loyalty was to himself. He worked with us for money, favors, protection and for Annie. Eventually we realized he was not trustworthy and a terrible risk, so we fed him low-grade information and misinformation to keep his connection. We found another contact at My Tho who delivered messages to Annie orally, no written documents, only word of mouth."

I began to understand the constant tension and bitterness between Annie and Major Trang. Trang was no fool and must have known he was being finessed. He must have been furious at being shunted aside and then exacted his revenge. Annie was faced with the impossible dilemma of needing Trang's help while denying him information and favors.

"Trang must have known what was happening," I said. "He must have been angry and vengeful."

Bao was looking obliquely at the briefcase twins who kept glancing our way. "I can tell you this," he said, "just before the coup that toppled Diem, when we needed our contact the most, he disappeared. I could no longer contact Annie. If Annie was arrested with NLF documents, it was a setup to catch Annie and others in a sweep. That's what happened. Dozens of our agents were executed. Maybe Trang deceived Truy as well. She could be very gullible. Maybe he fooled all of us, even you."

I had seen combat soldiers return from Vietnam with the thousand-yard stare, a frozen stare as emotionless as an X-ray that goes through and beyond to something else. That was the look I saw in the eyes and face of Bao Duc Binh. I wasn't surprised when he left abruptly without shaking hands or saying good-bye.

The briefcase twins followed him out the door.

Bao Duc Binh radically altered my perception of Annie's persona. If she was a committed VC as her brother claimed, Annie's affair with Colonel Rowe was subversively political. She was his worst enemy. But their relationship was so stormy and stressful, and so charged with emotion and feeling. Was it all play-acting on Annie's part?

Of course, much of Annie's emotional strain must have resulted from her forced relationship with Major Trang and perhaps having to live a lie. If Major Trang suspected he was being used he must have threatened Annie mercilessly and perhaps exacted payment in flesh as her sister suggested.

Annie had been exploited, as well, by her brother, in spite of the sister's defense of him. As Bao himself admitted with obvious guilt, the individual was always sacrificed to the greater cause.

Perhaps Annie's great conflict was that she was committed to a cause and to her lover at the same time. That conflict was destroying her before she was killed.

In the destruction of Annie's persona and in her death, I still firmly believed Major Trang was the guilty party.

A month after I'd returned to the States, I bought several magazines catering to militant vets and super-patriots: *Call to Arms, American Comitatus,* and *Soldier of Fortune.* There were a dozen ads from ex-Berets, Seals or LURPs promoting their talents as security specialists, which might also be another term for hit man. I had already picked up the phone and dialed an area code before I came to my senses.

Now I wished I hadn't come to my senses and hung up the phone. If I'd taken care of the dirty business then, I wouldn't be facing the decision again. After I told Sybil about my encounter with Bao I said, "If Trang ruins your business or threatens you again, I'll take care of him permanently!" Sybil laughed and hugged me, as if she didn't believe me but loved what I'd said anyway. She took me to bed and then abruptly turned her back. *Jesus! She's jealous, jealous of a woman who is only a ghost!* I grinned and promptly fell asleep.

The next morning I remembered that Mr. Hu, owner of the Mekong, had once spoken to my class in Asian studies. He'd been a neutralist leader during the Diem regime and had been forced to flee for advocating a coalition government. He would have known Lu Duc Binh and others of his family.

The Mekong was back to normal, exuding a greasy spoon familiarity with its aluminum pipe, Formica top tables and 1940s motif. Mr. Hu had purchased art deco napkin holders, salt and pepper shakers and Depression-era Coca Cola trays at an auction. His *piece de resistance* was a monster jukebox playing 1960s rock and croon. The only whiff of Asia came from overhead fans and kitchen aromas. Mr. Hu was famous for his Vietnamese noodles called *Pho*, which he had recreated into a garlic-inspired Cajun-California classic. On weekend nights, the line stretched outside for half a block.

Mr. Hu greeted me warmly, though, except for the previous night's encounter, I'd not seen him for six or seven years. His small, pinched face had become more prune-like, a dried prune partly mildewed with gray hair. I ordered a light meal and then broached the reason for my visit. "Do you remember the university chancellor and politician named Lu Duc Binh?"

"Of course, outside of the president's family and the military, he was probably the most influential person in South Vietnam at that time."

"He was, I understand, a neutralist like yourself."

Mr. Hu laughed somewhat cynically, "That's hardly a compliment. He was first and foremost a political manipulator, a neutralist in name only because it gave him more options, more flexibility to wheel and deal."

"I saw him as a very devoted and protective father," I said. "I remember how ferociously he defended his daughter against the U.S. military."

"How successful was he?" Mr. Hu challenged.

"Not very," I said. "Ultimately her involvement with the American officer, an affair that her father failed to prevent, cost Annie Binh her life. Maybe it was her connection with the NLF."

"If that was the case, it was a horrible tragedy. Unfortunately, Chancellor Binh may have brought it on himself."

"How so?" I asked. I was astonished by Mr. Hu's comment.

"By not being an honest neutral. If Chancellor Binh had not intrigued and manipulated he and his daughter might still be alive."

"Really," I said, "that's difficult to believe."

"Let me tell you something more disturbing and more difficult to believe. I think Lu Duc Binh may have arranged his daughter's arrest as the only way to keep his daughter safe from the American officer. That became the consuming passion of his life, more important even than the violent political events, partly, I think, because he felt so humiliated by American authorities who refused to discipline the guilty officer; also, because his daughter's affair destroyed his faith in himself as a father and as a man. He even arranged for a young army officer of unimpeachable character to be his daughter's chaperone and chauffeur."

My God, he must mean Trang!

"Why then did she commit suicide or perhaps suffer torture and murder?"

"I don't know," Mr. Hu replied. "The officer couldn't be with her all of the time. Once dishonorable dogs, the lackeys of Ngo Dinh Nhu, had her under their thumbscrew, she became a hostage to their political and, most surely, personal designs. Nhu could use her vulnerability against her father, to force his support for Diem or at least to keep him neutral."

"What happened, then; why did she die?"

"Everyone involved was, I think, overtaken and overwhelmed by events surrounding the overthrow of Diem. In that situation, violence becomes gratuitous and endemic. I've seen it happen many times. Anything can happen when things are out of control."

Mr. Hu poured some lukewarm tea and cleared his throat. "In the larger view, the way we Vietnamese might interpret the situation, Annie was willing to sacrifice herself for the good of the family, to secure her father's survival, as in our classic *Tale of Kieu*. From the time of the Trung sisters who led the resistance against China in the first century up to the present, Vietnamese women have sacrificed themselves for family and country. It's a long tradition. Annie's connection with a high-ranking American officer kept Nhu's killers at bay. Her links with the NLF protected him against assassination by the Vietcong."

I was stunned, trying to recover from Mr. Hu's verbal hardballs when his face wrinkled into a wide grin. He rose to his feet quickly and walked past me toward the entry.

"*Chao ong Trang. Moi ong vao.*" (Good evening, Mr. Trang, please come in.)

I twisted in my seat. It *was* ex-Major Trang. *What the hell? Was this a setup? It couldn't be. I'd arrived unannounced. Hu had excused himself to check the kitchen. Had he called Trang?* Mr. Hu was effusive and ingratiating. "Please allow me to introduce my friend, Mr. Nam Van Trang. Without his help my restaurant would have failed a dozen times."

Trang laughed. "Without your restaurant, life would not be worth living." Trang extended his hand. "The Mekong is the best Vietnamese restaurant in Santa Clara County, maybe the best outside of Vietnam."

A waitress brought hot tea. I felt I needed to clear the air. "I've met Mr. Trang before," I said. "He was a major in ARVN intelligence when I was in Vietnam. He was involved with the deaths of the people we were talking about, Annie Binh and Colonel Rowe."

Trang looked upset. "You've been talking about me?"

Mr. Hu frowned at me and broke in quickly, "No, no, nothing about you. We were talking about Senator Binh and his daughter. I said Senator Binh was a dealer and manipulator, not an honest and forthright neutralist, a true believer in compromise."

"I think you are completely correct," Trang said. "That's why our families, once very close, drifted apart."

"Is that why your promised marriage to Annie Binh was nullified?" I asked.

"Yes, yes, I suppose so," Trang replied. Trang's face suddenly hardened. He glared at me. I had caught him in a lie. Trang cleared his throat, but I beat him to the punch.

"You told me before it was your brother."

Trang's laugh was as brittle as broken glass. "Did I?" he asked. "I think it could have been either one of us. It was a family affair."

Mr. Hu was looking fearful and disturbed, like he really wanted this conversation to end. I didn't want to put his restaurant in financial jeopardy, but I needed to inflict one final jab. "You were also, I think, a double agent. I discovered that in Vietnam." Ex-Major Trang did not change his stony expression.

When I rose to leave, the two of them stayed in their seats. "Your brother, the bonze in Hue, sends you greetings," I said.

Trang didn't look at me nor did he respond. Neither did Mr. Hu.

What at first I took as a snub, I realized was a reaction to a deep, pervasive fear of exposure. Within the American-Vietnamese community were belligerent cold warriors, militant anti-communists who imposed an ideological straitjacket on their clients as rigidly as their communist counterparts in Vietnam. That's why Trang had ingratiated himself with the Vietnamese community, so he could control his destiny, hide his past and intimidate those who might threaten him. If ex-Major Trang's VC past were exposed, he would become an instant pariah, excommunicated, his business career and reputation ruined and his life endangered. The knowledge I possessed about his past gave me the power of life and death. Taking care of him would be easy—a few phone calls, a couple of letters, a fax or two to Vietnam. Of course, there were Vietnamese hit men, gang gunmen that Trang might unleash on me, but that was a risk I was willing to take.

I had already turned to leave when a scowling, elegantly dressed Vietnamese woman loaded with boxes and bags from Nordstrom's walked through the entry. She entered through an efflorescence of monoxide left by an angry taxi driver peeling rubber and the smog of her own expletives. The woman's mid-life customized chassis was as sleek as a Jaguar classic. Her short hair, complete with spit-curls, was topped with a perky box hat which matched perfectly the two-piece dress with wide shouldered jacket. With art deco lips as bright as red neon, she looked and acted every inch the Hollywood bitch goddess straight out of a 1940s movie.

"Fat ass wouldn't move his butt an inch to help and still wants a tip. I told him to find his tip in a fucking toilet." When she caught a spike heel on a chair, I lunged to retrieve her packages and spread-eagled over her custom pumps. I looked up into the unscarred mirror image of Madame Truy Duc Binh, into the bold face of a much older and angrier Annie Binh.

Annie Binh. She was still a knockout.

"Annie got your gun?" I asked. It was instinctive and I felt like a fool.

For a second she reared back with a puzzled frown, then struggled to free her foot. "Dammit!" she snapped. "You're on my fucking foot!"

"Dammit!" I said in reply. "I thought you were fucking Cinderella!"

"Smartass!" she hissed and high-stepped over my chest. She nailed my hand to the floor with a spiked heel and left a bouquet of Opium perfume.

I turned to Major Trang. His mask of hard-nosed confidence had collapsed into the malleable face of a suppliant transmogrified by thirty years of suffering, by love and pain and humiliation, by desire and repulsion, as fatally attracted to the woman who straddled me as the male spider victim is to his voraciously demanding black widow mate.

Perhaps because I was still splayed awkwardly on the floor, Major Trang said rather pointedly, "Before you leave, Mr. Parker, let me introduce my wife."

Annie Binh, or Trang, had already walked away and turned her back on us to redo her facial. A single, luminous eye glared at me from a tiny hand mirror and then winked provocatively.

Mr. Hu took my arm and steered me to the door. "Never have I seen a man so in love," Mr. Hu said quietly. "Perhaps because he's been through hell, many hells. He saved her life, you know. She owes him her life."

I turned to ask a question, the first of a thousand questions, but Mr. Hu drew a finger across his lips. "No more questions," he said, "no more questions. We must stop asking questions."

"I understand," I said. "I understand." But I didn't understand, nor would I ever understand how the duplicitous Major Trang had been able to manipulate the serpent's nest of rivals and factions in the monstrously corrupt and dangerous Saigon death machine to his advantage. To have destroyed his American rival, and to have rescued and escaped with his queen of hearts in the sudden death draw brought about by the coup of gunslingers was a triumph whose margin of error must have been narrower than a razor's edge.

There was, of course, another scenario. Annie Binh was no Madame Butterfly or Miss Saigon, willing to suffer her Asian female fate with passive endurance. Perhaps she had, with the fury of a woman scorned, been the agent of her own revenge and liberation. She had, after all, seized a fragment of the American dream promised by her hero and lover, Colonel Rowe.

What I did understand or at least surmise was that Major Trang was trapped by his absolute obsession for Annie Binh, that he was being ground exceedingly fine by the mills of the gods, and that those mills turned on the obsession of his goddess, Annie Binh, for her lost knight in shining chinos, Colonel Rowe. Perhaps that was *his* fate, *his* karma.

That was enough for me. Ex-Major Trang did not need another executioner. And, quite frankly, neither did I.

Glossary

A. Players

Bao Dai—last emperor of Vietnam. Cooperated with the Japanese during World War II. After briefly joining the Vietminh in 1945, he ruled as head of state under the French from 1945 until 1955 when Ngo Dinh Diem ousted him in a referendum.

Ho Chi Minh—born Nguyen Tat Thanh in 1890, Ho left Vietnam as a youth and traveled the world. He joined the Communist Party in Paris in 1920. After training in Moscow, he traveled in several countries under various aliases as a Communist agent. In 1941 he returned to Vietnam and created the Vietminh to fight against the Japanese (with the help of the American OSS) and for Vietnamese independence, which he declared in 1945. As the leader of North Vietnam, he fought the French colonials for nine years and after them the United States until his death in 1969.

Ngo Dinh Diem—fierce anti-communist, devout Catholic and nationalist, hand-picked by the U.S. to lead the Republic of Vietnam (South) after the Geneva Accords of 1954 divided Vietnam North and South. His dictatorial methods and isolation from the people led to his overthrow and assassination in 1963.

Ngo Dinh Nhu—Diem's younger brother and advisor whose use of security police and national police against dissenters spread dissatisfaction with his brother's regime.

Madame Ngo Dinh Nhu—daughter of a westernized Hanoi family and wife of Diem's brother; she became first lady because Diem was a bachelor. Her aristocratic airs and insulting speeches also provoked opposition to Diem's regime.

Trung sisters—Trung Tre and Trung Nhu led the first major insurrection against Chinese rule in A.D. 40. They have been revered as goddesses and models of resistance ever since.

Vo Nguyen Giap—modern Vietnam's greatest general and military strategist who defeated the French at Dien Bien Phu and the Americans by a combination of military and political strategies.

B. Military and Vietnamese Terms

Agent Blue—a toxic herbicide used to destroy rice fields supplying the VC.

Agent Orange—highly toxic herbicide used by U.S. military to defoliate forest vegetation used as cover by the VC.

AID—Agency for International Development. A branch of the U.S. State Department responsible for advising the government of South Vietnam on a wide range of policy and security matters, including the notoriously corrupt national police.

AK-47—Soviet-made military assault weapon used by the VC and NVA.

Ao dai—traditional form-fitting Vietnamese dress, high-necked and long-sleeved, worn with pants and overblouse split high on the sides.

ARVN—army of South Vietnam.

B-52—strategic high-altitude bomber able to carry twenty-seven tons of high-explosive bombs.

Bonze—Buddhist monk.

Body bag—plastic, zippered bag used to retrieve dead bodies from the field.

Body count—U.S. military term for number of enemy killed. Eventually it became the measure of military success in the field.

Butter bar—slang for second lieutenant.

Bush—informal term for jungle. Synonyms include boondocks, boonies, Indian country, the field.

Chieu hoi—South Vietnam's program to persuade VC to defect. Also refers to defector.

Chopper—slang for helicopter.

Civic Action—pacification program aimed at winning the hearts and minds of Vietnamese by upgrading the quality of their lives and eliminating VC.

CIA—Central Intelligence Agency. In Vietnam the Agency engaged in a wide range of covert activities besides its main function of gathering intelligence.

CID—Criminal Investigation Division. A branch of the U.S. Army charged with investigating crimes committed by U.S. soldiers.

Cobra—army attack helicopter. Also called gunship.

C-rations—canned, individual rations used on military operations in the field. Also called C's or C-rats.

Cu Chi—area on the outskirts of Saigon layered with VC tunnels. Also the site of a large American army base.

Dien Bien Phu—the French mountain fort, supposedly impregnable, captured by the Vietnamese Communists (Vietminh) in 1954. The battle ended French colonialism in Vietnam, and led to a divided Vietnam and eventual U.S. involvement.

DMZ—demilitarized zone separating North and South Vietnam at the 17th Parallel.

Elephant grass—tall, sword-like grass growing in the central and northern Highlands.

EM—enlisted man. Generic term for non-officers whether drafted or enlisted.

F-4 (phantom jet)—McDonnell Douglas' fighter-bomber used extensively in Vietnam.

Firebase—a temporary artillery base located in the field to provide fire support for ground operations.

Firefight—a small arms battle.

FNG—fucking new guy. A new arrival, also called a Twinkie or cherry.

Frag—fragmentation grenade. Also refers to murder of officers and NCOs by disgruntled grunts using fragmentation grenades.

Free fire zone—area designated by U.S. military in which any Vietnamese might be killed.

GNV—government of South Vietnam.

Gook—one of several derogatory names for Vietnamese and Asians. Others include: slope, dink, slant, zipperhead.

Grunt—common term for infantry man.

Hamlet—a small rural village.

Ho Chi Minh Trail—famous NVA supply trail running through Laos and Cambodia which, despite massive, continuous American bombing, effectively supplied the NVA and VC in South Vietnam.

Hooch or hootch—refers to either the tent-shack of the military or the thatch-bamboo hut of the Vietnamese peasant.

Hot—area under enemy control.

HQ—headquarters.

Huey—Bell UH-1. The utility helicopter used for transporting men and equipment.

Huoat Vu—notorious security police directed by Ngo Dinh Nhu, brother of President Diem.

In country—GI term for Vietnam.

Indian country—area outside the protection of a U.S. military base.

K-bar—military knife.

KIA—killed in action. Other terms include wasted, bought the farm, got his shit scattered.

Kit Carson scouts—former VC turned *chieu hoi*, serving as patrol guides by U.S. forces.

Lifer—a career soldier.

LURPs or LRRPs—members of Long Range Reconnaissance Patrol. Also called recon.

LZ—landing zone for helicopters, usually in a combat area.

M-16—the standard American rifle used in Vietnam, often cursed for frequent jamming.

M-60—light 7.62-caliber belt-fed machine gun used by U.S. forces in Vietnam.

MACV—Military Assistance Command Vietnam. Agency in charge of all U.S. military operations in Vietnam.

MEDCAP—Medical Civil Action Program. Agency providing free medical treatment for Vietnamese villagers by U.S. and ARVN medics.

Medevac—medical evacuation helicopter. Also called a dustoff.

MIA—Missing in Action.

Montagnards—aboriginals of central-northern Highlands who worked with U.S. Special Forces.

MOS—Military Occupational Specialty. Job designation.

MP—Military Police.

NCO—non-commissioned officer.

NLF—National Liberation Front. Official name for the Vietcong or VC.

Nuoc mam—strong-smelling fish sauce used by Vietnamese.

NVA—North Vietnamese Army.

PBR-Navy River Patrol Boat used to safeguard the rivers and channels in South Vietnam.

Phoenix—CIA-directed program designed to eliminate (terminate) VC leaders.

Point—the forward man in a combat patrol.

POW—prisoner of war.

PX—post exchange. Combination supermarket/drugstore where soldiers and their families buy needed items at reduced prices.

Puff—short for Puff the Magic Dragon. Affectionate slang for the C-47 aircraft equipped with three 7.62-millimeter machine guns capable of firing fifty-four hundred rounds per minute. Also called Snoopy.

Punji stakes—sharpened bamboo stakes hidden in pits or underwater. Designed to cripple or kill American grunts.

REMF—rear echelon motherfucker. Insulting name applied by combat troops to rearguard support personnel.

Renovation—official term for Vietnam's new economic policy incorporating capitalism with socialism.

Rock and roll—slang term for a weapon on full automatic.

Rome plow—giant earth mover whose front plow could topple trees, strip jungle to bare earth and cave in VC tunnels.

R&R—rest and recuperation. A grunt's temporary (three to seven days) vacation from the war.

RTO—radio telephone operator. The man assigned to carry the PRC-25 (Prick-25) radio while on patrol.

Sampan—a simple shallow peasant boat used for transporting enemy men and supplies during the war.

Sapper—a VC or NVA commando-infiltrator armed with explosives.

Search and destroy—the mission of most combat patrols was to find and kill the enemy. Also called humping it.

Strategic Hamlet Program—President Diem's plan to convert South Vietnam's hamlets into fortified villages.

Seals—the navy's special forces. Letters stand for sea, air, and land.

SOP—standard operating procedure.

Special Forces—known popularly as Green Berets. Combat soldiers specially selected and trained to operate behind enemy lines and undertake hazardous assignments.

Stars and Stripes—U.S. military newspaper.

Strack—term denoting ideal in military dress and demeanor.

Tan Son Nhut—large airbase on the outskirts of Saigon used by both civilian and military aircraft.

TET—Vietnamese lunar New Year festival, celebrated as a national holiday.

Tiger cages—underground cages used by the Diem government to imprison opponents.

TOP—short for topkick or first sergeant.

Triple canopy—mature jungle or forest with a third layer of ancient trees more than two hundred feet high that effectively blocks out the sun.

Tunnel rat—volunteers small enough and brave enough to crawl into VC tunnel complexes to kill or capture the enemy.

VC—Vietcong term for Vietnamese Communist in South Vietnam. Also called Victor Charlie, Charlie, or Sir Charles, out of respect.

Ville—short for village.

Wasted or zapped—GI terms for killed.

World (the)—GI term for the U.S., in contrast to "in country" for Vietnam.

Reading and Discussion Guide

The discussion questions and topics in this guide are designed to focus your reading and thinking about the most controversial and divisive event in America's recent history—the Vietnam War. The writer hopes these questions will enhance your empathy for and understanding of a tour group of Americans trying to reconcile with their painful pasts.

When the protagonist-narrator, Cole Parker, confronts his nemesis, ex-Major Trang, with Trang's possible complicity in the deaths of Parker's commander and his mistress, Annie Binh, Trang replies, "We were all victims, victims of American policy, government and military corruption, personalism, history. I can't feel sorry for her, or for him. Their deeds determined their destiny. Karma."

Parker concedes Trang's point but holds to the proposition that "with victims there must also be executioners, and few Americans wanted to face that reality. Neither did the Vietnamese, and certainly not Major Trang."

These two points of view—Trang's acceptance of the past as past, and Cole Parker's resistance to the idea of the past as fixed by fate—*without fixing personal responsibility*—recur throughout the novel as dramatic theme and reference point, as Americans and Vietnamese struggle to reconcile themselves with their shared history and with each other.

These questions and topics follow the sequence of chapters. Many of the stories, however, can be read and discussed separately if the reading group or class so chooses.

Prologue: Loose Cannons

When Trang delivers his tirade about "drug-crazed and sex-crazed American soldiers" and declares "It was the failure of purpose and will that destroyed my country," he evokes anger and insults from the veterans. Why? Was he too close to being "on target," as Nurse Noonan suggests? When former President Reagan told a group of decorated war veterans, "You did not lose the war in Vietnam," who was he implying did lose the war?

In *History Wars, The Enola Gay and Other Battles for the American Past*, several writers note that Americans have difficulty accepting a version of history that questions the heroic or official view, especially when it concerns World War II. Might this factor of "American innocence" explain former President Reagan's statement—or the difficulties Americans have in dealing with the Vietnam War?

Hearts and Pawns

Is Major Trang correct when he says of Colonel Rowe and Annie, "their deeds determined their destiny"? What early decisions taken by Colonel Rowe or Annie might have "determined their destiny"? Was Annie a pawn, as she said, "of a much bigger game I can't seem to escape," or did she choose to become a pawn? Does this chapter support or dispute Trang's claim that "we were all victims"? Do you agree with the assertion that "with victims there must also be executioners" (persons responsible for acts of violence and war)?

In *The Making of a Quagmire*, David Halberstam documents the series of decisions that eventually trapped Americans in an "unwinnable war" in Vietnam. Is "Hearts and Pawns" an accurate reflection of this thesis?

Karma is the Joker

What caused the narrator to conclude after his conversations with the bonze and Madame Binh that "In the game of life, karma is the final arbiter. Karma is the joker"? Did Madame Binh or the bonze offer new insights and information, or did they confuse the narrator's search? Do you think either of them was covering up, misinforming or withholding information? Do you think the narrator is "concocting (his own mental) scenarios"? Does Madame Binh agree with Trang when she says, "Let the gods take care of Trang; don't become his executioner"?

Lucien Pye, among others, writes in *Remembering and Forgetting, The Legacy of War in East Asia* of the difficulties of restoring historical memory after experiencing wartime trauma. He notes, "There is, however, a difference between remembering to forget and a conspiracy of silence, between choosing to ignore and a state of paralyzed imagination stemming from blocked memories."

Which of these, if either, might apply to the testimonies of the bonze or Madame Binh?

Out of Body—English

How do we know early on that Steve Solberg's story may be more subjective than objective? Why did Ms. Hung urge Steve to read *The Tale of Kieu* and what lessons did Steve eventually draw from his reading of the novel? How do you interpret Steve's remark, "It couldn't be Ms. Hung. But it was Ms. Hung or her double"? What was the key to Steve's reconciliation with his father? Is the reality of Steve's experience any less "real" because he was using his powers of imagination?

Lucien Pye again observes that "memory and imagination are intimately associated in a complex . . . relationship. The two can be mutually supportive in that memory calls for the fantasy play of imagination and imagination searches memory to get its building blocks." Is Steve applying "the fantasy play of imagination" in trying to connect or reconnect his past and present?

Replay

What do the first four paragraphs tell us about Vic Carlson's character—especially his hang-ups and problems? How did Vic's experiences in Vietnam affect his postwar relationships with women? Was Vic's sexual impotency symptomatic of a larger problem—or problems? How does Vic try to reconcile with his past? Is he successful? What does Vic need to do in order to come to terms with his Vietnam experience?

Tunnel Vision

In his study of Post Traumatic Stress Disorder (PTSD), psychiatrist-historian Robert Lifton asserts that "unresolved death guilt" over having survived the deaths of one's buddies may lead the survivor to violent actions and eventuate in a "mission of revenge." Does this phenomenon of "survivor guilt" help explain Tommy Neville's violent reaction to the *60 Minutes* program? When Tommy first encounters his friend Bobby in Vietnam, he immediately recognizes him as a "macho greenhorn" and "innocent abroad." What new role does Tommy assume in their relationship and how might this new role have influenced Tommy's decision to return to Vietnam? At what point does Tommy have a change of heart—and why?

The Hustler

In what way is Ben Hubbard's return to Vietnam a fulfillment of his own philosophy that "what goes around comes around"? How different is Hubbard's philosophy from Trang's assertion that "their deeds determined their destiny"? What character trait mentioned by Cole Parker in "Hearts and Pawns" makes Hubbard oblivious or blind to his own failings? Is the story's conclusion appropriate given Hubbard's attitude and actions?

The Wall

Jonathan Shay notes in his perceptive study *Achilles in Vietnam* that "many combat veterans are denied compassionate understanding by civilians because so many people cannot comprehend a love between men that is rich and passionate but not necessarily sexual." How might this powerful factor of male bonding explain Andy Fetzer's guilty feelings about a crime in which he refused to participate? Why, after Ishmael Breedlove kicks in his ribs, does Andy rely upon Ishmael to help him through his traumatic experience? What role do the wives play—and why?

Turncoat

How might the warrior tradition of male bonding mentioned by Jonathan Shay have influenced Andy's negative reaction to Tran's use of the term *chieu hoi*—or his dreams of Ishmael's Vietnam experience? What did Andy learn by returning to his old battle sites with Tran? Has Andy finally reconciled with his past when he says, "Yeah, I'm sure"?

MIA

In what ways was Kate Noonan's return to Vietnam a "homecoming"? Does Kate's experience exemplify the thesis that Americans have difficulty accepting a version of history that questions the heroic or official view? Who or what caused Kate's turnabout decision on suicide?

The Seduction of Elvis

How would you explain the dreams (or fantasies) of Tina Brown and Vinh? Were the barriers to their achieving a compatible relationship personal, cultural, social or political? What or who enabled Tina to reconcile with Vinh and her father?

In *Children of the Holocaust*, Helen Epstein contends that children of holocaust survivors may "possess as their own" the emotional traumas experienced by their parents, feelings that may result in depression, alienation and antisocial behavior. Is it possible that Tina and Vinh were similarly affected by their parents' experiences?

Cinderella Gook

How strongly did Lily Okada's background and upbringing influence her decision to go to Vietnam? What experiences shaped Lily's opinions and attitudes about the Vietnam War? What accounts for the conflicting stories about Lily—as well as Lily's own conflicting stories?

In *The Marginal World of Oe Kenzaburo*, Michiko Wilson describes the novelist's style of "repeating narrative" to deal with events too painful and potentially destructive for the protagonist's family to confront openly: "The narration shows the father/son in a desperate struggle to open a dialogue with his parents, wife and son." Might this kind of "dialogic narrative" describe Lily's attempt to find solutions to her problems, and explain her conflicting and overlapping stories?

Kickboxing Spider Woman

When Sybil Patterson says to Cole, "Sometimes you have to reconcile with pain, anger, frustration," whose previously stated viewpoint is she reinforcing? Does Sybil follow her own stated philosophy? What led Sybil to rebel against her fate, unlike the national heroine, Kieu? Why would a strong woman like Sybil say to Cole, "I've got to trust you. I'm relying on you to make the right decisions for both of us"?

Queen of Hearts

Why did Cole dismiss Bao Duc Binh's version of events? Does Mr. Hu's account support any of the previous testimonies or does he present a different story? Was Cole able to resolve the conflicting versions of events and motives concerning the death of Annie Binh—before the surprising finale? Were you, the reader, able to reconcile the conflicting versions?

SUMMARY

Loose Cannons is, by definition, structured loosely. Characters and episodes are portrayed separately and individually. By and large this is an accurate reflection of how Americans often deal with issues or problems. Several commentators, including Jonathan Shay, have seen this loner stance as part of America's failure to deal with the aftermath of Vietnam: "Any blow in life will have longer-lasting and more serious consequences if there is no opportunity to communalize it."

But as psychiatrist and historian Robert Lifton suggests, there are inherent difficulties in the communal approach as well: "In the past, the warrior as hero could be a repository for broad social guilt. Sharing in his heroic mission could serve as a cleansing experience of collective relief from whatever guilt had been experienced over distant killing, or from the need to feel any guilt whatsoever. But when the warrior-hero gives way to the tainted executioner-victim, not only is this repository taken away, but large numbers of people risk a new wave of unmanageable guilt and a profound sense of loss, should they recognize what their warriors have actually become."

Do you agree with the premise of both writers that reconciliation must be communal? Do you agree with Lifton's point that Vietnam veterans are seen by themselves and others as "tainted executioner-victims"? If Lifton is correct, don't Vietnamese citizens also have to be included in the reconciliation process?

In sum, what do you think is the most useful approach in dealing with the postwar problems of the Vietnam War?

1. The past is past. It's over and done with. Let's look to the future and get on with our lives.

2. The past is present. The problems and issues of the war, of guilt and grieving and reconciliation, are still with us and need to be confronted as a community and as a nation.

3. Ultimately, whether within one's community or as a nation, problems and issues of the Vietnam War must be dealt with individually—with one's enemy, as in the case of Tommy Neville, with one's inner demons, as in the case of Andy Fetzer, or with one's God or conscience—as with all of us. Redemption, whether secular or religious, is an individual matter.

RECOMMENDED READING

Marilyn B. Young, *The Vietnam Wars 1945-1990*; David Halberstam, *The Best and the Brightest*; *The Making of a Quagmire*; Myra Macpherson, *Long Time Passing*; Gloria Emerson, *Winners and Losers*; Neil Sheehan, *A Bright Shining Lie*; William Prochnau, *Once Upon a Distant War*; Mark Baker, *Nam*; Wallace Terry, *Bloods*; Lynda van Devanter, *Home Before Morning*; Keith Walker, *A Piece of My Heart*; Charley Trujillo, *Soldados*; Robert Lifton, *Home From the War*.